THE
MARSH
HOUSE

Also by Zoë Somerville

The Night of the Flood

THE MARSH HOUSE

Zoë Somerville

HEAD of ZEUS

An Apollo Book

First published in the UK in 2022 by Head of Zeus Ltd
This paperback edition first published in 2022 by Head of Zeus Ltd,
part of Bloomsbury Publishing Plc

9 7 5 3 1 2 4 6 8

A catalogue record for this book is available from
the British Library.

ISBN (PB): 9781838934668
ISBN (E): 9781838934675

Typeset by Ed Pickford

Printed and bound in Great Britain by
CPI Group (UK) Ltd, Croydon CR0 4YY

Head of Zeus Ltd
5–8 Hardwick Street
London EC1R 4RG
WWW.HEADOFZEUS.COM

For Alex and Jessie

1

From the moment the house were built it looked like it belonged right in its place. Like the shipwreck it was; a boat run aground on the marsh.

It were timber-framed and finished up in brick and flint like most of the houses hereabouts, but it didn't look like none of the others. It were lopsided, curved, with too many small windows, like portholes. They'd built it from the salvaged timbers of the wreck of the Gunwale out in the Pit. Maybe that's where the bad luck come in. They say he built it for her, the young wife he'd brought over from the East, in the hope that she'd not mind being all the way out here on the edge of the creek and the sea, with only the view over the Pit for company; that she'd bear him pink-cheeked babbies reared on saltwater and sky. It didn't quite turn out like that though, did it?

He named it Swalfield House after the land it were on, but it soon became known as the Marsh House. He spent all his money on it – electrics, indoor plumbing, all of it

– *but the lights would go on the blink and the drains'd get clogged up, and the black rats'd come off the marsh, looking for food. By the time the daughter was turning from child to adult, the salt and the vapours from the marsh'd got into the wood, making the joints and walls swell and bulge, and the lane got overgrown, and no one come up here no more.*

No one had lived in the house for years afore they arrived last winter. Not since all that fuss in thirty-four.

I watched her from my window. Our cottage overlooks the Marsh House, you see. Not so much overlooks as looks up to, across the lane. You can't actually see our cottage from the road, it's hidden, sunk down, practically in the marsh. The back of the cottage is right on the edge of the creek. If you're in the privy you can feel the salt on your nether parts.

There's no other houses on our lane. Like I said, no one come up this way.

It were nearing Christmas when she turned up. The snow hadn't come yet but it were biting cold and I was stood next to the stove, right where I am now. Always was the only place you could be in the cottage and get proper warm. I heard a car engine and this garish orange beast come down the drive – nasty, bright orange, what you couldn't take your eyes off of 'cos everything else is losing colour as it's winter. She's wearing a fur coat and there's a pale, weak-looking child with her and a small, yapping, white dog. I watched her from my window.

The first thing I think is that the fluff-ball dog is going to upset the animals. Especially the hound.

I notice there's a dent in the car bonnet. And her eyes are all puffy and her cheeks are tear-streaked and there are black, spidery lines running down her pretty little face. The other thing I think is – here we go.

I weren't surprised to see her though. Oh no, it was her all right. We'd been waiting for her.

2

The Marsh House
21st December 1962

It came from nowhere. Malorie turned a corner and the road must have been icy because it felt like the car was skating. The low winter sun was in her eyes and she was squinting, holding tight to the steering wheel, leaning forward to try and see below the glaring light. As the road bent to the left, a black shape flashed in her vision, springing in front of the car. She swerved to avoid it – or it might have been that she was skidding already – but it was too late. The hedge smashed into the front of the car. She screamed. Franny shouted something from the back. An almighty crash juddered through her body.

When she opened her eyes, frozen brambles were crushed against the windscreen, icicles of light piercing them. The dog was whimpering. Her gloved hands were still gripping the steering wheel and her cheeks were pressed into the wool. There was a sharp pain in her neck. God, she thought. Oh God. Outside, a robin fluttered down to the hedge, so close she could see its black, beady eye and the feathers on its red breast. Franny? She turned, a vision of blood rising before her eyes – and she wasn't there. But the sound of Larry whining rose from below and then she heard –

'Mummy?'

Hoisting herself out of her seat, she twisted around and leaned over and there they were, her daughter and the dog, squashed into the footwell.

'Are you all right? Can you get up?'

From the gloom behind the front seats, the whites of Franny's eyes stared up at her. She would tell Tony about this and Malorie wanted to scream again.

She breathed very slowly through her nose and reached down with an arm to touch Franny, who shrunk deeper into the footwell. Larry began to bark.

'All right, it's all right. Lift him up, Franny.'

'He's heavy,' she said, but she did it and Malorie nearly wept in sheer relief.

Franny's eyes were red-rimmed and a tiny trail of snot dripped down from her nose. She was eight years old and had a permanent cold. Malorie gave her daughter a smile, but Franny stared back, her small face hard to read.

Malorie tried to reverse. The front wheels spun and the car didn't move. Clambering across the gearstick, she opened the passenger door and almost fell out onto the ground. It was quiet on the road, no one in sight, just the violent sun blaring out from above the hedge and the huge pale-blue sky pressing down on her. The front of the bonnet was badly dented, as if a heavy animal had smashed into it. But there was no sign of anything. Pulling a flyaway wisp of hair out of her face, she inspected the front wheel and under the car. She must have injured – killed? – something. But whatever it was had gone. What on earth could it have been? Searching her memory she thought she'd seen a black animal – not a bird – too large to be a cat, too dark to be a hare.

'What was that?' Franny had somehow managed to get out of the car. Malorie had slid down the side of the car and was slumped against it, the ground already hard with the coming night-frost through her skirt.

'I don't know,' she said.

Perhaps if she just pretended all this wasn't happening it would go away. It was unfair, all of it – the argument with Tony; his affair; the hideous car he'd bought her; the bloody dog he'd given Franny instead of a sibling or friends; Franny's silence, all the way from London. The cold. The emptiness in her head. Worst of all – that she'd brought them here, of all the places in the world. Here, near where she'd grown up and where both her parents were buried. But the flat was full of Tony's things. It was his flat and she could no longer bear to be there. And the house – this house – had been somewhere to go.

At the hospice, it had smelt of mildew. She'd wanted to open the windows, to let in the fresh air, but it was October and raining. Condensation trickled down the windowpanes and pooled on the windowsills. She didn't want anything to do with this deathly place. She just wanted to get it over with. There had been a phone call the week before.

Can you come up, Mrs Cavendish? Your mother is asking for you.

Are you sure?

Her mother was very small and white in the bed, a shrivelled arm attached to a drip.

'Oh, you're here. Mary.'

'No, Mum, it's Malorie.'

'No one ever comes to see me.' The corners of her eyes were wet, and Malorie couldn't remember if she'd ever seen her mother cry.

'Mary. You were such a scrap of a thing. Come here. Come closer. I promised your father I'd – Oh –'

Her face was distorted in agony. She looked so old and helpless. Malorie knew she couldn't be that old, but the cancer had aged her, rotting her from the inside out so now she looked shrunken, as if the life had already been sucked out of her. Her mother's thin hand reached out and snatched at hers. Her voice scraped.

'Take this. Take it.' She stuffed a small plasticky square like a photograph into her hand.

'I can't tell you. It's too late. I can't, Harry, I can't.' She looked up at Malorie with a curdled expression of shame mixed with resentment. Her mother's brain was so addled with the morphine, she was talking to her dead husband.

Malorie looked down at what her mother had thrust into her hand. It was a photograph. A black and white square picture of a house. It seemed familiar but she didn't know why.

'I gave the rest to that nice man.'

'Who? What man?'

'Your nice man. He was always better than me.'

'Who – *Tony?*'

But she seemed to be talking to herself rather than to her daughter.

'He found it easier than I did. It should have been him that carried on. He was better with you than me. He was a good man, Harry. He was a good father.'

'Dad? Did Dad want me to have this, Mother? Why did Dad want me to have it? Have I been here?'

But her mother had slipped back into a morphine-induced stupor.

'Coffee?' Tony was in the doorway with a cup of the vile liquid that passed for coffee at the hospice. At his voice, her mother's eyelids flickered.

'I'll stay with her for a while,' he said. 'You go and have a break.'

'Yes,' she said, 'all right.' In her hand she still had the photograph.

Why hadn't her mother just talked to her after Dad died? Why all the bloody cloak and dagger? So there was some shameful family secret. So what? She didn't care. Her dad was dead. It didn't matter anymore. She could feel herself seething, boiling with a rage that seemed to have no source and no outlet.

Tony had been evasive on the way home. No, her mother hadn't said anything.

'But she said she had. She said she'd given you something.'

'Oh that. It was just some papers, Mal. I haven't looked through them, they're in the suitcase. She was hardly making much sense, was she?' He put his arm around her. 'Now isn't a good time.'

Malorie had sulked, angry at her mother for making her feel bad, angry at her for making her angry. Then her mother had died. And by then, she was consumed with the death of her marriage. The funeral had only been in November, a washed-out, sepia-tinted day. It had been like the negative of a photograph, just the shadows left.

She had felt – what? It was not exactly that she wanted something to fill the emptiness, that was too simple, but the image of that house wouldn't leave her alone. She'd wished her dad had been there to talk to. Her dad had wanted her to have the photograph. It must have had some meaning for him, something that her mother hadn't wanted her to know about. On the back of the photograph in old-fashioned writing, it said *The Marsh House, Stiffkey*. No date. The front showed an awkward, asymmetrical house with a porch in the middle and a gable at one end, a drive curling up to it, the foreground in shadow and dark trees on either side. It was a village on the North Norfolk coast, she knew that, but nothing else. She had no idea what connection – if any – there was to her parents. She'd thought they were both from Norwich. But she could no longer ask them.

In the fogged days after the funeral, she called up an agency that dealt with rental properties. It seemed hardly likely to be available, but she kept trying until she found someone who said yes, it was empty and she could rent it if she really wanted to. The way they'd said it made it sound like madness. At first, she'd only meant to go and have a look, but an idea began to form and to grow until it became everything she wanted. They would go there, for Christmas. They would have a proper family Christmas, she and Franny. She had to do something, something *good*. Away from the grime and grit of London, and the stale, poisoned air of her failed marriage. They would be able to breathe, to stretch, to be together.

She hadn't meant for it to be like this.

She felt a hand on her knee. It was Franny, with the dog in her arms. She looked so alarmed at the sight of her mother, crushed, weepy and broken, sitting in the middle of a country road, that it made Malorie laugh.

'No one's dead,' she said, and a voice in her head whispered, *Yes they are*. But she drew Franny's stiff little body to her and piled them back in. She ignored Franny's mumbling. By the time she'd heaved and shoved the car back on the road, the sky had turned a deep fuchsia pink. 'Look at the colour!' she cried. The house was not much further along the road. The car turned into the lane, and on the left-hand side, the trees rose straight and dark like sentinels. In her imagination, the sunlight filtered through those trees and she'd walk under the branches through a tunnel of bright green light. Near the end of the lane, the house was on the left, the only house. The lane continued on to the marsh. Into her head came an image of the house glowing with light, inviting her in. She leaned forward in her seat, suddenly desperate to see it.

3

The Sampler

There were no lights. It was a dark presence. Malorie had a sudden, crushing sense that she'd made a mistake. The house's many small eyes – she counted eight windows at the front at least – were blinded and in the gloom, the flint and brick face dull and forbidding. It was the time of day, perhaps. A jutting-out porch, concealing the front door, gaped dark like an open mouth. She switched off the engine and nightfall came rushing in. A dog was barking madly from across the lane somewhere. The back of her neck prickled as though she were being watched, and she turned to see who it was. She thought something moved in the trees across the lane. Grabbing her coat, she got out of the car to look, but the trees gave nothing away.

She tried to remember what the man at the agency had said. Was he supposed to meet her here? It was getting dark; soon, it would be even colder. They had to get inside. There must be a key.

'Mummy? What are you doing?'

Franny was standing behind her, with the dog in her arms.

'I need to find the key.'

'Where's the sea?' whined Franny. 'You said it was the seaside.'

'It's nearby,' she said.

Where would it be? Under a doormat? There wasn't one. Next to the door was an old terracotta pot. It would be there. It was – a rusty old key underneath the damp pot. Her shoulders relaxed. It was going to be all right.

The door was a heavy wooden one, with a small grubby window and a tarnished knocker in the shape of an anchor, which gleamed dully in the dying light. The long key stuck slightly in the lock and for a horrible moment she thought it wouldn't turn. The fluttering of panic came again but she made herself breathe out. She tried again. It turned and clicked and the door swung open. It was not much warmer inside. A smell of dust and age wafted over her. There was electricity though, thank God. She flicked the switch and the pale glow of the old-fashioned brass sconces flickered and shone on the worn carpet, low panelling and flowery wallpaper. On a dark-wood side table with ornate legs was an upright telephone with a separate earpiece – like something from an antiques shop. At least they'd entered the twentieth century. But further inspection revealed that the house had got stuck some years before. The ceilings were low and beamed and the wallpaper, densely covered in a pattern of twisting vines with little yellow flowers and green leaves, was peeling at the edges. From the walls came the musty smell of lack of use and damp, and Malorie wondered when the windows had last been opened. She made her way through to the kitchen at the back of the house. It contained ancient cupboards, an old gas range and a cracked butler sink under a small window. The clouded pane looked out onto a long garden and Malorie could tell, even in the gloom, that the marsh was just there, beyond a low wall at the end. Tomorrow, they would go to the marsh. They would walk along the paths by the creeks and see the sleek heads of seals.

'I'm hungry,' said Franny, standing in the kitchen doorway, still holding the dog, whose muzzle was buried in her duffle coat.

Malorie sent her to explore and busied herself lighting the gas oven (she found matches in a drawer and thanked God – or was it the agency? – again) and putting the kettle on the hob. On a shelf above the oven were dusty brown bottles, like the ones you'd find in a chemist's. The liquid inside one was dark and treacly. She picked it up and opened the stopper but it smelt rancid and she quickly put the stopper back in. There was no toaster but she'd brought some sliced bread and she could toast it under the grill. She could cope. But there was no milk and no butter and for a moment, she felt herself waver and rock in the middle of the cold floor.

Their supper was two mugs of black tea and toast with jam but no butter, and there was no coal to make a fire so it was freezing too. Franny made a face at the cup of tea and left it, but she ate the toast, feeding the crusts to the dog who sat begging by her chair.

'Mummy, if we're having Christmas here, we need decorations and a tree.'

Today was what? The twenty-first. Midwinter. Tomorrow was Saturday. All the shops would be shut on Sunday and then it was Christmas Eve. She couldn't bear the thought of attempting anything then. And if Tony did come and there was nothing, the turn in his mouth would be another failure. They would have to go tomorrow.

'And Mummy,' said Franny, 'when's Daddy coming?'

'Soon,' she said.

'Tomorrow?'

'Not tomorrow. Sunday. Or Monday. Soon.' It was only two days before but she could hardly remember what had been said. She'd snatched at his arm but he'd pushed past her. *I need to go. Go then.* And he had. Gone to her, the girl at the club. She wondered how old she was, whether she was the age Malorie had been when she'd met him, a young body unmarked by childbirth. He hadn't come back and she'd lied to Franny, told her he was working.

Franny looked like she would cry. She had grey circles under her eyes. Her daughter had nightmares, and rarely slept through a night.

'Bedtime,' said Malorie with false cheeriness, and took her upstairs. Larry padded up close behind them. The ceilings were low there too, and the landing seemed to curl upwards. The walls on the landing were panelled in dark wood, like the ground floor, but here it went all the way up to the ceiling, which made it feel like being in an upturned boat.

'This is my room,' said Franny, 'I already found it.'

It was a child's room with dusky pink wallpaper and a single bed with a pink-sprigged bedspread. The tiny, low window overlooked the lane.

'Look at this,' she said, and pointed above the bed.

Nailed to the wall was a yellowing sampler, depicting a house with the tufts of marram grass behind and the sea beyond. It was the house they were in, the Marsh House, beautifully stitched in grey for the flint and red for the bricks. Malorie craned to get a closer look and drew in her breath. In front of the house was an image of a strange woman, standing beside a large wolf-like dog with yellow eyes. And next to her was a young girl with long black plaits and tiny green crosses for eyes, holding a small chestnut-brown dog in her arms. On the other side of the house, a short, dark-haired woman with her mouth turned down. At the top, a motto was stitched in red thread: *May I strive for innocence and truth my every action guide. And guard my inexperienced youth from arrogance & pride.*

At the bottom, Malorie read aloud, 'Worked by Rosemary Wright, aged eight.'

She thought of her fair, plump father and it seemed a stretch to think these people were any relation of his. But she tried to tamp down the initial disappointment. The connection to the house could be anything. He could have worked here, he could have been a friend. There had to be something.

Franny had a curious smile on her face. 'She was my age. And she had a dog like Larry too. It's this house, isn't it?'

'Yes, it must be,' said Malorie, relieved at least that Franny seemed happier.

Franny didn't complain about brushing her teeth or her long hair. She took the pill for her nerves without complaint, and went to bed clutching her teddy bear, Frederick, quite compliant. She had Malorie's colouring: wan with dark hair that looked copper when the light caught it. People always commented on the two of them together – 'Oh, she's a spit,' and so on. But it wasn't really true, it was just the hair that tricked people, and the winter-sallow skin which turned a muddy brown in the summer. In reality, Malorie had sludgy-grey eyes and small features in a round face that made her look childish, and her hair was dull and dead straight. She had it backcombed up and pinned on the top, but it was hard to do anything with it. People always thought she was younger than she was, but her daughter looked older than her years. Franny's eyes were green and searching and there was a frown-crease between her eyebrows that Malorie wished she could wipe away.

Larry was curled up in a ball of cream fur at the end of the narrow bed. At least Franny had the dog for company, and for warmth.

On her own in the kitchen she opened a bottle of sherry she'd brought for Christmas, poured herself a glass then sat, huddled in the fur coat Tony had bought her, drinking the sherry and chain-smoking the last of her Rothmans. The small window reflected the kitchen lamplight back at her. Beyond it was darkness, the emptiness of the countryside, only the house between her daughter and all that lay beyond. The vastness of the unknown – her isolation – she felt as something physical, a great crushing embrace of darkness, and she had to rest her head on the table. She imagined reaching into her handbag for the Luminal the doctor had prescribed, swallowing one down with a draught of sherry. The ease of it, the relief. But she'd forced herself to stop all that. She'd begun reaching for them too much, needing them, sinking back down into the stupor she'd been in when Franny was small.

A few years ago, when she was diagnosed with 'nerve strain', the doctor had assumed it was her father's death that had been the catalyst but it went back further than that. She simply did not have the gift of happiness. She was afraid that if she started taking them again, she'd never stop. She was too tired to move from the kitchen, too tired for anything, and after three glasses of the sickly sherry, she was even too tired to drink. Maybe she'd be able to sleep tonight after the long drive.

The back of her neck tingled. There was something – just out of her hearing – that she couldn't quite place. She held herself still and closed her eyes; strained all her other senses. Nothing. It was deathly quiet, that was all. She was so unused to the country, it was unnerving. If she concentrated very hard she could just hear the creaks of the walls as they shifted and settled and a faint wind breathing in and out of the chimneys. Then a scratch; a thin, scratching sound coming from above. Mice.

In the bedroom at the back of the house, Malorie rubbed her feet together in the lumpy cold bed and tried to dig into the scratchy sheets to gain some warmth. There was another, larger room – she'd opened the door to see – but decorating cloths covered the furniture and what light there was didn't seem to penetrate it. It felt more like a funeral parlour than a bedroom so she'd taken this east-facing one instead. Eventually she gave up trying to warm her frozen feet and found a pair of socks to wear and a heavy wool blanket to cover herself with. It was not so bad. They were here. They'd made it. If they could have this one thing, a family Christmas, it would be all right. It would be different in the morning. Tomorrow would be better.

That night she was woken from a dream where the figures in the picture were alive and their faces changed into hers and Franny's. She and Franny walked in the dream down to the marsh.

A gull cawed and woke her. Her feet were cold again. The curtains were white and thin and the shimmer of the moon gave them a glassy sheen. There was a noise in the dark, like a child crying. It must be the gulls in the dream; she was still half asleep. There it was again. The window banged against its frame. It was the wind. She closed her eyes, tried to sink back into sleep, but the sound came again and then she was awake, sat upright. It must be Franny. Clutching her dressing gown tight around her, she crept out. On the landing, she paused: the crying had stopped. But she should check anyway. She opened the door and stepped in. The moonlight was stronger in here and gave a surreal quality to the room, like a room in a painting of a dream. Franny and Larry were both asleep but her daughter was twisting in the bed, moaning. This was what she must have heard. As she turned to go, her eyes were drawn to the strange sampler above the bed. It was half-lit by the moonlight. A cloud must have passed over the moon because a shadow crossed the cloth and the figures almost appeared to move. Then the moon was blocked again and the room was returned to shadow. She shivered and rubbed her eyes.

Back in the chill of the empty bed, Malorie couldn't sleep. The wind had dropped and now she could hear a rustling from above. It was probably the mice again. The old woman in the sampler flickered across her brain. As her mind reached for stillness and quiet, all she could see was the large black dog with the stitched yellow crosses for eyes, like a creature from a nightmare.

4

Temperature was dropping. You could see it in the birds'
puffed-up feathers, in the scurrying of the squirrels, and in
the rats, scuttling for warmth in the rafters of the house.
She wouldn't like that, I'm thinking. All them nasty, bloated
city rats give a person funny ideas about animals. Our rats
are small and black, not like those fearsome beaver rats
what escaped from the fur farm running mad over Norfolk,
they're little and harmless. Mostly, anyway.

5

Stiffkey

22nd December

Through the ice-crusted window, Malorie could see there was nothing but a thick grey mist. She pressed her forehead against the pane and closed her eyes. Her throat was sore and at the back of her head was a dull ache. She must not succumb to despair. After scraping at the ice on the window with her fingernails, she wiped a patch of condensation with the sleeve of her dressing gown and peered through the smear of wet droplets. Across the lane from the house and sunk in the mist, there were the shadows of trees, but apart from that it seemed deserted. Around the edge of the garden, the black arms of bare trees and a dark clump of firs. The mist merged with a dull sky and nothing else was visible. She'd imagined flinging open the window onto a sparkling view of the sea but it might as well not have been there. She cranked open the old window and sniffed the air. Yes, the sea was near all right. There was a faint tang of salt and a wet smell of damp earth and something else sharp that she couldn't name. Opening her mouth she tried to suck it in and swallowed a mouthful of moisture and seasalt. A low black shape moved in the distance along the lane. Was it the dog she'd heard last night? A taller figure moved behind the animal. A brown, stout person in some kind of hat. She wanted to call out but a gust of wind slammed the window shut and she jumped back. It only just missed smacking into her nose. When she looked again, the figure and the animal were gone.

From downstairs came the sound of Franny crooning to her dog. Her poor, lonely girl. It had been Tony's idea to buy Franny a pet, and Malorie, unused to animals, had resisted. But now she was glad. The little dog was the only being Franny warmed to. Malorie had a memory of her daughter thrashing in her sleep but wasn't sure if she'd dreamed it. She should try to find some friends for her. There must be village children. But she already knew this was hopeless – the idea of her silent little girl making friends with anyone was laughable. At the school in London they said she was 'shy' and 'well behaved'. She 'keeps herself to herself'. She'd felt as if their eyes contained a rebuke for not producing a happy, carefree child, for leaving Franny without siblings; their mouths set hard against her as a parent, that her daughter was strange and it was her fault. Tony told her she was being ridiculous; no one thought that. But she didn't trust anything he said to her.

The argument repeated itself. Another child, another baby. But she'd been ill, she couldn't cope, her father died. There was always something. And then, she began to suspect he was sleeping with other women. She had withdrawn even further into her private hurt. It was too late now.

'I might go to Norfolk for Christmas,' she'd said. He hadn't cared. He'd stopped listening to her years before. He'd care now, she thought.

She tried to picture his face when he found the flat empty and his daughter gone. It gave her a nasty bubble of pleasure. He would mind about Franny. Well, sod him. She saw him revving the engine of his Austin and speeding off back to the flat above the club. And the curvaceous body of Barbara. He would call her *Babs*, the way he called her *Mal*. Babs's beautiful body. She put her hands to her forehead and squeezed. This was no good. She shouldn't think about it.

And she was here now, wasn't she? She'd done it. Got out of London. Away from him and his blatant lies, from the empty flat and the pills. It wasn't at all how she'd imagined, but nothing was. Not her marriage, motherhood, her work (what work? There was no work. All her secretarial contacts had faded away since Franny). Her parents, both now dead. Her daughter. All of it had ended up somehow wrong. Defective. Broken. She drove her nails into her palms to staunch the flow of inky blackness cascading through her head. She would not take a pill. She would not. The window banged and she started. She hadn't put the catch back on.

Never mind the mist and the cold, they would take Larry for a walk down to the sea.

She dressed quickly in the freezing room, thinking of how they'd need food supplies and coal for the fire and how she should have thought of all of this before she'd piled them into the car in London. On the landing she hesitated. There was something about the night that she only half remembered. She looked into the pink bedroom but neither Franny nor the dog were there. Above the bed, the odd sampler. There was the severe woman, there was the old lady with the fierce-looking dog and there was the little girl with the plaits holding a book. Malorie's head hurt. She squeezed her eyes shut. It was just a creepy old picture. She needed a cup of tea.

On the right of the hallway as she came down the stairs was the living room, on the left, an empty room. The door to the living room was ajar and inside she found Franny curled up on a tatty old sofa, swaddled in blankets, reading a book, with Larry at her feet.

Franny looked up at her with reproach. 'I'm hungry.'

'Right, darling, yes I'm sure you are. What time is it?'

Franny shrugged.

'Mummy,' she said, 'what about a Christmas tree? We have to get a tree. Daddy would get me a tree.' In London, they had a small fake tree that Tony had bought in Harrods. It had been stupidly expensive but Franny loved it. Malorie knew his family had always had huge, real trees but he said they couldn't fit one into their little flat so this was the next best thing. Her parents, in their Norwich suburb, had always thought the tree they'd bought from Woolworths was perfectly good enough, thank you. Malorie had always wanted a real one. It was part of her vision of a perfect life. In her childhood books, children gathered around a towering, glittering tree. She somehow felt that if she could achieve this image – of them sat round the Christmas fir in their dressing gowns, the children's stockings over the fire – then she would have created something good. For this vision, she had to have a real tree. That was it: she could cut one down. There were loads of firs along the edge of the property. No one would notice if she chopped down a baby one.

'Mummy?'

'I'll get you a tree,' she said, smiling.

The kitchen was at the back of the house, cold on the flagstone floor, even through her socks and slippers. The clock on the wall said nine o'clock. Time stretched and warped here: she had somehow slept in. Larry followed her through, whining, and she opened the back door to let him out. The air was heavy and damp with the mist. At the threshold, the little dog bristled and hesitated, uncertain about the grey-shrouded garden, but Malorie gave him a shove with her foot. Outside, he began to bark. He seemed to be barking at the hedge and while she was looking at it, something dark slunk along the bottom. She caught a glimpse of a long tail – a rat – and shuddered. She doubted Larry would do much about it but she shooed him further out into the garden anyway, relieved that he was here.

Back in the living room, with two more mugs of black tea and toast with jam but no butter ('I'll buy some today, Franny, I promise'), she remembered the lack of a fire. She swallowed down the sob rising in her throat and washed down the bitter tea with a mouthful of strawberry jam.

As they were putting their coats on, the ancient-looking phone rang out in the hall, startling them both. Her first thought was Tony, and her heart leapt. He was going to say sorry, he'd made a mistake, he loved her. But she hadn't left a phone number, she didn't even have one. He had no idea where they were. The phone kept ringing, echoing around them, mocking her.

'Are you going to answer it?'

'Yes, yes,' she said, unhappily. She put the earpiece to her ear. 'Hello?' There was a knocking sound at the other end. 'Hello?' she said again, but the knocking sound was replaced with the monotonous dialling tone. 'It must be a bad line,' she said, and replaced the earpiece on the stand.

It was warmer outside, though the frost crackled under their feet and their breath blew white in the air. Through the frost, weeds poked, and in the thin misty, winter daylight she could see that there were tiles missing from the roof and cracks in some of the windows. The pale grey flint blended with the mist and it seemed as if the house had somehow grown here organically. She looked up at it from the same vantage point as the photographer must have done. But the photograph appeared to have been taken in the summer and the neglect, if it were visible then, had been disguised by the glow of sunlight. Now the house revealed the extent of its dilapidation. There was broken guttering, with weeds growing out of it. The bricks crumbled like flaky skin. One of the windowpanes was cracked, the wood of the frames speckled black with rot. It needed light and warmth and people. Not the dead of winter.

She glanced at the hideous car. The vivid orange had appealed at first. Why not? It looked jaunty and fun in London. But it was incongruous here, like something from a modern, gaudy world thrust into an old one. And the dent looked worse in the day – an ugly mark of something wrong. The car windows were thick with frost. She should wipe it down, scrape off the ice. But how far was the village? It couldn't be far. The dog needed a walk, and she needed more cigarettes on top of everything else. She felt inside her purse with pink-cold fingers. She had the week's housekeeping money and some left over from last week. It would have to do.

'Come on, Fran, we're going to walk into the village and get our Christmas supplies. It'll be an adventure.' She could ask in the village if anyone had known her father.

Franny squeezed her forehead in a frown but nodded. She was not lazy, you could say that.

As they were leaving, Malorie heard the same howl of a wolf from across the road. It must be the dog she'd seen earlier that morning, and if it was a dog there must be someone living there. Crossing the lane, she remembered the figure in the sampler with the wolf-like dog and half expected to see an old woman and a black dog emerging from the trees. It didn't look like there was anything there, just a dense, high hedge of knotted ivy and hawthorn. But then she saw there was a gap in the hedge, a small iron gate overgrown with ivy, and a narrow path that led to a squat brick single-storey dwelling, more of a hovel than a cottage, with a roof hunched so low it looked as if it would collapse in on itself. There was no sign of life or light through the thick, dark grime on the small window. Yet something about it made her want to turn around immediately and rush away. Its misshapen, lumpen form seemed to be scowling at her. She tried to laugh.

'*Mum.*' It was Franny, bored of waiting.

Malorie finally turned her back on the cottage. She was strangely relieved when they were out of sight of it down the lane.

At the end of the muddy lane a flint and brick wall appeared on the left, and behind it there was an old disused chapel from early in the century. The broken glass windows stared blankly. The mist kept low for the entire walk to the village. They trudged along the road that linked the village with Wells on one side and Blakeney on the other, dissecting the village between marsh and field, and only the dull brown of the low winter hedges gave any colour to the day. It was a respite to get to the village and see something other than the relentless grey-white mist. The village seemed to consist of an old whitewashed pub called the Townsend Arms and further along, on a little street just before a bridge over a low river, a shop that also functioned as a Post Office, judging by the sign outside. Stiffkey General Store and, underneath, a smaller sign that read Prop. G. Bayfield. In the leaded bay window of the shop, old boxes of Persil and packets of Bovril were stacked neatly, faded to pastel colours from years on display, under enamel signs for Fry's Chocolate and Capstan cigarettes. It was like a shop from the sodding war. From before the sodding war. The bell rang as they entered and there was a fluster of crashing and a voice shouted, 'Coming!' from the back. Out of the rear emerged a red-faced young woman of about Malorie's age, though it was hard to tell as she was wearing a blue headscarf and her brown hair was curled in what Malorie thought of as an old-fashioned style. Poor thing, stuck out here.

'Oh!' said the girl, her full mouth in an oval of surprise. 'I thought you were someone else. You must be the visitors with the orange car. What can I get for you?'

Malorie suddenly felt the stupidity of what she was trying to do. What would she do when the housekeeping ran out? Ask Tony for more? A bubble of panic tightened her chest and she had to breathe out and compose herself before she spoke. She consulted the list she'd hastily made that morning and the pretty girl (Malorie decided she was younger than she was, it was the get-up that made her look older) worked through it, slicing and cutting and stacking up tins. There was a tiny meat and cheese counter and Malorie bought a few slices. There was no Stilton, only Cheddar and Red Leicester but that would do. There was no ham or pâté, only luncheon meat, and the bread was rock hard. But they had some margarine and fatty-looking sausages, some dirty carrots and potatoes and the girl said she'd ask her father about a turkey or a goose. She disappeared out the back of the shop. In the gloom, Malorie could just about make out a short man with a cap and a gruff voice with the slow rhythm of Norfolk. In front of the counter, Franny stood sullenly next to her, scuffing her shoes on the sawdust floor.

'He'll see about killing one for you,' the shop girl said, returning from a door at the back. Malorie winced at the thought. She prayed the man would pluck it as well. It wasn't something she could face. Franny sniffed loudly.

'Blow your nose,' Malorie said under her breath, thrusting a hanky at her.

The shop girl leaned over the counter and said kindly, 'What's your name then? What about some cochies. Would you like some?'

Franny peered up at her and said, 'Frances,' very quietly. The young woman chuckled and got up on her ladder to fetch the sweet jars down from the top shelves. She handed Franny a barley sugar and then put a handful of other sweets in a cone twist.

'Thank you,' her daughter said to the shop girl, then to Malorie, 'Can I go outside?'

She waved her out.

The girl was wrapping the last of the 'provisions' in paper. Malorie realised there was no point asking the girl whether she'd known a Harry Skinner – she was too young – but she wanted to ask her about the house and if there was a woman living in the cottage with a large dog. She was framing the words when the girl spoke.

'You're up at the Marsh House, aren't you? There aren't been anyone living there since before I was born. Mother says it's a rum place. All kinds of funny things going on up there.'

Malorie was going to ask – what things? But the girl laughed at her expression.

'Ah, it's all tales, I reckon. People round here love a story. You hear her last night? She was wailing something rotten.'

'Hear who? I think the wind woke me up, but I went back to sleep.'

'Weren't no wind. That was the lost girl. Girl that got stuck out in the roke.'

'The roke?'

'Fog. Sea mist. She screams louder when the roke's in.'

'Who does?'

'The girl. Nancy her name was. My mum says she was out cockling with the others far out on the Blacknock sandbank on the Freshes – best place for Stewkey Blues – when the roke came in and she got separated. Mud's treacherous out there. Tide had turned, you see. She started to scream. All the fishermen, all of the village folk heard her blarring but no one could find her in the fog and the mud. Body was found the next day, seaweed in her open mouth.'

'That's horrible.'

Malorie had hardly understood half of the words the girl used but she felt the grimness of the story. She thought about the strange noises in the night and felt goosebumps prickle on her skin. It had been the *wind*, she wanted to say to her.

'Anyone told you about what happened at that house yet?'

'No,' said Malorie. The girl was annoying her. Why didn't she just spit it out?

'Yeah, probably all nonsense, but my dad says there was people what died there.'

Malorie smiled to herself. For God's sake, people died everywhere.

'Thank you for all of this,' she said, shaking herself out of this conversation. 'I'd better be going. And the turkey or the goose . . . I don't think my husband will be able—'

'Dad'll come round with something day after tomorrow. Christmas Eve. He can slaughter one today. He'll be round Christmas Eve.'

'Thank you,' she said. 'And I forgot to ask about coal or logs. I'm so sorry.'

The girl nodded. 'We'll see what we can do and drop some round. Right cold it is.'

She should go now but she had one more question. 'Can I ask – is there an old woman with a black dog who lives on the lane?'

The girl laughed again. 'Maybe it were Black Shuck,' she said, rolling her eyes comically. 'No, I'm only kidding. I wouldn't worry about that old one if I were you. She's always been around here. Belongs to the place, you see.'

Malorie didn't see, but Franny was waiting outside.

The bell rang as they left the shop and the girl called out, 'Snow's coming though. Do you watch out!'

As the three of them – Malorie, Franny and the dog – walked away from the shop and the village, she felt her back tingle with the gaze of the girl. She was relieved to get away. It wasn't fair but she was fighting against an uncomfortable sense of revulsion towards the girl. And with all the talk of *black shuck* and *roke* and hideous noises in the night, she'd forgotten to ask about the figures on the sampler.

She tore open the first of the two packets of cigarettes she'd bought and smoked one, inhaling the smoke deep into her lungs as they walked, adding her own curls of grey to the mist.

6

I was back at the stove when they returned. They looked lost. Especially her, the mother. There was something wrong with her. She didn't look like a grown woman, though I knew she must be with the child how old she was. She looked sort of stunted, like a tree that's not had enough light and air. Something'd got hold of her and stuck her in the city where she couldn't breathe. The child though, the child was sharp. She heard what the girl didn't tell her, she saw what she wasn't supposed to see. It was the mother who was looking for something but it was the daughter who'd find it. I wondered how long it would take her.

7

The Attic

When they got back to the house there was a small pile of cut logs by the front door. Malorie didn't understand how the grocer could have got here so quickly. There'd only been a couple of cars on the road, but it could have been him. She looked across the lane expecting someone to be watching but there was no one out there, just the dark hedge. Still, it was a relief to have the logs.

In the kitchen, she put her transistor on the windowsill and fiddled with the tuning knobs through the frequencies. Snatches of the shipping forecast broke through the static then disappeared again. Bells chimed, a Christmas carol burst through the hiss and faded away. Then a man's voice, suddenly loud and serious in the kitchen.

Snow is expected in most parts of Britain. Falls are likely to be moderate or heavy in Eastern regions with strong to gale-force easterly winds. Widespread frost is expected tonight.

The girl was right. It could be a White Christmas. Her heart jolted. It would be magical – a Christmas Franny would remember forever.

After a meagre lunch of yesterday's bread spread with margarine and some of the cheese and luncheon meat from the village shop, Franny disappeared to the pink bedroom, Larry close behind. Malorie set about finally stoking the fire into life. The cold was becoming unbearable and the two of them were each wearing a vest, a blouse and two jumpers. She managed to coax some pale, weak flames that gave off no warmth.

If Tony were here, he could have at least *helped* her make a fire – but the thought of that was quite absurd. Tony Cavendish had never laid a fire in his life – he had people to do that for him. And her parents had always had a gas fire. She was just going to have to do it on her own.

Flames were finally licking the wood, smoke was rising and Malorie was holding her hands to the faint warmth, when Franny came in. 'Mummy, I found a secret door.'

She followed her up to the landing. There was a little door in the panelling at the end of the landing that Malorie hadn't registered before. She must have looked at that wall several times and missed it. The door opened onto another narrow, winding staircase and Franny disappeared up this. She stood looking at the bottom of the stairs that led up to darkness, remembering the sound of rodents scuttling the night before.

'Come on, Mummy, come up!' came Franny's voice from above.

Crouching, Malorie squeezed up the tiny staircase. Her head came out into the low attic of the house, dim and dusty but neatly piled with old trunks. She listened carefully but couldn't hear any scraping or rustling. Her eyes fell on a wooden cot, the white paint peeling.

'Over here,' said Franny, and Malorie snapped out of her daze. She followed her daughter to the middle of the attic where you could see the misty sky through the cracks in the roof. Franny was digging in an open trunk. 'These are pretty.' On a bed of straw nestled beautiful tree decorations of angels and stars and apples and lanterns. Even in the dim light they shone, and where they caught the thin misty rays from outside they glittered.

Malorie picked up each piece and held it in the palm of her hand, feeling the delicacy of each one in wonder. They were made of fragile glass and painted in glorious bright colours of green and gold and red.

From another trunk Franny drew out a wooden box carved in an intricate leaf pattern. 'Look!' she said. Malorie itched to grab it from her and open it but she made herself wait. When Franny passed it to her, Malorie gasped in delight. Inside was an entire nativity scene made of wood, tiny and delicately carved, each feature carefully scored. There was a wooden Mary, a Joseph with a beard, and a baby Jesus the size of her smallest fingernail. There was a sheep and a donkey and a cow and a cradle with wisps of real straw and of course a stable, as lovingly carved as everything else. It was perfect.

'Mummy, look at this. Look what I've found!' Franny spoke from the other end of the attic, where she was tucked under the low slope of the eave. Malorie had been so intent on the nativity scene that she hadn't even been aware of where her daughter had gone. There was an enthusiasm in Franny's voice that she hadn't heard for a long time.

Sideways and bent-backed, Malorie edged along the attic and saw that she was holding up a piece of paper. It was a cutting from an old newspaper with brown, curled edges.

'Look,' said Franny again. 'It's the girl, it's the girl in the picture. Rosemary.'

Malorie took it out of Franny's hand. The cutting showed a photograph of a young woman staring into the camera, hair tucked under an ugly cloche hat and dark smudges around her eyes. It was a mug shot, Malorie thought, a defiant stare at whoever was taking the photograph – at the world. Underneath, the caption said *Rosemary Wright aged 19*, but there was no corresponding newspaper report. The girl's eyes seemed to look into her own as if she knew her.

'Where did you find this?'

'In here.'

It was a small, beaten-up, brown leather suitcase. Inside it was empty apart from a mess of paper, but behind the elasticated cotton pouch for underwear, Malorie thought there was the shadow of something. She stayed silent. 'I wonder what happened to her,' said Franny. From downstairs came the sound of Larry barking.

'You make a start taking these Christmas things down,' she told Franny. 'And go and see if Larry's all right. I'll be down in a minute.'

Being in this attic full of other people's history was like rooting around in someone else's memories. She realised she wanted to be on her own with the suitcase. To afford it a kind of privacy.

She quickly rifled through the paper. At first it was disappointing – nothing but old bills of sale, advertisements for political meetings, a few pamphlets on aged yellow or faded pinky-red paper saying things like *BRITONS AWAKE!* and *TRADES UNIONS – YOU ARE THE VICTIMS*. The dates were all in the early thirties. It was creepy. A little flash of insight into how fascists used to think. All that felt like ancient history now. He was still carping on though, Mosley – he'd been out that summer in London. She remembered seeing it on television. *MOSLEY SPEAKS* said the banners. He'd been knocked to the ground, all the stuffing knocked out of him. 'They cried Down With Mosley and down he went,' said the newsreader. This was his heyday though, the thirties. He'd been on the up then.

But she didn't really care about Mosley, he was on the way down now. If the people who lived here had supported him, that was unfortunate, but British people had rejected fascism, it was in the past.

Behind her, at the other end of the attic, she could hear the rustling of mice – or was it rats? She remembered the rat she'd seen, and prayed it didn't appear. She shoved her hand into the underwear pouch expecting more of the same. But she touched something different; hard-edged.

It was a book of some kind. A sheaf of high-quality paper, with a dark red, stiff leather cover, not much bigger than her hand, held together with hard brass tacks, with the name *Rosemary Wright* embossed in gilt on the front. It seemed to be handmade. At least it wasn't more fascist nonsense. Malorie opened it. There were pages of almost-illegible handwriting in black ink. She flicked through the pages with jittery fingers, feeling like a voyeur into someone else's life, then shut the book and thrust her hand back in the pouch. With a small lurch she felt the outline of another slim, red volume. The mug shot of the girl from the newspaper. Something had happened to her. And it was unlikely, but there might be some clue here to help her find out what it was her father had wanted her to know.

The attic space seemed to be waiting to see what she would do. There was only the quiet scraping sound. *I'm just borrowing it*, she thought and, gripping hold of the suitcase handle, descended the stairs quickly, banging the suitcase on the steps, before any animals emerged from their hiding places.

Franny had laid some of the decorations out on the wooden floor and they sparkled in the firelight like treasure found in a cave. With Franny and Larry curled up in front of the fire, the glow of the flames lighting her daughter's face and warmth in all their bones at last, she felt that perhaps it had been right to bring her here after all.

Malorie sat awake in the gloomy bedroom. Although she'd filled two hot-water bottles for them to warm the beds, the fire had long since died out, her bottle gone cold and she couldn't sleep. She listened out for Franny's night wakings or the screaming cockler, but it was still and quiet. She switched on a lamp and opened her library book. It was a modern novel called *Marnie* and was quite thrilling. Marnie was a bad girl, a liar and a thief with multiple identities – and troubled. She liked her. But tonight, she couldn't read. It felt too much like her own life, without the crime. Instead, she took the notebooks out from under her pillow and flicked through the pages of the first. Inside, written in black ink in large, cursive script: *The Journal of Rosemary Wright.*

But someone had obviously ripped out the first few pages of the journal. Malorie sank down into the bed. She was strangely disappointed. Then she turned the page and in the same handwriting but much smaller, more cramped, the girl had written *Holloway, London. March 1935. An account of the events of the period July 1931 to August 1934.*

Malorie did a quick calculation. She had no idea how old her father had been when she was born – he'd always been the same gentle man with the creases around his eyes. He'd been in the war – that was what had caused the heart attack according to her mother. *He never got over it.* So he must have been a young man in the 1930s. It was conceivable, then, that he could feature in this journal. Her pulse quickened.

It was a kind of diary. She flicked through the pages then opened the second notebook. This too was embossed with the name *Rosemary Wright* in gold-coloured script and full of the same cramped, black script. Pages upon pages filled with inky handwriting. She hesitated. Was it wrong to read someone else's personal journal? But it was a long time ago and the compulsion to escape into someone else's life – a real one – was too strong. She'd just skim it and if it was boring or salacious or too private – or if it had nothing whatsoever to do with her family – she'd stop. She started at the beginning.

THE FIRST NOTEBOOK

THE JOURNAL OF ROSEMARY WRIGHT
Private and Confidential

Holloway, London. March 1935

An account of the events of the period
July 1931 to August 1934

8

I will try to set down as faithfully as I can what has led me to this cell. I asked for these notebooks to be sent to me as soon as I was brought here but they've only just arrived. I think it's because they've begun softening towards me. I intend to fill the books with my story so if you ever read this, you will be able to understand it from my point of view and make up your mind about me, regardless of what the newspapers and gossip-mongers say. I always rather liked the idea of writing and now I finally have the chance. I suppose there is the vanity of leaving something behind. I don't intend for this to be a diary. This happened, then this did. Instead, I want to give you a sense of how it really was.

I was going to start with the arrival of the Lafferty family in the village because that was what changed everything, but I've decided I need to tell you about my family first, because how will you understand me otherwise?

All my life I lived there, on the marsh, in the house Father built for my mother, but by then it was only us: my dog, Perdita (shortened to Perdie, although Mrs Fairbrother called her Pesky and kicked her when she went near the kitchen) and the gardener, Rogers, who had been there forever, waging a running war with the rats that came off the marsh. Janey always said he was here when Mother came, as was plump old Fairbrother, who was as severe with me as she was with my dog.

Nearly four years ago, on my birthday, my father gave me a set of three leather-bound blood-red notebooks. I never wrote in them apart from childish scribbles and a number of beginnings of detective stories. I was obsessed with the novels of Mrs Agatha Christie. How my young self would be agog to see me now. The writer and main character of my very own mystery tale.

I was disappointed with the notebooks at first because I wanted a copy of The Murder at the Vicarage but Father said it wasn't suitable reading. This was utter nonsense because I'd already read The Murder of Roger Ackroyd, The Mystery of the Blue Train and The Mysterious Affair at Styles. I borrowed them from the library in Wells and hid them from him. His idea of a good book was Walter Scott or Trollope or another man who wrote long novels with a lot of characters and lots of morals. He thought Mrs Christie or Dorothy L. Sayers were 'for women'. For someone who prints words for a living he didn't really like proper stories at all. But he said as I was constantly stealing his papers for my scribbles, I was to have books of my own with which to do what I wanted. I liked the way they looked all together, the dark spines hiding the blank pages, waiting for me to fill them with ink.

That birthday I was fifteen, and my body was changing although I didn't want it to. My monthlies had started but no one knew. They were an ugly ache in my belly and sheets I washed myself and no one, not even Janey to tell, though she discovered it quickly enough. If my mother were there I could have told her. My birthday often made me feel melancholy when I thought of her. They told me she died of tuberculosis when I was an infant, but I knew it wasn't true. Sometimes I heard them talking about 'Mistress' and it made me think she wasn't dead but hidden somewhere.

I can't remember her at all. No, that's not entirely true. I have one memory – it's of us sitting on the sand in bright sunlight. I can feel the sand between my toes. My mother hands me a shell and I hold it in my tiny hand. At least, I think it's a memory. I might have imagined it.

Another memory, a more recent one: once, not long before the events of this account, I overheard Fairbrother tell Rogers that the master was going to Norwich on business. The printing press is in Cromer so that was a clue that it was something other than usual.

'Mistress Louisa business, I reckons,' she said.

I was in the chestnut tree, which was in full leaf and covered in soft yellow catkins and a good hiding spot. I gripped hard on the bark of the tree and it cut into the palm of my hand, but I couldn't call out or otherwise they'd see me and I'd be in trouble for spying. Louisa was my mother's name. Father said when I pressed him that I'm named for his mother, Marie, and for my mother. Rosemary Louisa Wright. I like to think that my mother gave me the name Rosemary, as her way of trying to steer my fate away from my father's. She must have known by then what kind of man he was. And Janey told me it means the dew of the sea, and I always liked that too.

'Reckon so,' said Rogers, but he didn't look up from his digging.

I don't think Fairbrother was very happy with that because she stomped off back to the house.

As soon as they were out of sight, I shinned down the tree and ran over to knock on Janey's door, Perdie trotting after me on her short little legs. Janey was our only neighbour, and the only person in the world who cared for me. Janey's cottage was smaller, darker and damper than ours. Where the Marsh House was winding and confusing, full of little rooms and wood panelling on all the walls, Janey's cottage was squat, sunk down and hidden by a line of thick trees, just one main downstairs room where she ate and cooked and slept, and the privy out the back of her garden, down by the marsh. It was crammed full of bottles of various sizes, herbs hanging from the rafters, chipped crockery and straw dolls she made from the marsh reeds. The air was always moist with the salt vapours or whatever she had cooking on her old range. There were always animals – her black dog, Smutch, frogs (she called them hopp'n toads) in the pond, the white mice she laughingly called her imps and the bees in the hive. It was cleaned rigorously but the animal hair, the marsh mud and the salt would get in anyway. There were so many books higgledy-piggledy you couldn't see the floor. The whole building was ramshackle, warm and stunk to high heaven, like Janey herself. I loved it.

I asked her straight off, what had happened to my mother and she said, 'I don't right as know if yer father wants you knowing but I see you knows suffin already. She were awful fierce after she had you, Rosie, and she weren't never right after that. I had to take you on meself for a time.'* That's how she talked.

*I know I can't remember all the words people said so you'll just have to believe me that it was something like this.

'Fierce how?' I asked, determined to get an answer.

'Frazzled is how. It were like she had a misery in the head. And I couldn't help her, no matter what I did.'

'But if she didn't die, where is she?'

'That I can't tell you,' said Janey and she put her old hand on my head. 'But don't you go blaming yerself for any of it. It weren't nothing to do with you. It were a bad birth thass all.'

But what she said made me think it had been my fault that my mother had become unwell, that it had been my birth that had made her sick. Janey had delivered me, hadn't she? She'd told me the story many times – of the 'filthy tempest' that night and the doctor being called but him not arriving in time. She said I'd been stuck and Mother lost a lot of blood and when I came out I'd not made a sound. She and Fairbrother, who'd come to help too, had thought I was dead.

I still ask myself, what really happened to her to get her sent away? The children at the village school used to taunt me, saying that she'd gone to a madhouse.

Another memory, from early on that summer. I was scuffing my boots down the street towards our lane, when coming the other way were a group of children from the school. One in particular, the ringleader of their grubby gang, a wiry mean-faced boy called George with pretty curls, always sneered when he saw me.

I remembered him from my long-gone school days. George Bayfield hated me. And I him. So when I saw him and his gang, I began to run.

'There she is,' he said, pointing at me, 'the mad marsh girl. Where's your ma, Mad Mary?'

Another of the children, a snot-nosed little girl, chanted back, 'In the madhouse, that's where she is.'

I didn't slow down. I kept running at full pelt towards them, heart banging hard with excitement, and as I drew up level with the boy, he drew back from me as if I were a scythe come to cut him down. And I was. I came at him with my fists clenched, and would have punched him right in the jaw if he hadn't veered away just in time. My fist caught the end of his chin, and at the same time, someone else grabbed one of my plaits and yanked me back until I was lying on the hard road. Above me the sky was a clear dome of pale blue. Then into the blue dome came a ring of dark heads. They had made a circle around me and were peering at me like I was a strange creature from the bog. At first I thought they would throw stones at me or poke me with sticks and I steeled myself to jump at them, snarling. But they whispered between themselves and held back. Someone spat near my head, then the ring expanded and they began to skulk off. I raised myself onto my elbows. They were at the edges of the street now, each of them a safe few feet away. Apart from one. The grocer's boy, George.

He was hovering a foot from my head and suddenly darted forward and hissed in my ear –

'I'll get you, you mad witch!'

But before he could get away, I snatched his hand.

'No you won't,' I said. I dug my nails hard in and he yelped in pain like a dog.

I let his hand go and he sprang back, glaring at me.

'You can't even catch me,' I said. And I flew home, not looking back, exultant and hurt all at once, cut off from the rest of the world.

Why didn't I ask my father about her? I did when I was younger.

Once, in a dark rage I yelled at him, 'The children say Mother is in a madhouse!'

A dark look of anguish crossed his face but he said calmly, as if with great restraint, 'Your mother is dead, Rosemary. The sooner you accept that, the better it will be for you.' Then he turned away.

So you can see that before it all began – the events that led to me being here – before all of that, I was almost alone in the world. I had my dog, Perdie, I had Janey. That was all. Father wasn't cruel to me, but neither was he much bothered about me. When I was younger he'd sent me to the village school, but by then I hadn't gone for an age. No one liked me there and I didn't like them. They thought I was snooty and strange. They used to call me 'Marsh Girl' which was true enough. I had a governess, Miss Cannadine, for a while. I liked her and she was sweet to me, but she left all of a sudden because of an accident, according to Father. I cried and cried when she left. Periodically, he'd threaten to send me away to school but he never did. I don't think he had enough money. Either way, by my fifteenth birthday, I'd been rather forgotten about.

My days were spent exploring, reading or with Janey. Janey used to call me her 'Wild Rose' and I suppose I was. I had no lessons, I barely did any chores and there was no one to supervise me. I could read and write passably because of my early, tormented days at the school – and because sweet Miss Cannadine used to force me to study my letters – but I was appalling at sums. Sometimes I would run into the house and startle Father, and he would peer at me as if disgusted by the feral child who lived in his house. 'You look like a half-breed,' he'd say, or he'd call me a wild animal. He'd shout for Fairbrother who'd try to take a comb to my hair, and failing, cursing, would chop it off to my shoulders and slather it with grease so the comb could get through the knots. She'd pull at my hair, yanking it until my scalp smarted and tears came to my eyes. Every week on Saturday, she'd wrestle me into the bathtub – in front of the fire if it was winter – and scrub at me until I was flayed and raw like a gutted fish.

On Sundays we'd troop to church and I'd squirm on the hard pew, not listening to the fat-lipped rector but imagining myself far away from all of them, up a tree, or walking for miles along the beach beyond the marsh. The rector himself has his own fantastic tale, and does not stay long in mine, but more on that later. Every other day I'd be away, Perdie yapping at my heels, crossing the marsh by the bridges, picking up pieces for my collection. I collected the world around me. The hollow shell of a bird's egg; a sprig of seablite or sea lavender; a stone that looked like a heart. I lined them up on the windowsill in my room and I would name them and touch them every day for luck. Janey said I started collecting when my mother went away, and I have no reason not to believe her. The first item in the collection was the shell I thought my mother had given me. I know now that it could have been any shell but in my childish mind it was hers, and as she'd given it to me it was special. From then on, anything that caught my eye was inspected and either discarded or chosen. By the time I was fifteen, it ran along the whole windowsill and covered the top of the chest of drawers as well. Now and again, Fairbrother would threaten to throw it all out as it was filthy and probably carrying diseases. But she never did – afraid, I think, of my anger.

If I wasn't collecting, I could be found in Janey's dark cottage. She'd tell me stories of hyter sprites, phantom dogs and travellers lost on the marsh; the moon trapped by wild creatures and a girl who outwitted a ghost. She told me all the names of the birds in the garden and the ones that came to the marsh at different times of the year, and the ones with names that she and Rogers used, but which weren't to be found in my British Book of Birds: spinks and buttles, hedge betties and King Harrys, hornples and Jill-hooters. We'd drink tea that she brewed from the herbs in her garden and eat cakes made with honey from her bees.

And if it hadn't all changed, perhaps I'd still be there where I belong, under the wide, open sky, rather than locked up, an animal in a cage.

9

The day it all really began was the Friday after my birthday, when I still believed that the greatest drama of my life was my mother's disappearance. It was the day I followed Father to Old Hall.

Fairbrother had been full of the arrival for months and months. A family was coming and I'd been planning the adventures I would have with the children. Children who would be my friends.

'There's a boy with them,' I'd overheard Fairbrother telling Rogers while he was laying rat poison at the threshold of the kitchen. 'A tall, sharp, blond boy. Older than Miss. Reminds me of the Prince of Wales he does. Handsome as anything.' Even I knew who the Prince of Wales was, everyone did. But he was an adult, not a boy. Whenever I tried to ask Father about the new family, whether there were any children, how many they were, exactly how old they were, he shooed me away, said we mustn't bother them and they'd invite us over soon enough. But I saw the boy first.

Father left the house soon after breakfast. He told me he was meeting important people in the village, but wouldn't tell me who. That was suspicious because there weren't any important people <u>in</u> the village. He despised the rector and there was no doctor in Stiffkey.

I waited on the drive for him to leave, until he disappeared down the lane into the little swirls of morning mist. First I had to shove Perdie quickly into the house otherwise she'd trot after me and might get squashed by a motor car.

After Father left, I ran down Green Way and saw him cross Church Street to the river. He stuck hard to the river all the way along, with me following behind, just fields on one side and trees shielding us from the street. I thought he might be going to the church, but instead he went down the little path that leads to the big house. Only it's not a house, Old Hall. It's not like the Marsh House with its windy stairs, tiny windows and warped walls that look like the sides of a boat, and the dark bedroom where she gave birth to me which no one goes into. It's more like a castle. A medieval, fairytale castle.

Old Hall. It's a rather boring name, isn't it? But it's not boring, everyone knows that. It has turrets and a courtyard and loads of windows and is really rather grand. I'd always played in the gardens. When I was little an old lady lived there and she was too slow and infirm to chase me away. She'd peer out of one of the top windows and bang it with her cane and I'd run away. Then it was empty and, along with the marsh, it really became my playground.

I was quite tempted to knock on the front door and ask to introduce myself to the new family. But I lost my nerve.

Instead, I saw the boy from the churchyard of St John the Baptist's. There was the old oak in the graveyard next to one of the ruined turrets which I could climb quite easily, and I could see right into the east side of the courtyard. I waited and waited, but I didn't mind as I was used to entertaining myself. I'd taken a slice of pork pie and an apple from the larder and I munched on those while I waited. He was sure to arrive at some point. A blackbird took up singing loudly above me, but it was mostly very quiet. Up there I could see the purple haze of the sea lavender on the marsh behind our house. The sun had burnt off all the sea mist from the morning and it had become a hot day. I took off my stockings and bunched them in the pockets of my dress. Father would be angry if he caught me like this. He was forever telling me to cover up or I'd look as brown as a gypsy. He didn't seem to realise that without school and without a governess or a mother there was no one else to tell me what to do. 'She's a wild thing,' Fairbrother used to say, but she didn't think it part of her job to tame me, and Dolly, the girl that did the laundry, was a meek little bird and would no more tell me what to do than she would an ogre.

I was tired after the pie and, leaning on the wide branch of the tree with leaves for my pillow, I thought I could close my eyes and have a little nap, but of course as soon as I did, I heard a shuffling sound across the courtyard below. There was the boy. He was tall and fair-haired as Fairbrother had said. He looked like he was thinking quite hard about something because he didn't look up. In a kind of rush of madness, I threw my apple core at the back of his head, and he did look up then because it whizzed right by his ear. I was quite a good shot, I should have got him, really.

'Hey!' he said. 'Who are you?' He was really very handsome, though his ears stuck out. And my mouth was stopped. All my clever retorts died on my tongue.

'Come down here at once, you nasty little monkey.'

Then – oh horror – he started walking towards me perched up my tree and I saw belatedly that he had a shotgun in his hand. He stood under the tree, raised the gun and pointed it in my direction and for a horrid moment I thought he was going to shoot me like a bird.

'I ought to shoot you out of that roost you're in. Spying on me, are you?' But I saw he had a funny smile and his eyes – very blue – were flashing at me as if this was all a great hoot.

'Go on then,' I said, my heart thumping.

'Ha,' he said, then he did shoot, and my ears rang with the crack of it. I felt the air whoosh and the leaves in the tree ripple out. The blackbird squawked, flapping up into the sky. I screamed, I'm sorry to say, and fell backwards, thumping onto the hard ground below. I was fine – nothing but a sore arm and a scraped leg – and I was up and running.

I ran away across the graveyard as quick as I could, past the entrance to the church, heard him shout as I ran but I knew I must run fast to be home before Father was alerted.

'I know who you are!' came the boy's voice from behind the church wall.

But I didn't stop running. I kept on, head down, straight into the rector, nearly toppling him over since he was so short.

The rector grabbed my shoulders. 'Slow down there, Miss Rosemary, what are you doing running like a boy in a holy place?'

I recoiled from him and shrank away. I looked back. The boy hadn't followed me. 'I need to get home, Mr Davidson.' The rector was a funny man – he had fat, fleshy lips that looked like they were about to gobble something up and eyebrows that were like furry caterpillars crawling over his forehead. Fairbrother maintained that he was a wonderful preacher, which made me dislike him even more. His fingers dug into my shoulder-blades and I wanted to scream.

'Father wants me,' I gasped. And I wriggled like an eel out of his grasp and away off down the lane and across the street to our lane and our house. I knew he wouldn't follow as Father was not a churchgoing man. Not since I was born.

But I only had one thing in my mind, and it was the blond-haired boy at the Hall, though I was bound to be in awful trouble with Father if he found out.

10

In my memory, distorted though it might be, that summer is filled with the dazzling sunshine brought into my life by the family who came to Old Hall.

Hilda was the daughter. She was eighteen then and I thought her quite a lady. Franklin was seventeen. He was the blond boy with the ears, the one I saw from the churchyard. They spent most of the time in their house in London and came to the Hall for weekends when I went to visit them. I needn't have worried, he couldn't have told Father I'd spied on him from the churchyard because Father came back that evening and told me we were both invited for tea at Old Hall. Father made a great friend of their parents, Colonel and Lady Lafferty, and so I finally had companions. I no longer cared that the village children hated me.

I remember all of us on an outing to the sea in Cromer in the summer, soon after they arrived. They had a motor car! I loved listening to the putt-putt-putt as it approached our house and watching the clouds of smoke billowing from the back. Perdie wasn't allowed to come and ran after the car barking until Fairbrother yanked her back into the house. I felt a twinge of guilt but they were out of sight so quickly, it was hard to dwell. I was off on an adventure! I sat in the back, squashed between Hilda and Franklin, and Lady Lafferty sat in the front with Father and the colonel, who loved to drive wearing a special outfit of flying helmet and driving gloves. Lady Lafferty wore an enormous straw hat tied underneath her chin and the purple ribbons flew out behind her in the wind. Hilda was dressed in London fashions (this is what she told me) – wide trousers and a pink floppy sun hat atop her short, bobbed hair – to which her mother raised her eyebrows but really, they allowed Hildy and Frank to do what they liked. Hilda wasn't as handsome as Franklin, but she was tall like him and had a bold look and rolled her eyes a lot and made me laugh. Franklin (he said to call him Frank) was dressed all in white and the rush of air as we drove along the coast to Cromer made his sandy hair rise up. He was shoved up close to me so I could feel his leg pressed hard against mine. I looked past him at the fields whizzing by and marvelled at the feeling of speed and at the red poppies nodding in the breeze in the wheatfields near Cromer.

Then I felt his hand on my leg. It crept up my skirt and he rested it on the inside of my thigh. I stared at him and he stared right back until I blushed and looked down at the floor, quite dizzy. He kept his hand on my leg for the rest of the journey and I wasn't sure what I should do.

We promenaded along the front and took lunch at a hotel high up overlooking the pier called the Hôtel de

Paris, but I found it hard to concentrate on anything at all with the memory of his hand on my bare skin. I thought of my mother and what she would have me do. He was so lovely and they were all so kind to me and I did like it, but I was afraid of what Father would say if he knew.

'You young ones should go on and have your fun,' said the colonel and Father frowned, but Lady Lafferty took hold of his arm and said, 'Come on, Richard, you can leave Rosemary to my Hilda, and you gentlemen can discuss the ills of the world without fear of interruption. I must tell you about my work with the Girls' Friendly Society.'

'Mind you watch your manners, Rosemary,' Father warned me, but he couldn't very well not let me go after that, could he? He was already far away, listening to Lady Lafferty and I imagined him later, head-to-head with the colonel. He had finally found someone else to talk to about the Problem of Capitalism or Communism, the Inertia of British Democracy and the Problem of What To Do About It. Although he talked about 'the integrity of the farming man', he never actually went to the Townsend and drank with them. We were isolated, Father and I, in our own ways, and both of us took to the Laffertys like thirsty men swallowing water.

On the front, Hildy took my arm and Frank walked on ahead of us. As soon as our parents were out of sight, he ducked back and began to run down the ramp to the seafront. 'Come on girls, let's feel the sea air!' He was grinning and it made his face shine. How beautiful he was, with his golden looks and white suit. I noticed that his lips were a dark pink colour like the grazing of skin and I wondered how it would feel to touch them. The only other boy I'd ever liked was Rogers' son, Billy, but Father wouldn't let me be friends with him because he was 'from a different background', and he never came to the house anymore. Whenever I caught sight of him picking samphire or cockling on the marsh for his mother, I'd wave and he always smiled at me and waved back but he never came close.

Down on the beach the sand was hot, and we took our shoes and stockings off. Frank rolled up his trousers and I could see the gold hairs on his slim calves. I had never been so close to a boy's body since Billy and I went splashing in the creeks when I was little. I always loved the feeling of sand under my bare feet, the way it oozed between my toes. Frank ran down to the sea and Hildy and I followed, holding hands and laughing. The sea was freezing cold and splashed against our legs and Frank, teasing, sprayed seawater over us. We squealed and laughed and the sun was hot on our heads. After a while I felt faint as we'd left our sun hats back with our shoes.

'Oh, if only we had bathing costumes with us, Rosemary. Next time we must. We absolutely must. Before the autumn comes and it's too cold.'

I thought of wearing a costume showing my pale legs and arms in front of Frank and I must have reddened because Hildy squeezed my arm and said, 'You have a lovely figure, dear Rosemary, you'd look wonderful. I know it. And you should think about bobbing your hair. You could carry it off, you know.' She picked up one of my braids and twirled it between her fingers. 'It's very lovely, this colour, you know, but you would set off your face if you cut it off and got rid of these childish plaits.'

How I wished I could go bathing with Hildy and Frank but the idea of Father letting me gad about in public with bare flesh showing was laughable.

'She has unusual colouring for an English girl, don't you think?' Hildy said to Frank.

He narrowed his eyes and cocked his head to one side, sizing me up. I blushed. 'We can't call her Rosemary, it's far too frumpy,' he said. 'Let's call her Rosie, in honour of her rosy cheeks,' which made me blush even more.

Later, Hildy and I lay on the sand letting the sun warm our feet, her with her trouser legs rolled up, me with my skirt hitched just above my ankles. Frank sat and smoked, and when I thought he wasn't looking, I sneaked a glance at him. Hildy took up gentle snoring, her neat chest rising and falling.

'What do you do in London, Frank?' I asked, emboldened by the sea air.

He looked down at me and blew smoke out of his nose. 'What do I do? Nothing of importance at all, dear Rosie. My mother would like me to do good. My father wants me to be useful.' He said this with utter disdain. 'He was, you see. My older brother was too. Army and all that. The war. Before my time of course.'

'You had a brother?'

'Two. Hildy and I are our father's second family. The others are all dead and gone.'

'Oh,' I said, foolishly, unable to think of anything to add, trying to imagine how old the colonel must be.

'But I have never been good at anything at all,' he went on. 'Father is thinking of standing for Parliament, you know. Wants me to join him. But I can't think of anything worse.'

I puzzled over this. I couldn't see how you could do nothing at all with your life.

'But don't you want to do anything?' I knew he didn't have to earn his living, unlike Father who was always worrying about money, and all the other people in the village and hereabouts, but it seemed so dreadfully boring.

He laughed. 'I'll help my father with his campaign as he says I must, but the sort of men we have coming to our house are so dull I shall hardly bear it. They are terribly serious, and I'm afraid I have never been able to muster much care about anything apart from sport. I think your father will join us though.'

'Join what?'

'The party,' he blew out a plume of smoke from his mouth towards me and I coughed. He reached over and tousled my hair and I felt all the skin on my scalp prickle. 'You'll see soon enough, dear Rosie. Father's organising a supper party for them at the Hall at the end of the summer, and your father is invited. I imagine he'll bring you. Hildy will insist upon it. And so will I.'

Then he leaned down and kissed me on the mouth. A chaste kiss, a mere peck, but nonetheless, the taste of his cigarette, the warmth of his breath and the sea breeze on my face was a blur of wonder. I was so shocked I jerked back and bashed into poor Hildy sleeping behind me, and she yawned and stretched. Frank caught my eye and, smiling with his eyes wide, put his finger up to his lips (the lips that had touched mine!).

'Lord, how long have I been asleep?' Hildy said. 'I'm absolutely famished. Time for tea, surely.'

As we walked back along the promenade to the car, he played with a shell in his hand, his long fingers caressing its ridges and smooth interior.

'It's beautiful,' I said.

'This?' he said, holding it up as if he'd hardly thought of it. 'You should have it.'

I smiled shyly and put it at once in the pocket of my dress.

We had a cold supper of an egg pie and lettuce when we got home, Father and I, laid out by Fairbrother. I gave half of mine to Perdie as they're always mean to her when I'm away. Dolly, the help, would give her titbits if she dared but Fairbrother always said she was spoiled.

'You'd do well to keep the company of people like the Laffertys, Rosemary,' Father said to me, and I went hot although he hadn't said anything bad. 'Lady Lafferty asked me to invite you to a meeting they're hosting for some important people from London, and I declined on your behalf because I said you were a motherless, simple girl and not used to society.'

'Father –' I started, hot with indignation. 'I'm not simple!'

But Father gave me one of his rare smiles, more like a grimace, but a kind of smile nonetheless, and he held up his hand and said, 'Hold fire, child. She made a firm case for your inclusion and I assented. But you must behave like a lady, Rosemary, not your usual wild self.'

'I will!' I cried, and jumped up to wrap my arms around him, although he pushed me away.

My heart was whirling. Did Frank love me? Were we courting? I didn't know. All I knew is that I'd dearly love Hildy as a sister and Frank made my heart hurt with longing. But he was older and much more sophisticated than me and I wondered if the two of them had joked about me when I'd gone back to our dark house on the edge of the marsh, with my country ways and no knowledge of London society or politics or anything at all. I was scared that in front of all the London people I would be shown up as who I really am and Frank wouldn't love me.

That night when I undressed, I found the shell he'd given me and laid it carefully on my windowsill with my other treasures. Its inside was pink and pearly and it reminded me of an open mouth.

Before the supper party we had a chance, Hildy and I, to wear our bathing suits. Franklin suggested a boating trip on the Broads, and this time it would be just the three of us. All the previous week I could barely eat or sleep for excitement. The summer was having a last fling, and the day was bright and warm. Thrillingly, Hildy drove her father's motor car and I sat next to her, with Franklin in the back. I had to hold onto my sun hat so it didn't fly off my head and I couldn't help but turn to see the road streaming out behind us, the locals gawping at the smart motor car and Franklin, leaning back against the leather of the seat, grinning at me. It was impossible not to smile back, I was so full of joy.

At the helm of the boat, Franklin wore a white sailor's cap and an open-necked white shirt and steered. Hildy wore a cap too, and a singlet with long trousers that made her look impossibly tall and elegant. I had a long cream dress on of course, because I had nothing else but dresses, but underneath so Father had no idea, a mustard-coloured swimming costume Hildy had found for me, that she'd long ago outgrown. I had never worn one before. When I swam in the river or the sea I would wear my drawers and underwear, or, if no one was around, which was most of the time, nothing at all. I wanted the feel of the water on my skin, it made me feel like I was a water baby, a sea-nymph, a mermaid. Hildy's costume was a striking cornflower blue like the deepest summer sky, and she had a swimming cap of bright pink so she stood out like an exotic flower among English daisies.

They'd hired a kind of boat I'd never seen before, a motor cruiser called *Dancing Light* which was like a yacht but with an engine rather than a sail. Franklin laughed and said it was a 'Damn sight easier than sailing,' and I could have a go if I wanted. 'She's a bit sprightly,' he said. The trick was not to rev her too much or the other chaps on the river would get uppity with their old sailing boats and wherries, according to Frank.

We'd picked up the boat at Wroxham marina and then cruised along the river Bure towards Horning where we ate lunch and drank beer sitting on the grass at the Swan Inn. I'd never drunk beer before but the others said it was just the thing on a hot day, and although my mouth puckered at the sharpness of it and the foam went up my nose and made me cough, I drank it all down and they cheered.

Afterwards, Hildy and I lay on the boat while we puttered on along the river. We were in our swimsuits now, and I was acutely conscious of my thin arms and legs sticking out and exposed, my body not quite a woman's. Hildy's limbs were long and pale and shone in the sunlight. But Franklin's arms, visible from the elbow where he'd rolled his sleeves, were golden. From my position, lying on the front of the boat (the 'hull' I was informed), I thought I could spy on him at the wheel, unobserved. But once, while I was gazing at the curve of his jaw as it met his neck, he caught me. For a long second our eyes connected, and I felt quite certain he knew I'd been looking at him.

'How do you like it?'

'Marvellous,' I said, using one of their words.

'Yes it is, isn't it? I think this is what my father calls the bucolic idyll. He feels that the modern man ought to get back to nature rather more and away from the sickness and depravity of society.' I had no idea what he meant but I sat up straight and tried to look as if I did. 'He rather thinks I'm a symbol of this modern malaise,' he said, with a strange smile. 'And maybe he's right. It's why he bought Old Hall after all. It's why he likes it up here, cut off from civilisation.' His voice sounded sarcastic and teasing but his eyes were wistful. 'It's the real England he's after. No foreigners, no degradation.' He seemed to notice me again. 'And if we hadn't come up here, we'd have never met you. It's someone like you, dear Rosie, who makes the world seem good with all your unspoilt loveliness. You don't even know how special you are.'

My head was buzzing with his words. How did I, of all people, make anything good? But he was looking at me with such hot, sweet tenderness, I melted under it.

'She's a beauty, isn't she?' he went on, stroking the gleaming wood of the helm. I imagined his hands caressing me the way he touched the wheel, and although he said nothing more after that, he kept his eyes on mine until I felt my skin burn and had to lower my gaze.

Luckily, at that point a sailing boat with a chattering group of young men and women came into view. They were smoking and laughing, the men in black bathing suits and the ladies in brightly coloured suits like Hildy's. They waved at us as we cruised by above them and as I waved back, one of the men dived into the water, making a huge splash. When he rose up through the water, his hair was slicked back and water dripped off his tanned skin like a water god.

'My,' said Hildy, who I'd thought was hardly awake as she sunbathed, 'Frank, we ought to find a spot to bathe, don't you think?'

Franklin agreed and soon we came to a sheltered place on the river, with only a windmill for company. She and I jumped in and swam in the cool, reedy water, although Franklin declined, saying he didn't have a suit, and sat smoking, watching us from the boat. Blue dragonflies flittered in the reed beds, sunlight danced on the cucumber-green water and it made me think of the boat's name, *Dancing Light*.

Hours later, as the sun was setting, we drank tea to warm us up, took the boat back to the boatyard and vowed we would take her out for longer next time. <u>Next time</u>, I thought, hugging the idea close. Frank drove the car back to Stiffkey, and I sat next to him, damp and sagging in the wet woollen suit, still tingling from the feel of the cool water, tired and euphoric, wishing the day could go on forever.

I've never forgotten it. That day has become a shining image of the past, of carefree youth and promise and glamour. Of course, I didn't see it like that then, I didn't know it would retain its lustre for so long. I thought there would be many more days like that to come, and there were – but now, looking back, it's that one first time on the Broads that sticks out as the most radiant, a tantalising glimpse of a life I could have led.

11

Not long after that trip to the Broads the weather turned, ushering in a dreary start to the autumn, but I didn't care because the long-awaited party at Old Hall was approaching. It was a nasty, blustering day with the mizzle coming off the marsh and barely any light. The walls of the house were damp and the floors cold. I snuck out and spent all day with Janey, preparing a love potion in the dark mugginess of her cottage. When I arrived, she was picking money spiders from the roof beams. She plucked each one delicately with her fingers then cupped them in the palm of her hand. She kept the spiders in her thick shrub of wiry grey hair 'because they're lucky'. I always loved that. The potion was supposed to be a tincture for a sniffle I had, but ever since I was a child Janey seemed like a miracle worker to me. I believed she could cure anything, even a stricken heart. Along with being a midwife and a layer-out of the dead, the villagers came to her with all kinds of afflictions, including love.

Her shelves were full of dusty glass bottles of brown and green with dark liquids inside, but I only knew a fraction of what they contained. I've remembered some of what she taught me though, and I can recite them now, like a spell with no outcome. There was dandelion for blood disorders, comfrey for sprains and wounds, nettle tops for coughs, aloe for burns, yarrow for diarrhoea and digestion, mandrake for the skin. And there were empty bottles too, into which she'd put bits of human nails and hair for people who thought they'd been bewitched. 'Hardly any of them nowadays, though you'd be surprised how many still come for something.' Because although the belief in witchcraft was waning as the century progressed – so she said – people were still afraid of things they didn't understand and would come to her with cases of melancholy and unexplained illnesses which had no cure. She would try to help with a herbal potion and she might also have said some words that sounded like a spell, though I don't know if it really was. Still, if the people who came to her believed in the remedies and if they helped them, then what did it matter?

She gave me some yarrow that day. She said I had to take one of the serrated leaves and tickle the insides of my nostrils repeating this:

Yarroway, yarroway, bear a white blow,

If my love love me, my nose will bleed now.

I blew hard into my handkerchief but all that came out was a sticky mucus, and not a drop of blood. Janey chuckled and said that was to be expected as he hardly knew me. I think she was teasing me.

These were the ingredients for the cold/love potion:
Verbena
Burnt juniper
Honey

all of which she got from her garden or her hive, along with a secret ingredient Janey said was an 'elixir', which smelt a lot like camphor. The potion tasted bitter-sweet and left a woody, pine coating at the back of your throat.

But by the time the evening of the party came, I was certain it had worked and Franklin would find me quite irresistible. My nose was no longer running and I felt as if I was glowing with good health.

It might seem strange to other people, brought up in other ways, that I still clung to these beliefs and superstitions, even as the modern world was opening up for me. But time is different up there in a village like mine, on a forgotten bit of the coast, isolated from day trippers and city ways and the so-called march of progress. There are still people there who follow a different lore to those of commerce and man-made time. There are ways older than motor cars and electricity and telephones that persist, like the black layer of mud on the marsh, concealed beneath the top layer of rationality. I'm not saying those ways are better, but they are there, whether you like them or not.

I've almost run out of space and besides, I've been writing this for two days now in between gardening duties, and I'm tired. 'What are you writing, Miss?' they ask. But I won't tell them. Tomorrow I will start the next notebook. I have lots more to write.

12

The Church
23rd December

A gust of wind caught at the window, making it rattle, and something pale fell to the floor with a faint thud. Malorie's head shot up from the book. In the dim room, nothing stirred. Slowly, she realised that the night had returned to eerie silence, as if all noise had been muffled in some kind of fog. Half asleep, she looked at her watch on the bedside table, its face lit by the lamplight. It was just past midnight.

She rubbed her eyes in the dark of the bedroom. Through the curtains there was a silvery glow. It must be the moon. She should try and shut the window, so she slid out of bed, gasping at the cold. As she moved, she felt a slight jar at the back of her head, like the beginning of a migraine or a hangover. On the floor by the window was a shell, with a pearly-pink interior, which must have fallen from the windowsill. She held it in her palm and tried to think why it seemed familiar. Outside, snow was falling silently, and everything was cloaked in a thin shroud of silvery white.

Malorie gripped the edge of the windowsill and cried out an incoherent sound. Something – someone? – was moving in the snow. A shadow. Her hand rose as if to reach for it. A vague, pale shadow, a slight darkening of the endless white, like a figure dressed in snow. Then, nothing. She felt foolish – she was so unused to the countryside, to the noises and creeping shapes of the night, far away from the familiar safety of streetlights and shops and bars. There was just the snow gently falling in great clumps, white flakes through the dark. Standing dazed at the window, she pinched her bare arm and it hurt. Bed. She was delirious. She had to go back to bed. Stumbling, she dropped back onto the covers and pulled the blankets tight around her. The pain at the back of her head had eased but her mind was crowded with this girl – the girl from the picture in the paper, the girl in the notebook who seemed to be speaking directly to her. The book had ended abruptly. There were pages left but they were empty, as if the writer were withholding. This couldn't be the end of the story. It wasn't, she already knew that. The mug shot of the girl from the newspaper cutting – that challenging gaze, straight into the camera.

A few hours later, surfacing from fitful dreams, Malorie woke to a chilly light washed over the room. There was no sound from anywhere. No birds, no wind, not even the sea. Nothing but a slight creak in the bowed walls of the house. She was thirsty but her water glass was empty. The quiet had a dense quality like cotton wool. Before she opened the curtains, she knew why. The entire scene below her was muffled in white.

As she turned from the window, there on the floor by the bed was a thin oblong package, tied in a red hair-ribbon. It must have fallen out of the notebook. She picked it up and unknotted it with fumbling fingers.

Inside were two photographs. It was strangely surprising, as if she'd been reading a story rather than a record of someone's life. One was of a boy – an attractive fair-haired young man in a pale suit, leaning nonchalantly against the wall of an old building. She felt a bubble of recognition. He reminded her of Tony when they'd met – someone used to getting what they wanted. But this boy had a harder edge than Tony and a haughty look with narrow, laughing eyes, a slightly pouting mouth and a supercilious expression on his face. Tony never meant to be cruel. This one did. It was obvious who he was. On the back, someone – it was Rosemary, she knew her from her handwriting – had written *Franklin, August 1931*.

This Franklin made her skin prickle with a weird combination of attraction and repulsion. What came into her mind was Tony, sliding down a sofa at a party and cupping his hand on her breast. He hadn't even known her name. She'd pushed him off but he hadn't seemed at all bothered. Here she was now, cold in a lumpy bed in an isolated house on the edge of Norfolk and what was Tony doing? She couldn't bear to think of it. Some other party, no doubt, some cool little joint in Soho. That was Tony's kind of thing. He returned to it each time. He went back to the emptiness of dark basement bars and whisky. And a fawning woman making him drinks. It had been a mistake to think he would ever have wanted a life with her and Franny. He would have loathed it here – this cold, dark house by the sea.

The other photograph was of a young woman. At first she thought it was Rosemary herself. But it was an older photograph from a different era. The woman was wearing a long, pale dress with a high lace collar and was seated on a rattan chair with palm trees around her. Perhaps it had been taken in a studio. She was small, pale and dark-haired, drowning in the stiff, voluminous dress, a child really. With an uncomfortable jolt, Malorie knew who she was. The absent mother, Rosemary's lost mother, Louisa. And sure enough, on the back, in a different hand, someone had written *Miss Louisa, February 1912, Delhi.*

She tucked the photographs back into the notebook, stuffed both the books under the pillow, before fetching a cardigan to put over her nightdress and going out onto the landing. No sound came from Franny's room. Downstairs, she managed to coax the fire into sputtering life and, squatting in front of it, waited for warmth to spread across her skin. The heat prickled her fingers but she didn't withdraw them. Her back, exposed to the room, was cold and a shiver like someone's finger tracing the line of her vertebrae tickled down her spine. *Somebody walked over my grave.* She snapped her head round. Nothing but the sofa and a badly painted seascape of a storm. A memory flared – someone, something – whiteness in the garden. The middle of the night. She must have been dreaming of the girl from the notebook. *Rosemary*, she said to herself. It was like peering into someone's mind, reading her words. She shouldn't have read it. *Private and Confidential* it said. She was a voyeur, a Peeping Tom. But why write it at all if you didn't expect people to read it? And Rosemary *did* want someone to read it – she'd even written something to that effect. At the same moment she was also wondering when she could slip away to read the second notebook. She wanted to know what happened to the girl. She felt a kind of responsibility for her, as if in reading her words she had a kind of duty to her. And it was possible, yes it was possible, that in those words there would be some clue as to why her father had kept a photograph of this house. She realised that while she was reading she'd completely forgotten about her initial reasons for reading the notebooks. There'd been nothing though, no mention of a Harry Skinner or anyone who could have been him. But there might be. *I have more to write.* She heard footsteps and froze. Facing the door, she had a vision of a girl in a white dress coming into the room. She called out in alarm.

It was only Franny, holding a snow-flecked Larry in her arms.

Malorie breathed out, her limbs trembling.

'What's the matter?'

She laughed, a mad, snorting laugh that made Franny stare at her in suspicion.

'Nothing, darling. Nothing. Just a terrible night's sleep. Have you been out? Where've you been?' Franny was wearing some kind of dirty yellow dressing-gown, the colour of an old banana, over her nightdress, and big thick socks. Her pale face was reddened with the cold.

'Larry needed his morning walk, Mummy. The garden's completely covered in snow. I'm freezing.'

She came and sat next to Malorie with the dog, who stretched out in front of the fire. 'Look what I found.' She held it out for Malorie to see, a piece of flint in the rough shape of a heart. But when Malorie moved it in her hand it no longer seemed heart-shaped. It was just a stone.

'We need to put the decorations up, before Daddy gets here,' said Franny.

Malorie winced. She didn't have the heart – or the courage – to tell her.

All morning, Franny strung up the decorations they'd found in the attic, setting up ancient, faded paper chains and old painted lanterns on every ledge, hook and door handle, then she trailed outside in her coat and wellingtons, with Larry, almost camouflaged in the snow, skittering beside her and barking at the hedge, to make a snowman and cut down holly and mistletoe. At first, Malorie didn't leave the house. She tried her transistor radio again but she couldn't find a station through the thick static so she turned it off. As she moved around the rooms – feeding Larry, helping Franny with the decorating, tidying up – she kept coming back to the girl in the notebook. It struck her that this village had been Rosemary's home and it, too, would hold traces of her life. And maybe – just maybe – her own life as well.

'Franny,' she called from the back door. 'I'm going to the village, do you want to come?' She never knew what tone to take with her daughter. It sounded false the way she spoke, the jollying tone. And Franny sensed her discomfort, like a dog senses weakness. Whereas Tony, feckless bloody Tony, somehow knew how to be with her, how to make her laugh. He picked up his daughter and spun her round as if it were nothing. I am not really a mother, she thought. I'm just acting.

From the other end of the garden, in the shadow of the snowy trees, she could make out Franny's brown woolly hat, navy duffle coat and yellow wellingtons. 'I don't want to.'

'Please,' she said. God, the stubborn child never did what she wanted. She had no power over her. Franny stood immovable in the snow. Her hair stuck out from beneath the hat that Malorie's mother had knitted before she'd begun to fade away. Everything was covered in snow crystals.

'Fine,' she called, 'I won't be long.'

Malorie found the fur coat and the fur-lined boots Tony had bought for her in the autumn. She took a different route this time. She thought if she walked to the end of the lane she might see the sea. But when she got there, the marsh carried on until the horizon, frosty and bleak, pockmarked with holes where God-knows-what lurked. Defeated, she looked about her, unsure which way to go. Above her on a ridge was a line of bare trees with their gnarled fingers curling to the air. A shiver across her back and she felt she should follow the trees. It was what Rosemary would have done. Nothing disturbed her walk. It was a consolation to be alone after her failure with Franny. The snow was untouched and pristine and squeaked as she stepped on it. No people, no animals. The frozen and still landscape could be apocalyptic, or medieval or prehistoric. Not of this time. She picked up a clump of snow-feathered grass, thinking it must be the marsh grass that Rosemary had run through. It was coarse and pricked at her skin. It wasn't long before she found a lane that she thought must go towards the village. It was an ancient path, with no sign whatsoever of modern life. Peering down its dark recess she thought that it could be any time in the last few centuries. The 1960s hadn't reached here at all. It was narrow and sloped down, as far as anything sloped around here, and as she crunched along the virgin snow of the track, the jagged trees high on either side felt claustrophobic, as if anything could be lurking there and pounce on her. She walked quickly, not looking left or right but straight ahead.

The lane came out beyond the shop, next to a war memorial to both wars and a tired-looking village hall with a peeling green roof, but no sign of any people at all. She slowed her pace. Now, she was conscious that she was once again following Rosemary's footsteps towards the other end of the village where the church was. As the road curved out of the village, she glimpsed on the right the turrets of a large house behind a high wall and, next to it, the grey flint tower of a church. In front of the churchyard gate stood the village sign with a metal silhouette of a bird, and behind it what must have been the school, now boarded up.

The wall to the big house was too high to see over, but she knew it must be Old Hall. She felt a buzz of excitement at walking where Rosemary had thirty years before, being in the same place as if no time had passed. There was an iron gate with a driveway to the Hall and on the pillars on either side, the crumbling stone sculptures of two ugly boars with their tusks stuck in the air. But she could hardly see further than a few feet down the drive as the trees overhung and created a thick screen. Following the wall a few steps on, the stiff gate to the churchyard was free of snow so she was afraid there would be a churchwarden or someone else around, but she went through anyway. Inside the churchyard, she could see the imposing building next door more clearly. Straight ahead, behind the far wall of the grounds, was a ruined tower. There was no tree next to it as Rosemary had described. They must have cut it down. From what she could see on her tiptoes above the wall, the house was a vast, elaborate manor with a snow-covered tiled roof and knapped flint walls, further towers and numerous mullioned windows, but it was hard to see fully behind the trees lining the outer wall. She was sure it was a deliberate ploy to stop prying eyes. She strained to see, but there was no sign of life.

Inside, the church was bare, and mercifully empty. She searched in vain for any reference to the Wright or Lafferty families; it was as if they'd never existed. Neither were there any Skinners. Returning outside, she scoured the graves. There was a strange, weathered gravestone with two skulls and a cross-bones carved on it, but the writing at the bottom was so worn by time that she couldn't read it. In a far corner of the church, underneath a yew tree, she found a stone cross, half-covered in yellowing moss and the white-grey blooms of lichen, dedicated to Harold Francis Davidson, the rector mentioned in the notebook. On the plinth at the bottom of the cross, a quotation had been carved. It said:

FOR ON FAITH IN MAN
AND GENUINE LOVE OF MAN
ALL SEARCHING AFTER TRUTH
MUST BE FOUNDED

She had no idea where the lines came from or when he'd died, but he at least was a real person. Now she'd found this headstone she was even more determined to find evidence of the Wrights in this churchyard. There must be some. But as she looked, peering at each half-erased name and faded epitaph in the weak, overcast light of the winter morning, it became colder and colder, and soon she realised that she'd been in the churchyard for far too long, leaving Franny in the lonely house.

As she was leaving, she noticed ivy crawling along the wall of the graveyard and hanging down from a hawthorn tree in the corner. She pulled a tendril and more came with it, sprinkling snow over her face and arms, until she had an armful of it. She could hang it in the house. As she stuffed it into her shopping bag, a stone detached itself from the mass of vines. It was a piece of flint, shiny, smooth grey on one side and a rough sand colour on the other. It reminded her of the Marsh House.

She struggled through the snow as quickly as she could, seeing only a solitary walker – an old man who nodded at her under his cap – and one passing van. It was strange how empty it was. When she was younger, children would have been out in a snowy winter throwing snowballs. A yellow light was on in the small window of the shop and she slowed down her pace.

'Morning,' the shop girl said as she entered. Already she felt she was known and discussed by the villagers. 'What can I get you? No little girl today?'

'Good morning. She's playing in the snow. I just wanted to say thank you for the logs that your father left at the house yesterday. It was very kind.'

The girl looked up from her ledger with a blank face. 'Logs? I thought he was bringing them with the turkey.'

'Oh. I wonder—'

'Someone's looking out for you, any road. Snow's come in fast, ent it? Going to be a bad one, they say.'

'Do they? Can I ask you a question – I wonder – did you or your family ever know a boy called Harry Skinner?'

'It don't ring a bell. Why's that then?'

'I wondered – I thought – he might have something to do with the house.'

'What, the Marsh House? Might've done, I spose. I'll ask my dad.' Malorie sighed. The name wasn't known here and there were no Skinners in the graveyard. The photograph must have had nothing to do with her father. So why the hell had he wanted her to have it? There was something she was missing, like a name you couldn't remember at the far reaches of your brain. The more you grasped for it, the deeper it sunk into the shadows.

'And – and I was wondering about the people who lived in the house.'

'That place is right strange. All I know is that when I was a kid, it was empty and boarded up. We'd dare each other to go up the lane, but no one ever went inside. Funny, ent it? It's just a house. Our parents never told us what was wrong with it, just that it was a bad house. I'm sure it's nice now though,' she added, seeing Malorie's frown. 'You sure you don't want anything?'

'I'll take a newspaper,' she said, picking up that day's paper. She did a quick calculation in her head. She only had a few shillings left and might need petrol. 'And these –' she passed over two cans of tomato soup. 'I've been wondering,' she added. 'Where are all the children?'

'Oh, they go sledging down Devil's Hole.'

'Devil's Hole?'

The girl shrugged. 'An old path out of the village. There's some old tale about it. They say it can't ever get wet because of a crime done there. Gets lots of snow though. We always used to slide down there when it snowed.'

Walking home, she saw the headline of the local gazette was *BODY OF FISHERMAN FOUND IN SNOW*. She picked up her pace, wanting to be inside.

13

I saw her walking to the village and I knew she'd found out something and what she was looking for. She wanted evidence. Proof. Facts. As if it would all be there for her and she could lay it all out and it would make sense. But it's never as simple as that. The graves are elsewhere. The bones are dust. It's not graves that tell you a history, a story of a life. That's much harder to find, but if you know where to look, you can find it. It'll reveal itself. It's all still around you if you're ready to see. It's in the crumble of a wall, a scratch on a beam, the sound of a tread on the stairs. Most people don't though, do they?

14

The Snow Girl

They ate a lunch of one of the cans of tomato soup she'd bought from the shop, heated up, and toasted half-stale bread. The ivy was in a pile by the back door. Malorie followed her daughter out again to the snow-covered garden to see the snowman.

The sky was still laden, no sun had appeared, but the white blanket covering the lawn and trees reflected a dull sheen back at her. By the back door there was a large bush of rosemary, flecked with white. It was old and woody but still alive, with thousands of sharp, dark green needles in sprays. She leaned down to pick some sprigs and the deep, sweet scent filled her senses. *Rosemary, that's for remembrance.*

'Mummy!'

In the middle of the lawn, Franny was standing like an angry pixie next to a snow-girl. She had created a young woman with hair of dead leaves and eyes of coal and a long dress sculpted out of snow.

'That's clever,' said Malorie. 'Where did you get the idea for that, darling?'

Franny frowned. 'I don't know. I just thought of it.'

Malorie gave her a hug. 'Well, it's very unusual.' Standing in the centre of the garden she was taken back to the night before, looking out of the window. It was dark, snow was falling, someone was looking up at her. A shape – the shape of a girl in white.

'Stop squeezing me, Mummy, it hurts.'

'Sorry.'

'When are you going to get us a tree? It's Christmas Eve tomorrow. We have to have a tree to put the presents under.'

'A tree?' Oh God, she'd forgotten. And she had to wrap the presents she'd shoved into the car – all the extravagant gifts that Tony had bought for his only child. She wondered if he was cursing her now, or relieved that he was shot of them. Shot of her, at least.

'You promised.'

'I did. I'll cut one down. There's plenty of them.' She had no idea how to cut down a tree. And what with, anyway? 'Are you going to help me?'

'I'm cold.' Franny had turned inwards, her face closed down. Malorie had failed her again. She felt a small surge of undirected anger but stifled it. It was *Christmas* – she had to make an effort.

She sent Franny inside with Larry at her heels. There was a falling-down shed on the left side of the garden with peeling brown paint. The door was warped but not locked and she prised it open. Inside, in the dim winter light, at first all she could see were spiders' webs and lines of pots. It must have been a gardener's shed. In her head, her father emerged from his beloved shed into the clipped and neat rectangle of the garden in Norwich, their pride and joy. He looked upwards and crumpled onto the lawn. Her mother had called her, in the digs in London, her voice hesitant and small. The funeral had been tortuous. Tony had come with her, ballasted her with his certainty. She'd tucked herself in against him and felt an uncharitable relief that she had him now, that she didn't belong there anymore. Her mother had let Tony hold her hand in his and looked up at him with such beseeching gratitude that Malorie had been glad to get away. Even her mother would rather Tony comforted her than her own daughter.

If what her mother said was true, her father had wanted to tell her something. As she peered into the shed it was as if she could see him in the shadows, hunched over and working on something as he always had been. If only she could talk to him now. If only she'd been a better daughter. There it was again, the inky blackness behind her eyes. If she let it, it would spread through her skull, seeping into her brain, sinking into her whole self as it had done after Franny was born, until the weight was so heavy she couldn't move. Tony had found her once, when he'd come home from work, her teeth unbrushed, sleeping in her nightdress, the baby soiled and crying, unable to wake her. She blinked quickly. She had to focus on now, on Christmas.

As she adjusted to the darkness inside the shed, her father's form evaporated. She began to see the shapes of tools hanging from the back wall. A couple of spades, a rake, some large scissors – secateurs – various trowels and something she didn't know the name of with a long handle and a small half-moon metal head. And, most pleasingly of all, an axe. She couldn't imagine wielding such a thing, let alone chopping a tree down with it, but she had to.

It was incredibly satisfying, she discovered. The axe was heavy and hard to keep a grip on with gloved hands, and the first time she tried to take a swipe at a suitable-looking pine tree on the edge of the garden, she only managed a small nick in the side and the head of the axe almost fell onto her boots. But then she practised swinging it back and forward a few times. The third time, she angled it horizontally into the trunk and it sliced into the wood and stuck there. She had a hard time yanking it out, but when she did, the first cut had been made and it was easier after that. When it fell she had to jump out of the way. It sprayed snow into her face but she grinned, feeling the flakes on her tongue, pleasantly aware of the ache in her upper arms.

'You did it.' Franny had been watching from the back door. Malorie felt a childish rush of pride. She had done something on her own. No Tony. No parents. They exchanged a fleeting smile. Her daughter came over and began trying to pull the fallen tree over to the house. 'We need to get it in a bucket,' she said, but Malorie still had the axe in her hand.

'I'm just going to chop some wood for the fire,' she said.

Franny seemed to be waiting.

'Just leave it there. I'll bring it in, in a minute. I won't be long.'

The rhythm of the swing, the hissing thwack of spliced wood on the trunk she used as a block, the tingle of pain in her arms – it was addictive. Her father, sprawled on the lawn. Thwack. Her mother's closed-off face. Thwack. Tony, she thought, who is not here. Thwack. Thwack. Franny, who she didn't understand. Thwack. She was a bad mother. A failed mother. Thwack.

A dark shape moved on the edge of her vision. Someone was watching her.

Malorie shouted out and the axe fell out of her hand, carving a wedge into the snow by her foot. The sky had darkened, the only light now coming from inside the house, a single square of yellow. Across the white lawn and through the trees, an old woman was standing motionless outside the cottage.

Had she spoken aloud? Had the old woman heard her?

'Hello!' Her voice croaked. Who was she? She should thank her for the logs – it must have been her who'd left them, after all.

The words from the journal came back to her – *Janey delivered me*. She had an image of the woman watching over the house from before it was built. Watching over this girl, Rosemary, and her mother. Still here, still watching.

'Janey?' she called out uncertainly.

She thought the woman dipped her head in response. Then she turned and disappeared. Malorie watched the brown shape slip back between the dense foliage. Now she'd gone, she felt foolish. It was probably not the same woman at all.

Malorie sorted out the tree – finding a bucket to put it in, sending Franny off to find stones to weight it, tidying up the ends – until it looked almost like a reasonable Christmas tree, but bare. The whole time, Larry sat by the fire, his hackles up. She wondered why he didn't sleep there like a normal dog would.

'There's candles for the tree in the attic, I think,' she said.

'Fairy lights?' said Franny.

'Hopefully. I'll go. You stay here and finish the decorating.'

Crouching low and shuffling along on her knees, she came to the cot she'd seen the day before. Without meaning to, she raised her hand to the bottom edge and felt along it. Their cot was not much different. Her tiny starfish body splayed out in the middle; her red mouth open, mewing; swaddled, tucked in, asleep. Then it had been kept up in her room for ages, waiting for Malorie to be well enough to have a second child, until finally, reluctantly accepting there wouldn't be another baby yet, Tony dismantled it and bit by bit took it up to the tiny attic space above their first floor flat. It was the symbol of one of her failures.

She let her hand drop.

On her hands and knees she nudged towards where Franny had found the old suitcase. She found a box that was stuck under the eave and had to be yanked back with some force before she could open it. Puffs of dust floated up and she coughed. This box was heavy. It contained books. Her heart jumped a little but they weren't notebooks or even Agatha Christies, they were mostly exercise books from when the girl had had her governess. She flicked through them but there was nothing interesting. Just the scribbles of an intermittently obedient pupil, the declensions of Latin verbs, arithmetic, violent crossings-out. She leaned back on her heels, her head touching the roof, irrationally, crushingly, disappointed. She'd felt so certain she'd find something.

A faint rustle made her twitch. Sure enough, she heard again the scraping of claws above her. God, she hoped she didn't see one. She loathed rats. Tony used to tease her about all the rats in the London gutters.

There were no treasures up here, no secrets, just the boxes of books and the rats.

But she had to get the fairy lights. Dejected, she scrabbled through one of the Christmas boxes and pulled out a handful of small white candles. They would have to do.

Back on the first floor, Malorie glanced through the open door of the bedroom. Her fingers itched to open the second notebook, to lose herself in Rosemary's world. It was waiting for her under her pillow. But she couldn't read it now. She must admire the tree, make Franny some supper, get her to bed, wait, wait patiently. She stood there a moment, taking in the smell of something warm and sweet. It was the rosemary she'd picked earlier, in the pocket of her blouse. She smiled and placed it on the windowsill. It was the namesake of the girl in the notebook – her herb, her flower.

When she returned downstairs, Franny attached the candles to the tree with clips she found in one of the boxes of decorations, and lit them, sending golden spangles onto the lumpy, warped walls. Malorie had never seen a Christmas tree lit with real candles before and it was beautiful. While she made the tea, the window above the sink showed her face staring back at her. She imagined Rosemary in this room, or by the fire, like Franny in the next room, sewing her sampler. By the back door was the mass of ivy she'd taken from the graveyard. They could hang it around the house. Then she remembered the piece of flint in the pocket of her coat and quietly retrieved it, took it upstairs to the bedroom and laid it on the windowsill alongside the sprigs of rosemary, a tentacle of ivy and the shell that was already there.

That night, the fire was still burning and Malorie was curled up on the sofa with a bottle of wine on the rug, a packet of cream crackers and the first pack of the cigarettes she'd brought from the shop. Franny was asleep – or supposed to be – and Larry lay curled again at the bottom of her bed. He had taken to sticking closely to her, whining whenever she left him.

She'd brought down the second notebook. The last thing she'd read was the girl drinking a love potion. She thought of herself, meeting Tony at eighteen, married at nineteen. But at least she'd been eighteen – an adult of sorts. She'd certainly thought she was. Escaped from the stifling house in Norwich with its regulated eating times and only the *Reader's Digest* or the *Radio Times* for culture. She'd seen herself as oh-so-grown-up with her beehive, handbag and high boots. She'd been newly living in London, a job in a secretarial pool (she'd soon find something better; her dad always told her she was clever), in digs with her friend Clemency, who believed she had a foot in the aristocracy as her father had stumped up for Bedales. Clemency took her to an underground bar in Soho and introduced her to Tony. Oh God, he'd been so dashing in his tight shirts and Cuban heels. Not conventionally attractive – his lips were too full, his hair too high on his forehead – but he had so much confidence it radiated from him, warming her with its glow. She'd wanted so much to be part of the London scene, to shuck off Norfolk and her awkward relationship with her parents, and Tony had promised that, with his job in a hip bar, his flat near Soho and his easy way with money. He'd probably only meant her to be a fling. But Franny had stopped all that.

The wedding was a quickie in Marylebone Register Office, the only witnesses Clem and Tony's friend Seb. Her wedding dress a cast-off from Clem, a long custard-yellow dress she'd have worn for the season. Not white. How could she in her condition? It had felt like an adventure, a rebellion. She'd write to her parents and tell them when it was all done. It had happened in such a rush there hadn't been time to think about it – he was the promise of the life she thought she wanted, the glamour and freedom. They'd had drinks in a grubby bar after but she'd felt queasy, went home early. Tony had stumbled in the next morning and fallen asleep beside her smelling of brandy and cigarettes. It was nauseating. She'd felt a heave in her stomach and lurched to the bathroom. Slumped on the lino floor, she watched the water trickle down the side of the toilet bowl. On her finger, the cheap ring Tony said was only temporary. This was her life.

She had a better class of ring now. Not the family heirloom he'd promised her (she suspected his sister had kicked up a fuss about that), but a large diamond wrapped in gold from Bond Street. In the gloom of the bedroom, Malorie held the diamond up to the thin light to make it shine.

His parents had quite obviously disapproved of her – she was from a council house – but she tried not to care about that. It was part of the thrill of it, wasn't it, to be striking out from both their upbringings? Her parents had only met Tony a couple of times. Her mother had fawned over him, impressed by the car, the clothes, the cut-glass accent. Her father had been quietly disapproving, called him 'flashy'. And although she'd told herself that it didn't matter – Tony was her family now – it had hurt. She'd stopped ringing, unable to bear his disappointment in her. By the time Franny had come along, her father was already dead, collapsed in his beloved garden with a heart attack. And he'd never forgiven her for Tony. That was one of the worst things, the humiliation of her error. He'd been right about Tony all along.

That appalling night in London before he left, he'd shown himself to be who he really was. And she had too. He'd called her a bitch. And what had she done? Slapped him? Cursed him? Screamed and shouted? No. She'd cried, crumpled and defenceless.

'Don't do that,' he'd said.

'You can't leave me,' she'd said.

He hadn't answered, just picked up his hat and left. The shame she felt was like a cowl she wore.

Outside, an owl hooted and a draught made Malorie tuck her feet up under her legs. The window was completely black. Anything could be outside in the darkness. They were exposed, just the two of them, stuck out here on their own with only a silly little dog for protection. For God's sake, there was no one there, she chided herself and turned back to the notebook.

She'd begun to think there would be nothing in the pages that made sense of why her mother had given her an old photograph of this house. But the urge to read was overwhelming. She cracked open the second notebook. It was full, as the first one had been, of the same slanted, cramped handwriting.

THE SECOND NOTEBOOK

15

I think I will enjoy writing this part of my story. It will remind me that I was once a very different person and although I now reside in what looks like a castle with crenellations and turrets, there is a place like this far away on the coast of Norfolk, which once seemed like a fairytale palace.

Father and I walked to the Hall with a great umbrella. The rain had cleared but the sky was grey and looming dark. We didn't talk, but I didn't care. The darkness of the trees swaying in the wind seemed to be urging us on and I skipped so far ahead that Father complained I would lose my hat.

The hall was lit with a thousand candles in chandeliers and glowing electric lights and there was jolly dancing music coming from the drawing room. Their butler person (they brought their servants up from London) took my old black velvet coat that was far too small for me. I felt instantly foolish as the only smart dress I had was a hand-me-down from Hildy which was navy blue wool with a Peter Pan collar, but it looked awkward on me. On Hildy I imagined it would have been chic in an intellectual, bluestocking kind of way, accessorised with one of her lovely little hats, but it just made me look like an overgrown, gauche child. At home, on the marsh, it had seemed smart, even elegant, but here, it was all wrong.

Hildy was standing in a long satiny cream gown in the corner of the room, being flirted with by a middle-aged man with a luxurious moustache and a receding hairline. She looked bored and marvellous. She always did. I waved and she wiggled her fingers at me and raised her very arched eyebrows even higher.

'Darling, you look delightful,' she said, entirely unconvincingly. 'Excuse me, Gerald, I must get this poor child a drink.' She extricated herself from the wet-lipped, moustached man and, steering me by the elbow, led me to one of the tuxedoed staff they must have hired in addition to their own staff (from where? In Norfolk?! I'd never seen anything like it) and took two glasses of champagne from the boy. I'd never had champagne before – it made me splutter and bubbled up my nose – but I rather liked the taste, and very soon it had all gone.

'God,' she sighed, 'that man is so tiresome. All he talks about is his horses.'

'He seemed to like you,' I said.

'He's in love with me, always has been,' she said. 'Poor Gerald!' Then she looked at me as if she'd only just seen me.

'You look like someone's let you out of school for the day in that outfit,' she said, peering at me down her long, straight nose.

'It's yours.'

'I know that, silly. I see I'll have to give you something more suitable for the evening.'

'Who are all these people?' I said, looking around the room at the men in black tie and the women in backless gowns.

'Daddy's friends from London. Some of them are in the army, some are politicians. That one –' she pointed across the room, 'is married to Diana Mitford. She's a stuck-up old thing but considered quite a beauty. You must have heard of her. All the Mitfords are such gadabouts. Guinness is a bit of a bore but terribly rich. I've heard she's in love with someone else, but no one knows who. It's all terribly romantic.' I looked around at the perfectly sculpted heads and tried to see The Beauty, and there was one woman with golden hair and startling bright eyes who was holding court, but Hildy had already moved on.

'That one over there –' she was saying, pointing to a handsome woman with a green cloche hat, 'was a famous suffragette.'

Someone was playing a harp in the corner of the room. Canapés were passed around and I tried every single one of them. Smoked salmon, devilled eggs, stuffed tomatoes, I ate them all. 'Gosh, Rosie, do you never get fed?' said Hildy. 'You've become quite a squeaky piggy.'

'Snort, snort,' I said, helping myself to a chicken liver toast. I didn't like to tell her that I had never eaten anything like this in my entire life. It was all fatty pies and boiled vegetables at home.

All this time, I had my eye on Franklin but he was by his father's side, being talked at incessantly by one of these men or another. I could hardly get near.

'Oh God,' she said suddenly, lowering her voice to a whisper, 'let's make a run for it – it's Mummy.'

Sure enough, gliding across the room was the willowy Lady Lafferty. There was no escape.

'Darlings,' said Lady Lafferty, 'how are you?'

'Fine, Mummy,' said Hildy disconsolately.

'And Rosemary, dear, are you well? I'm afraid this little gathering might seem a bit ostentatious for someone unused to such things.'

'I'm enjoying it, thank you,' I said in my politest voice.

'I notice we don't see you in church very often, my dear.'

'Mummy!'

Lady Lafferty stiffened, but kept the patient smile on her fine-boned face.

'My father is not very fond of the rector.'

'Neither is the colonel, Rosemary, but God would rather you were in his church regardless.'

'Yes, Lady Lafferty,' I said at the same time as Hildy said, 'I don't think God has an opinion, Mother.'

'Hilda May,' said her mother sternly, and flashed a pitying look to me.

She put her long-fingered hand on my cheek, assessing me the way Franklin had done that time on the beach, and I realised that no one had ever looked at me properly before then, or touched me the way they did.

'Dear Rosemary, what a beautiful name you have, like the herb. And so unaffected,' she said, touching my jaw. 'Don't let my daughter change you, my dear.' Then she left us, patting me on the head.

A fearsome-looking woman approached us. 'What do you think about the unemployment situation?'

I stared at her. She was tall, with blue-black cropped hair, a severe, very glamorous suit, and a brooch in the shape of a scorpion on the lapel of her jacket.

'I don't know,' I said.

'No, of course not,' she said, 'you're just a child.'

'But a very lovely one,' said Hildy in her mocking voice, pinching my cheek.

I began to think I was the butt of some extraordinary joke, but I couldn't think what it was. These people were all I had dreamed of and yet they clearly knew I wasn't one of them. I was a curiosity.

My glass kept getting filled with champagne and my belly became full of bubbles. Hildy was laughing at one of the older ladies whose nose was stuck firmly in the air – she obviously thought she was very important. I began to feel quite tired and wished I could sit down, but then Frank appeared beside me like a rabbit from a magician's hat.

'Watch out, Rosie, you've got all squiffy. Why don't you come with me before someone notices?' The touch of his grip on my arm was like a firebrand.

'I'm fine!' I said, but I did feel dizzy.

I saw Frank and his sister exchange a look and I tried to pull away from him, but he held on tightly to my elbow and led me out of the drawing room along the corridor to a little conservatory at the back that held dozens of exotic ferns and cacti. I collapsed onto a wicker settee.

'That was mean of you,' I said, but I was glad he'd taken me away.

He lit up a cigarette and stood above me. 'You've had too much, that's all. Can't have you embarrassing your father. Not with all those old bores out there.'

'You didn't look like you were bored.'

'It's just playing a part, Rosie. Not something you're used to.' He sat down next to me and put his hand on my leg, and began to stroke it. 'That's why I like you. You're unspoilt.'

'I am?' I said. I was aware my voice sounded squeaky. He was close to me now. He smelt of a strong cologne, like something I fancifully imagined the princes of Arabia would use. I was certain he must be able to hear the pounding of my heart, which was beating so hard it hurt.

'At the moment you are, yes,' he said. 'You're exactly as you should be.' He reached up and felt along the length of my plaits, which, for once, had been pinned to my head, then plucked a hothouse lily from a pot and planted it in my hair.

I didn't exactly know what he meant. I for one wasn't at all happy with how I was. I wanted to be like Hildy, with a knowledge of the world and to travel, like all the Laffertys did, through the universe without doubt and dread. But here was a beautiful, supremely confident boy – a man now he'd turned eighteen – and he liked <u>me</u>. I closed my eyes and waited for him to kiss me and sure enough, he did, just lightly, like the brush of a peachskin. And for a while there, in that huge old hall, with a party going on nearby, I was the happiest I have ever been in my life. I don't think I realised at that glorious moment that I would spend the rest of the winter pining for him.

16

I must warn you that parts of this account might seem vulgar, even shocking. I'm not doing it deliberately. It might sound pompous, but I feel that now I have a duty to tell the truth. These places make you feel like that. It will be strange, perhaps even unpleasant to read, but I hope you will.

It wasn't until the snowdrops were out that I saw Franklin again.

Janey found me running down the lane the day the Laffertys arrived and called out –

'You be looking mighty pleased with yerself, Rosie.'

'They're back,' I said, 'the Laffertys are back.' Right then, the entire lane seemed to be budding with life and the birds had set up a chorus just for me.

She frowned. 'Look after yerself, child,' she said.

I stopped and put my hands on my hips. 'I'm not a child, Janey.'

'You are and yer not. Thass what I'm afeared of.'

I gave her a squeezing hug and leaned in to smell her particular aroma of marsh mud, salt and rosehip tea.

Over winter they hadn't come to Norfolk for weeks and I became quite morose. Father got fed up with me and told me I'd have to go away to school if I didn't stop moping about. I knew this was an empty threat. The printing press hardly made any money if Fairbrother's grumblings were true. I received letters from Hildy, never from Frank, telling me all about the shows she saw, the people she met and the parties she went to. She sprinkled her letters with names, like glittering jewels – the painter Augustus John, Harold Nicolson, the imperious Lady Astor, the marvellous Mitford sisters and especially Diana Mitford, now Guinness, shocking everyone by becoming Oswald Mosley's mistress. A year ago I wouldn't have known who any of these people were, they meant nothing to me, but through Hildy's letters they took on the feel of characters from a picture book, brightly painted and gaudy. I'd come to realise that Hildy, being untitled, resented and mocked this society, but yearned to be one of them at the same time. She mentioned Franklin in passing but they couldn't come up, apparently, as it was all too 'manic' with 'Oswald's new party'. I couldn't understand at all why this meant they couldn't come to Norfolk.

But when they finally came back to Old Hall, it was the same as before. We spent the whole time together, Hildy, Frank and I, playing music on their gramophone – jolly songs, jazz and show tunes, records from America; singers with names like Ozzie and Louis and Skip and voices that dripped with treacle and honey. Frank would twirl me around the drawing-room so I felt, if I half-closed my eyes, that I was one of the bright ones, the beautiful ones, always dancing and laughing and gay. When they weren't there, I would take long, freezing walks along the marshes and imagine the summer to come, which would be a more brilliant version of the one before. I could hear the music in the birdsong around me – the orchestra playing in the air and winding through the reeds on the marsh. I would hum the words I half remembered: dream of me ... sweet and lovely ... a bowl of cherries. I could <u>feel</u> spring coming, on my skin and in my heart. I was nearly sixteen and I could feel life blooming from deep within me, opening out towards the sun.

One Saturday morning, Hildy and her mother went to visit a lady friend of theirs who lived near King's Lynn, a viscountess no less. Frank told me he'd made up some bunkum about shooting and they let him off the trip. The colonel hadn't come up this time. Apparently he was needed by Mr Mosley to organise meetings for the party. I knew all this because Frank bicycled straight over to the Marsh House and rang the bell. Afterwards, I was relieved it was me who answered, though I should have known that Frank was the sort of person who'd be able to dream up some excuse.

'Frank! Why are you here?' I said, but he took hold of me and shut the door behind him, telling me to 'Ssshhh'.

'Is your father here?' he asked, but I assured him that Father was at the printworks in Cromer and wouldn't return until the last train. Since the summer of the Laffertys, Father had been having meetings around the county with various political people. Each time he returned, he would tell me that the meeting had been 'very satisfactory', but I only had a dim idea who these people were or why he was meeting them, just that they were something to do with Frank's own father, the colonel, and their dislike of the disastrous Ramsay MacDonald and Stanley Baldwin. And I knew it had something to do with the people we'd met at that supper party in the Hall back in the autumn – the London people in their beautiful suits – and Mr Mosley's new party. I supposed that he was hoping to make some money from them. He said they were the future of this country.

Frank relaxed then and we had a pleasant hour gossiping and drinking tea. He told me all the latest news from London, about the film version of Noël Coward's operetta Bitter Sweet, which he said was not a patch on the original, other farces and musical plays he'd seen and other details about London life. It all sounded very far away and glamorous, but I've forgotten most of it because as the morning raced towards midday, he professed himself ravenous. We foraged for a picnic in the kitchen and set out to the marsh. 'I feel like seeing a bit of the sky, little Rosie,' he said, putting his hands on either side of my face until my head tingled.

'I'm not little,' I said, catching the words in my throat.

He glanced down at me. 'No,' he said. 'You're getting to be quite grown up.'

We walked away from the empty house, with only the windows watching us, up the Green Way towards the marsh. His arm was in mine. I was becoming taller all the time and 'filling out' as Fairbrother said disapprovingly, frowning at my strained blouse. I was aware of every single movement of my body as I walked with him. My head came to his shoulder and he held onto my arm lightly. When we came to the marsh, he took my gloved hand and pulled me along to the edge and started to unbutton his boots.

'You too,' he said, grinning at me.

'But it'll be freezing cold, Frank,' I said.

'You're not a sissy, Rosie, are you?' he said, the dare in his eyes.

I could only obey. So there we were – our stockings stuffed in our boots and feet in the cold squelch of the marsh mud. He took me far along the creek where there was a spit of land. The spit was hidden by tufts of marsh grass you could hide behind and no one could see you. We ran over the little hill of sand and fell down the other side, laughing. The sun was out and it was almost warm – like the first day of spring. And I was surprised, though I had no right to be, but he pulled me to him straightaway and kissed me full on the lips. It was not the first time he'd kissed me, but this time was different. Our feet were caked with drying mud and our bare legs intertwined and I could feel him swell beneath his trousers and I wondered what on earth I should do. He kept touching me on my chest where I'd grown, circling his fingers, and putting his head there and making moaning sounds. Then he put his hand down his trousers and seemed to be having a kind of fit of spasmodic movement, until finally he threw back his head and howled at the clear blue sky above us. All the time he kept one hand on my waist which dug hard into my ribs. He fell back against the dune, panting, quite red in the face but with a look of ecstasy that was strange to see.

We didn't say much for a while, we just lay on our backs looking at the sky and I waited to see what he would do. I hoped it wouldn't be the same thing again, but I wanted something to happen. We were told so little and I'd stayed at the school for such a short time I had only a vague understanding of what he'd been doing – I knew it was something to do with desire but at the same time it was quite alien. I began to feel cold but I didn't want to break this feeling of being alone in the world with Frank. He moved his head close to mine and spoke softly into my ear so it tickled –

'Do you love me, Rosie?'

'Yes,' I said, hardly breathing.

'Good,' he said, 'because I don't know how much longer I can bear it. Dear little Rosie Valentine,' and kissed me again, slowly this time, his tongue flickering into all the crevices of my mouth.

And that was all, but as we waded back along the creek, the mud chilling my ankles and shivering up my legs, I felt that I was fully alive. The world was just the two of us, Frank and me.

Late in March, a day of fleeting clouds and sudden sunlight, Frank was alone for an afternoon at the Hall. Lady Lafferty was at the church as usual, the colonel was riding and Hildy was off for a drive with the persistent Gerald.

That day as I walked, tiny silver needles of desire prickled in my stomach and groin. The weekend staff were off too – it was just Frank and the cook there, and she was having a nap in the kitchen. He was eating an orange when he opened the door – the smell of it entered my body like a kind of sweet wine. He pulled a segment away and held it to my mouth. I opened it feeling silly, like a bird being fed by its mother, and he pushed it in, the juice dribbling down my chin and the tartness of it making me wince. He laughed. 'I bet you've not had many of those, have you?'

I shook my head, mute from my mouthful of orange.

Janey told me once that if a man wanted a girl, he must take an orange, prick the skin all over with a needle and sleep with it in his armpit. The next day he must make the girl he loved eat it. I remember thinking that sounded quite horrible, but standing there in the great entrance hall of Old Hall, I couldn't help but think of this with the sweet orange in my mouth, and imagine the charm-juice sliding down into me, making me love him.

He took hold of my hand and I followed him up the main staircase. I had only ever been to Hildy's bedroom, never to Frank's, but I knew that's where we were going. I didn't know exactly what for, except that he'd been saying for weeks now that our love (<u>our love!</u>) was natural and any expression of it was natural as well. I wasn't so naïve that I didn't know what men and women did in married beds. I knew how children were created – the rector himself spoke of such things. But I didn't know exactly what Frank had meant until then.

When it happened – it wasn't for very long – it hurt and I bled. Frank looked disgusted at the red blotches on the sheets and it brought tears springing to my eyes. He put his arm around me, told me to stop crying and wiped my eyes with the white edge of the sheet. But then he said I better get cleaned up quickly, and when I picked up my underwear and left the room I saw him tugging off the bedclothes and shoving them into a ball as if he couldn't bear the sight of my blood. They had an enormous upstairs bathroom that the colonel had had installed and which I always thought was luxurious, but it was draughty that afternoon. I sat on the lavatory and the stinging made more tears come but I wiped them away and wiped myself down there – it was sticky as well as sore. The whole room with its brass taps and curled bath feet and ruched curtains felt as if it were rebuking me for the horridness of my body, repelled by all this bodily matter, this grotesqueness.

When I got back to Frank's bedroom he was gaily smoking on the bed, propped up on the pillows.

'Come here, sweet Rosie,' he said, holding his arms open, and I wanted the comfort so badly, I did. I tucked myself under his arm and he stroked my hair. I had an urge to say something, to ask him not to do it again, but he kissed me on my head and said, 'There, it wasn't so bad, was it? You're my girl, now.' Despite the pain in my groin, it felt good to hear him say that. I was wanted by someone. I belonged to someone.

At home, I cocooned myself in tight with a hot water bottle, listened to the rats scuttling in the attic above me, and let Perdie nestle into my bed. I didn't know what to think. Afterwards, seeing my red eyes, he'd said I would like it when I got used to it, but I didn't like it then, I didn't like it at all and I wished my mother was there to advise me. But I wanted him above all else and that was more important than any discomfort I might have felt. The words of a song played in my head, a song we'd been playing all spring. 'Body and soul. I surrender'. I supposed that was what you did for love. You surrendered yourself.

17

It was Easter Sunday and we were all in church for the Easter service, the Laffertys at the front, Father and I behind. It had been gloomy and overcast all morning, and as we walked to the church it began to rain. It was the middle of the trial of our old rector, Mr Davidson. In my current situation, I've come to feel rather sorry for him. As I write, he has become a pathetic figure, an outcast. Back then, he was all over the papers. After the rector was late for the Armistice Day service, Major Marsden from the next village, who had been complaining about him for years, had finally succeeded in forcing the church to begin holding a trial against him, accusing him of using 'innocent girls' for his own ends on the streets of London. The rector was a fool, I think, more than anything. According to the rags and local gossip, he would find girls from Lyons tea shops or on the streets and offer to help them, often bringing them up to the rectory. Depending on your view, he was either trying to save them or lusted after them. Perhaps it was both. The village had been full of the scandal all year. In the meantime, the services went on, still sometimes held by the old rector and sometimes by some other poor man who had to deal with a divided village. They still loved him, you see, the rest of the villagers.

The service went on and on as usual, the stand-in rector talking about Jesus dying for our sins. Father muttered under his breath and I think if it hadn't been for Lady Lafferty's piety, we wouldn't have gone to church at all.

'She thinks she has a holy duty,' said Hildy, rolling her eyes.

But then I thought, too, of what Frank and I had done. I couldn't put it into words, I was too ashamed. It was me as much as him. Not at first, but by that Easter. I had begun to like the feeling of it. It's hard to think something can be wrong when it feels like an explosion in your insides, all the way through you to the tips of your fingers and the top of your head and you can't breathe, and your whole body feels alive for the first time, and you want it to go on and on and on. But I wasn't supposed to think like that, I knew it. I looked at Colonel and Mrs Lafferty and tried to imagine them doing it to create Hildy and Frank and I had to squeeze my eyes shut to stop myself bursting. Or Mrs Fairbrother with her fat bottom. It was a terrible thought.

As we left the church the rain had stopped, but the sky was still hung low and overcast. Hildy had her arm in mine while we waited for her mother. Lady Lafferty's elegant neck was bent down to the stand-in rector. Then she turned to me and smiled beatifically, as if she were about to perform some Christian miracle. There was a keenness in her look though, that made me squirm. I was afraid she knew – and worse, that she would take Frank away from me. I thought I must be damned and although I knew I should feel guilty and tell Franklin to stop, I wasn't sure I could.

St Mark's Eve is at the end of April and on that night it is traditional to perform divination rituals. Janey had taught me how to divine who we would marry. Although I didn't entirely believe it, neither did I want to bring myself bad luck by not going along with it. I hadn't met Franklin the year before, and had done it out of fun. I'd never seen anyone. That year, Janey gave me some hemp seed and said, 'You oughta find out who you're destined for since you're going on with the boy from the Hall.'

'Oh Janey, it's just nonsense,' I said, hiding my embarrassment, but wanting, needing, at the same time, for it to be him.

'That may be so but I reckon you want to try anyway, dunt you?'

'Oh all right then,' I said, feigning disinterest.

Janey herself always took herself to the church on St Mark's Eve because, as she told me, 'The next year's dead will walk.' This was a very old custom, she said, that no one practised any more, but she had the habit and couldn't get out of it or she might miss her own death. She told me the watcher must watch the entrance to the church at midnight and those who would die in the coming year would walk in and not come out. I didn't believe in this either, but she did seem to have a miraculous tendency to predict who in the village would die in the coming year. She'd predicated a local farmer's death the year before.

At just before midnight it was black as pitch in the garden and the ground wet with dew. I snuck out in my boots and threw the hemp seed at the end of the garden, where it meets the creek. I chanted in a low voice:

> Hemp seed I sow,
> Hemp seed I grow;
> He that is my true love,
> Come after me and mow.

I waited, feeling incredibly foolish, out in the dark garden with a cool dampness in the air, in my nightgown and boots. Nothing happened, merely a rushing sound from the marsh which sent shivers along my skin. There was a sliver of a moon and I thought maybe something passed by in the shadows, but it wasn't a man mowing with a scythe. It was probably a rat. Annoyed with myself, I stomped off back to the house. What exactly had I been trying to prove? That Franklin was my destiny? I was a country girl with a mad mother and he was a Lafferty. The most pressing concern for me should have been how to stop it before anyone found out. But already, my mind was twisting itself to justify our actions. Damned or not, I told myself, it wouldn't be entirely bad, would it, if he loved me? If we loved each other, surely we could be saved? It was natural, he said. And it seemed true. As natural as breathing.

The next day, I asked Janey who she'd seen out walking in the night and she gave me a funny look and said it were bad luck to name them but it were no one young. So that was a relief.

Later – it might have been the same day – I was walking Perdie along the path at the end of the lane that skirts the marsh, when I saw the smirking face of George Bayfield a mere foot away. I'd been daydreaming about Franklin and had hardly noticed anything around me at all. Now I felt like I'd emerged out into the open, undefended. To my left, the marsh was clothed in the light green of spring and to my right, the line of Stiffkey Wood was soughing in the wind and casting waving shadows across the muddy track.

'Perdie, heel,' I said, but she was already bounding up to the boy and he'd kneeled down and had something held out in his hand to her.

'She's a right pretty dog you got there, Rosie Wright.'

'Yes she is,' I said, haughty as anything. 'She doesn't need feeding.'

'She likes it,' he said, and sure enough, silly trusting Perdie was licking his outstretched hand.

'What do you want?' I said, as sure as I could. I didn't like the way he was smiling at me. He wasn't angry and shouting like before. He seemed calm, which was more worrying.

'To see you,' he said. He was closer now, in front of me.

'Why do you want to do that, George Bayfield? You called me a witch last time I saw you.' He should have been a handsome boy, George Bayfield, with his dark curls and symmetrical features, and I could once have imagined taking a fancy to him, but he was always amused at others' failures and his face often contained such callousness that it contorted his fine features.

He smiled as if it was a funny joke. 'Maybe you are,' he said. 'My ma says you've bewitched the boy from the Hall. The posh one. She says you've got gypsy blood.'

'She doesn't know anything about him,' I said. 'Nor me.' My neck was hot and I could feel the blush rising up my chest to my throat.

'Well, either way, I've heard a lot about you and him and what you get up to. The whole village knows it. But I thought I'd come and find out for myself whether it was true.'

Now my whole body was burning.

'Leave me alone or I'll hurt you,' I said.

'Oh come on now,' he said, 'don't be like that.' And very quickly, before I could run away or retaliate, he'd grabbed the back of my head and shoved his tongue into my mouth. One hand had my hair pulled back and with the other he was pawing all over my chest.

For a shameful, terrible moment I froze, I was so shocked by what he was doing. Then Perdie began to bark. I bit down on his wiggling, flickering tongue. He sprang back, yelping like a pig, clutching his mouth.

'Don't ever touch me again,' I stammered and picked up the yapping Perdie.

'You're a whore, Rosie Wright!' he shouted at my back. 'A whore and a witch.'

I should have known by what happened with the grocer's son on the path by the marsh that I wasn't meant to be saved.

18

The next month, the Marsh House saw something it never had before – a party to celebrate Father's birthday. Father was never one for birthdays and other trivialities, but he was forced into it by the Laffertys. They were that sort of people. Sometimes I used to think Father would ride around on a horse naked through the streets like Lady Godiva if the colonel or Lady Lafferty told him to.

The day of the party was a fine, spring day and the apple trees were in blossom. I always used to imagine my mother with apple blossom in her hair like confetti when she was married, but it was just a childish made-up thing. I would hide in the trees and shake it down over Billy, the gardener's son, when we were children. Lady Lafferty tried to get Father to hold the party in the Hall but he went rather red and insisted that if a party were to be held, we could certainly manage it. He, Fairbrother and Dolly got themselves into a huge flap after he announced it. Perdie was dressed up in a bow and pranced around the garden madly excited. Fairbrother made up a vast trifle and dozens of fancy little cakes and made me sew hundreds of triangles of cloth for bunting which poor Rogers had to string up all over the garden. There was a lot of fuss about impending rain. Fairbrother spent most of her time on the morning of the party muttering about 'threatening clouds' and making Rogers construct a kind of rain shade from sheets over the patio. It looked completely ridiculous, like some kind of safari tent, but in the end the clouds passed over and the afternoon was clear.

Now I think of it, the whole of that summer was remarkable for the lack of rain. Day after day, as spring turned to summer, the dew evaporated and the morning mists burnt off and the sun shone unrelentingly on the marsh. We were burnt up, the land and I, hot and fevered.

I was made to wear a white dress, a very old-fashioned one Father had found a woman in the village to make for me for the summer, with frills and ruching, which was not the fashion at all. I looked like one of the village girls, dancing around the maypole on May Day, something I'd long since given up. Hildy always brought me magazines she'd read and all the dresses in them were simple, without what we considered 'baby nonsense'. She would lend or give me her old dresses but most of them looked misshapen on stumpy little me. Or the colours wouldn't work with my complexion. I tried to imagine Mother getting married in a long, white dress but there were no pictures up anywhere. Father must have hated to be reminded of her. I had only two photographs of her, which I found in a drawer in Father's desk. I kept them in my bedside drawer and took them out sometimes to look at. They were like a pair: before and after. One was taken in India where mother was born – I'd been told she was an orphan then and I wonder if it was sent out to prospective suitors. She was very beautiful and serious-looking with large, deep eyes. She was in white, as in the next photograph, but it was a summer dress and she had a parasol. It was like the portrait of someone whose life has already been decided. In the next one she must have just got married but she wasn't smiling at the camera. The date on the back says May, 1912. It was very formal. She was seated outside the front of the Marsh House, which had just been built, on a high-backed chair and wearing a pale dress that, apart from the length (mine was shorter though not short enough), looked much like the monstrosity I was forced to wear to the birthday. Father stood behind her with his hand on her shoulder. He looked proud, as if he'd just landed the catch of a lifetime.

I wished I could climb into the photograph and put my head on her lap, for her to stroke my hair. But now I think what was in those sad eyes was fear. I often wonder if she knew what was going to happen to her. That her first baby would die within the year, then the next, and that they would take her away from me, her only surviving child. Janey had told me there'd been babies before me, ones that had barely survived, ghost brothers that no one spoke of. I knew this but it didn't mean much to me then because what girl thinks much of the time before her? I used to think about the madhouse though, and try to imagine what Mother did in there. Was she locked up as I am now? Had they shaved her hair? This is what Hildy told me. She was an expert as she'd visited a lunatic asylum in London. I still wonder about it. And I wonder if they've told her where I am.

'You look fair, Rosemary,' Frank said when he arrived, 'like a lovely, innocent country girl.' His lips twitched as if he was itching to tear the little bows at my breast off with his teeth right there. But perhaps I imagined that because he spent the rest of the party ignoring me, off talking to various other young men all dressed up in suits, and only now and again peering at me with a lascivious look so that I felt naked even though I was trussed up like a turkey. Hildy came to my rescue and took my arm and we paraded around the garden with glasses of rhubarb cordial, eating some of the little cakes with lemon icing that poor Dolly had churned out. Sadly, this wasn't for long. We'd barely taken one turn around the lawn when we passed a knot of the older people gathered around Lady Lafferty – men and women like Mrs Parkinson who's a nosey-parker from church. I caught snatches of their conversation.

'Oh, she is quite small,' said one.

'Her complexion is quite . . . dark,' said another.

'I always wondered if there was a touch of the – you know – about her –' This one lowered his voice and whispered something into the ear of someone else so I didn't know what it was I might have been touched with.

'I hear she's a reader of mystery novels,' said another, as if this was quite distasteful.

'She's not a beauty like her mother, let's hope she's not . . .' started one, but didn't finish the comparison.

'It must be because of Richard's support of the colonel's politicking,' said someone.

'It must be hard for her without a mother,' said Lady Lafferty, 'the poor child.'

I imagined them circling around me, prodding and touching as if I were a prize sheep being weighed up for a show. Hildy and I stood back from them unseen, and I could see her sardonic eyebrow underneath her jaunty little purple hat. I wondered what it would be like to have the kind but distant Lady Lafferty as a mother.

Finally, when we were away from the crowd, I said to Hildy, 'I can't think why they were so interested in me all of a sudden.'

'Oh Rosie, you are a silly thing,' she said, 'don't you see? You're like a vision of virginal girlhood. Everyone venerates virginity, even if they don't practise it themselves.' She took a sip of her cordial.

'What do you mean?'

She gazed at me with amusement. 'In my world, darling, it's rather a given that the men and sometimes even the women will roam. We can't all be staid as Mummy. It's not the modern way. But you – you should cultivate this –' She waved her hand towards me in my convent girl get-up.

My face felt hot and I worried I was blushing. Perhaps she would think I was a humble sort of person.

Hildy continued. 'Poor Mummy is awfully worried about Frank though. He's always been her favourite. She turns a blind eye to most of his shenanigans but I think she's worried he'll get syphilis or something. That would really be a shock, even for her beloved Frankie.'

I didn't know what 'syphilis' was and thought it was some kind of urban illness, but it made me feel queasy thinking of Franklin touching me and our relations in the bed. I had a picture then of how they would see me if they really knew. And while it made me feel giddy with a thrilling nausea, I couldn't let it continue. If they knew ... If they knew they wouldn't forgive me. They would blame me, not him. I must have reddened because Hildy suddenly grabbed my elbow and peered down at me with suspicious eyes.

'You haven't let anyone seduce you, have you?'

'No, of course not,' I said hotly, thinking of George Bayfield thrusting his tongue in my mouth; Franklin pulling up my dress with his fine fingers.

'Well you absolutely must not, whatever they promise you. Don't be a fool, darling. They are slaves to their instincts you know, even the well-bred ones.' She made a pointed glance across the lawn to the knot of suited men, which included her dogged suitor, Gerald.

'All of them?' I said. 'What about Gerald?'

She laughed, throwing her head back. 'Yes, Rosemary, all of them. Even dear old Gerald. Even my dear brother. Especially him.'

I looked down at my feet blurring below.

'Does your mother know about – Gerald,' I said, very quiet.

'Oh yes, she's chums with his mother. Rosemary, listen to me. You must understand that it's different for men.' There was a slight change in her voice then and I glanced up to see her face tighten and I wondered, for the first time, if Hildy had any doubts. Until then, she'd seemed impervious. Then she laughed again and took one of my plaits in her elegant, white hand. She peered at me curiously.

'This – this is your value. Without it –' she shook her head. 'I know you're fond of Frank, darling, but he's . . . well he's no different. In fact, I think he's one of the worst. Mummy is a fool about him, she always has been. Do be careful.'

'Hildy,' I said, 'I'm not feeling awfully well. I might just go and have a lie-down.'

'Oh,' she said, 'we can't have you party-pooping. Take some smelling salts or something. Or a nip of brandy,' she called as I ran off to the house.

But I didn't come out again and Father was angry with me later, telling me I'd ruined the party. I didn't care at first, I was tumbling with such a mess of feelings I didn't really think much about anything apart from Franklin and what we'd done and if he loved me and what to do. I had given my virginity willingly. I wasn't pure like they thought I was; I'd given myself to him. He couldn't just discard me.

After the awful party, the Laffertys went back to London. As the days passed, I thought perhaps Hildy had been exaggerating Franklin's appetites. Men ogled at women, I did know that. It didn't mean they did anything about it. But I resolved to settle it with Franklin when he returned, and to make it clear somehow that I was afraid and he must protect me.

But my life at the Marsh House was so empty of anything interesting, it was impossible not to feel a lift in my heart when Fairbrother told me the Laffertys were coming back to Old Hall for the Midsummer weekend. I practically threw myself at Hildy and she at me when we were reunited. And when I saw him and he smiled at me the sun came out, for all my resolutions. It didn't, of course, it was a grey day, but it felt like that inside. I knew it was sentimental and foolish. I told myself that Frank probably smiled at lots of girls like that and tried to burst the bubbles of delight I felt. But it was the devil in me; I felt the current of electricity running between us and wanted more than anything to fuse our bodies together. To touch him and to have him touch me.

We were in their drawing room for tea. My father, the colonel, Gerald and Mr Saunders – a thin man from the party, who Hildy said knew Mr Mosley personally – were playing bridge by the window. They were talking about Mussolini in Italy, and the Mitfords, the latest affairs of the Prince of Wales and various other people whose names were always in the papers.

I made an effort to pay attention as I thought that one day I might meet some of these people and I would look like such a bumpkin if I didn't know who they were.

Lady Lafferty was making plans for a church fête, Hildy was drinking tea with her feet up on an ottoman and I was next to her, greatly wishing I wasn't there.

'You look well,' said Frank, smiling at me from his position leaning against the fireplace with a cigarette.

At Franklin's words, I felt his mother turn her attention towards me.

'Yes, positively so,' she said. 'Come here and sit beside me, Rosemary.'

Again, the shiver of fear ran through me that she knew and was going to stop it. For all my good intentions, the thought of his attention being withdrawn from me was like the curtains being drawn on the day. But I moved across the room and sat on the settee next to her. She turned her ice-cold eyes on me, chilling my skin, although the room was warm. But then she said something that was unexpected.

'You're a true country girl, Rosemary, and you don't know the ways of the world, but I think of you like a daughter and I will do my best to protect you.' She laid a cool, thin hand on my arm and set my skin to goosepimples. 'There are things about this world that I don't think you understand, child. Things it took me too long to understand. Be careful, dear. You must keep your wits about you.'

It was an awkward little speech and I didn't know how to answer it. I mumbled, 'Thank you,' not understanding exactly what I was to be protected from. From Frank?

'We can't stay cooped up in here, Mama,' said Frank and, stubbing out his cigarette in his teacup, he took two steps across the drawing room and reached down for my hand. 'Rosie and I will take a little stroll.'

I tried to glare at him, but he had his blue eyes fixed on me and I was like an insect stuck in the sticky trap of a spider.

'Yes, go, darling,' said Lady Lafferty. In her voice was a weariness and nervousness that made me think Frank had some hold over her. As I left, the look she gave me was one I couldn't interpret, although now I think it was a kind of pity. They returned to their hands of bridge and Hildy to her magazine, and the two of us went out into the garden. It was cool and wet from a rare flash of rain that morning and my boots got soaked in the grass. I remember the lawn was sleek and wet – I kept sliding and he held onto me. We walked a long way across the grounds to the summer house overlooking the river and fields that ran south away from the Hall. I'd never been there before – it was round with a tiled roof and open windows entwined with ivy, and a stone bench that ran around it. I knew he'd brought me down there because it couldn't be seen from the house. In a rigid panic, I tried to hold myself stiff and unyielding to him.

'Hildy says you've done this a lot. Been with girls,' I blurted out.

'That was in the past, Rosie.' Frank was lounging with his feet up on the bench and I stood, jittering.

'Did you do with them what . . . what we've done?'

He didn't answer.

I felt the dreaded tears rise in my throat and sniffed them back down. 'You . . . you disgust me, Frank. You tricked me into doing it. I didn't know.'

'Now Rosie,' he said, smiling indulgently. 'That's not true. You liked it as much as me.'

'I didn't,' I said, but it was pointless because he knew the truth. Not at first, but soon after, yes.

He sighed and said, 'It's you that I want, little Rosie.' Reaching up, he pulled me to the bench and touched the nape of my neck. He put his lips to the top of my spine and with a great effort, I pulled away. He exhaled in frustration.

'What would your mother think, Franklin? She says I ought to be careful.'

'She likes you. She thinks you're a sweet girl.' He chucked me under the chin as if I was a child. 'She doesn't know you like I do. She doesn't know your true nature. Sometimes I wonder,' he said, putting his fingers on my face, tracing along my cheekbones and hairline, 'if you have Mediterranean or Arab blood. It would explain your wildness.' He bit my earlobe. I grimaced. 'Shall I tell her how you cry out? It's your nature, my wild, sweet Rosie. And mine.'

'We should stop,' I said, but the next moment all I said was some murmuring that became a moan because his mouth was on my throat and collarbone and down to my chest, and his hands were up my skirts. It was no use. I was going to give in. I closed my eyes and thought of the light playing on the water on the Broads in the summer and his hands on the wheel and how this, just this, was the most natural thing in the world.

19

At dusk on St John's Eve at the mid-point of the year, I went with Janey to pick fennel, rue and St John's wort to ward off evil and then, when night fell, to the creek at the end of our lane where she was going to perform the toad bone rite. Janey always took these rituals seriously. As I said, I told myself I didn't believe it but I see now that it was part of me, as the house was, as the marsh was. It was our world: Janey's and mine. A secret world that no one else entered. Not even my father. Actually, especially him. The funny thing was, every time we performed one of those rites, I felt closer to my mother than I did otherwise. When she'd arrived in Norfolk from India, before I was born – the year the Marsh House was built – she told Janey she'd left behind an ayah, a kind of nurse who looked after her while her parents were off ruling over India, and the ayah had taught my mother all kinds of magical rituals. So I could imagine my mother there with me on the bank of the creek.

Janey used a dead toad she'd kept specially (she would never kill a toad like others might). Behind the creek, away on the marsh, bluish lights danced on the bog. Janey always used to tell me stories of the will-o'-the-wykes that led travellers to their dooms, but I knew it was marsh gas and that people used to get sick from marsh fever. She lit a fire from the dry reeds and at midnight, under a pink Rose Moon (my moon, Janey said), and by the light of the fire and the marsh lights, we lay the little bones in the muddy water and let them float off. I knew that while you were watching the bones in the water you must on no account take your eyes off them. Janey told me she had to keep her eyes trained on the floating bones or her power would be lost. Even if the world was falling down around her, she couldn't stop watching them. When she finally came out of her trance, Janey fished out of the creek one of the bones, a little crotch-bone, she said it was. She would take it home, bake it, powder it and put it in a box; the oil from the bones made a powerful, old magic.

The rest of the tiny toad bones gleamed in the fire and moonlight and then disappeared into the glimmers of the reflections. I silently mouthed a prayer to God that Janey would always protect me from dark magic, that she would harness her powers, whatever they were, to keep me from harm. I thought about how Frank put his lips on my neck and the way George Bayfield had clawed at me. I wondered if the toad bone oil would be strong enough to keep them away and decided I'd ask Janey for a spell. I felt on the edge of something both desperate and absolutely humiliating.

That night, I added a bunch of the fennel, rue and St John's wort to my windowsill next to a sprig of seablite and the white, dry husks of whelks' eggs.

The next day, when I was helping Janey make some herb tea, she went out to give Smutch his bone and I took one of the little bottles of toad bone oil from her shelf. She'd laughed at me when I'd asked for a spell, saying 'I don't do that kind of magic, Rosie, and you know it,' and ruffled up my hair like I was a child.

I didn't think about taking it, I just did. I didn't know then what I planned on doing with it, until the following Sunday when I saw the grocer's family leaving church ahead of me and the glossy black curls of the back of George's head. I skipped ahead, sidled up to him and whispered into his ear.

'I wanted to say sorry for the other day.'

His eyes flickered towards me.

'I've got something for you, George.'

He looked askance at me, wary I suppose after that time when I bit his tongue. But he had a look in his eyes that was hungry and wanting. I could hear his breathing, shallow and raspy.

'Come to the marsh at dusk,' I said. 'I'll give it to you then.'

I held his gaze until he reddened and mumbled, 'Aright.'

The sun set late at that time of the year so after supper I said I had to take Perdie. I undid the top buttons of my Sunday best lace blouse to expose my throat. It was a warm night and I liked the feeling of the breeze on my skin. Sure enough, at the top of Green Way, with the marsh and the darkening sky spread out before us, there was the short, skinny figure of the grocer's son, squinting as the sun set in a blaze of orange behind me. He had his hands in his trouser pockets as if it was nothing to him to be waiting for me on the edge of the marsh.

'What've you got for me then?' he asked. He didn't come close like last time. And for the first time, it occurred to me that he would really expect something of me, and I didn't know what he would do if he got angry.

'You'll have to come a bit closer to see,' I said, and licked my tongue along my bottom lip.

He frowned and held his hand up to his eyes. 'How do I know you're not going to do something mad like last time?' he said. 'How do I know you won't bite me?'

'I wouldn't,' I replied. 'And anyway,' I added, 'I bet you liked it really.'

'You're mad,' he said, but his face had gone red like earlier, and I could see that mixture of hate and wanting that he'd had before.

'Come here,' I said. In the pocket of my dress, I fondled the unstoppered bottle of toad bone oil.

George took two paces towards me and as he did, I took the bottle out of my pocket and flung it straight in his face. The whole sloppy mess dripped down from his forehead to his mouth. His hands flew to his eyes and I watched while he shouted out and stumbled back, tripping over his feet, and fell onto his back on the path. Perdie jumped up and down, barking at him, startling the birds in the trees, who squawked off into the dusky sky.

He tried to wipe the oily substance from his face but it was still in his eyes. He was blinded.

I turned my back on him and walked home, Perdie capering about my feet. I thought that would be the end of the Bayfield boy, magic or no magic.

On the way back along the path by the creek, there was a shudder in the grasses and a silvery-grey adder slid out in front of us. Perdie yapped at it, but the snake seemed unperturbed. It turned its red eye to me and flicked out its forked tongue before slithering in a sinuous curve, back into the grass. I decided to ask Janey if an adder brought any luck.

But there was no protection after all.

A week or so later, not long before my birthday, Father and I received an invitation to a garden party at Old Hall. The day it was held was the hottest day of the year so far. As Father and I walked to the Hall, sweat prickled under my arms. I wondered if this was the moment when his mother would be waiting for me. When she would damn me.

It was not a garden party like the one for Father's birthday. This was quite different. There were glass bowls of strawberries and cream, a huge meringue with plump fruits and fat dollops of cream on the top, a real band in black tie playing jazz on the patio, and the beautiful people milling about with their cigarette holders and knees on show. I was wearing a pale primrose-yellow summer dress with white sprigs all over it and white stockings on underneath. Across the lawn I saw Lady Lafferty in a flowing pale pink gown the colour of the inside of a shell and she tipped her fan at me. I wandered about for a few minutes looking for Hildy and Frank, listening to the gossip about the rector and stories of rallies in London and Birmingham. But I was hardly there any time at all before Franklin took my arm and led me to the summer house. We are having a conversation, I said in my head. I won't let it happen. I can't. He held my hand and I wanted him to. That was the stupid thing about it. I wanted him to look after me, to take me away from my isolation. His skin shone with the heat of the day. His sleeves were rolled up, revealing the blond down on his arms, lit golden by the sun. I felt a film of sweat on my upper lip.

At first he kissed me on my cheek, and then my mouth. I felt the fluttering in my groin but held myself back. 'What's the matter?' he said. 'You can't be off again. It's impossible.'

'No. Nothing,' I said.

He played with the hem of my dress. He took a bunch of fabric in his hand and lifted it up to my thigh, exposing the skin above the stockings. I could hear the clinking of champagne glasses, the trumpet and the horn from the band, laughter like bells.

'Not here, Franklin,' I said. 'Someone might see.'

'There's no one down here apart from the gardener and I'm sure he's seen worse.

'Do you like this?' he added, touching the soft part of my inner thigh. Yes, I thought. I like it. Don't ever stop.

'We mustn't,' I said, screwing up all my will, and took his hand and held it away from me.

'Don't be a tease,' he said. And he kissed me again and this time he pressed himself on top of me too, so my spine was against the hard stone of the bench that went around the summer house. With one hand he had his fingers splayed on my neck and with the other, he pulled my underwear down and put his fingers inside me. It wasn't gentle and I tried to pull away.

'What about this?' he said, and pushed his hand harder into me. His fingernails scraped against me. His mouth was near my ear and I could feel the wet heat of his breath and the smell of alcohol.

'It hurts,' I said.

But he didn't reply. I told myself he hadn't heard me. He was breathing hard now and was fiddling with his own trousers. I tried then to push him but he was strong and he took both my arms and pinned them down, scraping the bones of my wrists against the stone.

When he pushed himself inside me I would have shouted out, only I couldn't because he had his hand over my mouth. The back of my head was pressed onto the rough edge of the bench. The trumpet blared and someone shattered a glass on the patio and everyone cheered. A breeze blew across my exposed thigh making me shudder.

Afterwards, he tried to kiss me and I turned my head quickly so his mouth fell on my cheek.

'What's the matter with you?' he said.

I was pulling up what was left of my stockings. 'Nothing,' I said.

'Come here,' he said, his voice soft. 'I forget sometimes how young you are. You make me want you, Rosie. I can't stop myself.'

And despite the humiliation, my pulse quickened and I allowed him to kiss me again.

I walked home on my own, the way I'd come, and the day was the same. It was the same hot, still day with hardly a breeze in the trees. I didn't run, I dragged my feet one after the other in a daze. Stifling, not a breath of air. I didn't understand how my shoes still clopped on the same dusty road and the sun still burned the back of my neck and the same dirty curtains hung in the windows of the cottages. The sun heated the top of my head and my neck the same way it had done on the way to the Hall. It all went on just as before. Except now I had a throb in the back of my head, marks on my wrist and a soreness in my groin.

I never wore that dress again.

I can still see it clearly though, that dress, the sunshine yellow, the tiny white flowers like stars scattered all over it. It would be pleasant to have something pretty to look at now I'm only ever in grey. Not that dress though. I'm thinking of the ones Hildy used to wear, in violets and lavenders and silky creams. They were beautiful clothes, bedazzling, the cloth and cut so fine they looked as if they belonged on her tall, thin body. I think of the roughness of the cloth I'm wearing now and it's like a penitent's. I suppose that is what they want from me.

20

Sitting on the edge of the bathtub, my cheek leaned against the cool porcelain of the upstairs sink. In the bowl was a pool of salmon-pink vomit. My body had produced something the colour of the dress Father had brought me for my sixteenth birthday.

I hated the dress, which was long and unfashionable. He had also given me Trollope's Barnaby Rudge and I did not think much of that either. Franklin had sent chocolate truffles from London in a beautiful embossed tin box with a pattern of blue flowers around the edge, but I had found them sickly and they made me gag. I was going to find out why.

From behind me I heard Fairbrother's hard, blunt voice –

'That's you fallen,' she declared with grim satisfaction. 'Up the spout.' There was no lock on the door and it was ajar. 'I always knew you'd come to no good.'

I understood her – I heard the way the villagers talked and I wanted to shout 'No, I'm not!' – but she'd already stalked away. 'Your father needs to know what you've gone and done.'

I shut the door then – too late – and sat with my back to it. What <u>had</u> I done? It couldn't be true. My body was revolting against something inside it – but not that, surely. I must be ill.

The doctor was summoned. He was an old man, not from the village, not our usual doctor. Fairbrother made me sit on the bed.

'You don't have to be here, do you?'

'Your father asked me to,' she said, and crossed her arms over her very ample bosom.

'Lie down please,' said the doctor. His voice was shaky as if he was disgusted at having to do such a thing. I wanted to scream at them all that I had no need of any of this. My Janey could have done it, she had <u>delivered</u> me. She had seen me come bloody and bawling out of my poor mother. She would know what to do. But Janey wasn't ever invited into the house, not anymore. Not since Mother was sent away.

I squeezed my eyes shut and clenched my fists and lay back on the bed. My thighs were clamped together but he put his hands on my knees and pulled them apart, chilling my parts. His cold fingers prodded inside me, his heavy face averted. I could hear his breathing, shallow and fast. Up he went, pushing right into me until he must have found what he wanted. There was a dull pressing ache in my stomach. I kept my mouth tightly closed and bit my bottom lip. All the time, he never spoke to me, only to Fairbrother, who stood watch like a prison guard in the room. Fat, stupid tears appeared at the corners of my eyes and fell down the side of my face and I wiped them away furiously.

When it was over, the doctor washed his hands in a bowl of hot water Dolly had brought up, washing me off his cold, white hands. He whispered something to Fairbrother and said to the wall behind me –

'You can get dressed now.'

It was the end of July and normally the Laffertys would be in London for the season. So it was a shock when very soon after the doctor's visit, on a dreary day, I heard the doorbell ring and Fairbrother go into a great clattering fuss.

'It's her ladyship, her ladyship! We've got nothing for her. Dolly – Dolly, get here now!'

I crept out of my room where I'd been reading, and waited on the landing, until Lady Lafferty had been let in and her umbrella stashed and her coat taken – it was drizzling outside – and she was shown into the front room.

Dolly was sent in with tea. When she came out, backwards, her head bent low (Oh Dolly, I thought. Don't!), I tiptoed to the door to listen. All I caught was this:

'Richard, I know you aren't terribly keen on the church after all the village has suffered, but please, for me ...' There was a scrape and a hush and I couldn't catch what was said. Then my father's voice, hoarse and in pain–

'... deeply sorry that my family should bring such shame –'

'No,' came Lady Lafferty's voice, soft and low, 'it's the least we can do for you. You know how much I value your loyalty to my husband, Richard.' She paused. 'And your kindness to me.'

There was a rustling. I caught the words 'lonely' and 'Louisa', then a hard scrape and footsteps and I flew, lightly and fast, back upstairs.

They were going to help me. Perhaps it would be a sanatorium, an exclusive place where unfortunate girls could go to dispose of awkward things. I pictured big, white rooms and a wall of glass overlooking a frozen lake. I didn't know how she'd found out, but I could guess – Fairbrother and her chattering mouth. By now, I knew enough of how people like the Laffertys lived to know that they had ways to smooth over something undesired. It was such a relief, I felt like singing.

When she'd gone, Father called me to his study. This was highly unusual – I was rarely allowed in his sanctum. Inside it was overflowing with paper – pamphlets and books spilling over his desk and onto the floor. Stacks and stacks of them. On his desk was a photograph from the party in the autumn. He was standing next to Lady Cynthia and her alarming husband, Mr Mosley, the man with the film star looks. Colonel and Lady Lafferty were in the picture too, but it was Frank I homed in on. He was beaming at the camera as if this was exactly where he wanted to be.

I hardly heard Father talking. He was saying that the colonel and Lady Lafferty and himself had agreed that it was best for all concerned if a marriage took place between their son – 'and you, Rosemary, given your condition'. Outside the study window rain was falling. The noise of it smattering against the pane drowned out his voice. So that was it. My future had been decided. For a strange, bewildering moment, I wished I could have melted into the floorboards and transformed into a rat with a fat tail on the marsh. It was a dream come true, a girl's best wish, the ultimate ambition. But it didn't feel like it at that moment. I didn't understand why I wasn't cock-a-hoop. Rather, I felt small and scared. I didn't understand how I was supposed to have a *baby*. I had prayed and chanted and dreamt of Franklin loving me but I had never thought of babies.

'Rosemary, look at me when I'm talking to you,' he said, cutting through my inattention.

I lifted my gaze to his. There was the trace of a sad smile on his face. Perhaps he was relenting.

'I feel responsible for what's happened. I should have sent you away to school to learn decent morals.'

I said nothing but looked out of the window at the rain lightly pattering onto the garden.

'I should have married again, a long time ago, and given you a mother –'

'I have a mother,' I said.

'– given you a mother who could have guided you, and perhaps you would never have lost your way so entirely.' His face clouded. 'But –' Here he glanced with a satisfied look at the photograph on the table, 'at least now you'll be entering the care of a good family. With time, you'll learn to be grateful. You'll be a wife and a mother.'

'I don't want to be either,' I said sullenly. From the window I saw the rain had stopped and the sky was clearing.

'Nonsense,' he said. 'There's no alternative.' The inevitability of it dropped like a stone into my stomach. It would happen, whatever I wanted.

'You're very lucky indeed that I haven't cast you out. That I kept you all this time. That I didn't send you away at birth. And now you have been offered a sanctuary which, frankly, you don't deserve. And you respond like this. You are an ingrate.' His voice was low and hard.

'I don't know why you kept me. I wish you hadn't. You cast Mother out, you should have got rid of me then too,' I said.

'If you don't want to turn into your mother, you should do as I say.'

'You said she was dead,' I said defiantly.

His face darkened and seemed to pulse with rage. I was afraid he would strike me and cowered in front of him waiting for the blow. But his expression shut down and he closed his eyes.

'Go!' he said.

I ran out of the study, letting the door slam deliberately behind me, and out of the house to Janey.

She ushered me into her all-in-one room, as I thought of it, her sitting-room-cum-dining-room-cum-kitchen. On the hob, a pot was simmering and the air smelt soupy.

'You want a cup a something?'

I never refused Janey. So we shared a cup of the tea she made herself. It was bitter-tasting, laced with sweet honey. It wasn't cold outside, in fact the day had heated up, but here in Janey's cottage the season was always the same – an indeterminate half-lit world, the only sign of difference being the herbs she had strung up, and what was in the pot.

'What's happened, girl? Spit it out.'

'The doctor says – the doctor says – I'm pregnant. And they want me to marry Franklin.' The words were heavy and I was still reeling from the force of them.

Head down, I felt rather than saw her move over to where I sat. I could smell the sea-smell she always had on her and I wanted to cry then, for things to be how they had been before, for my childhood. She let me fall into her and cry on her ugly old clothes and into her familiar, cushiony chest.

Eventually I heard her speaking from above me. I was afraid she'd say I warned you but instead she said –

'Now I'd have thought that would please you, the way you've been going on about that boy –'

'I am . . . I think. It's just I don't want to . . . I don't want . . .' I could barely speak.

'I know,' she said. 'But you think they'll want you to wed if you aren't with child no more?'

I sniffed. 'I don't know.' The idea of being married to Frank was a dream I hadn't dared to believe in. I couldn't see how the Laffertys would ever deem me suitable for their golden boy. A part of me knew it was only because Lady Lafferty saw me carrying his child that she wanted me. She had other reasons too, but I didn't know that then.

'And what about you? What do you want? Do yer love him?'

No one ever asked me what I wanted. I tried to think. I wanted the Franklin of the beach; of the early days when he was sweet to me. I wanted him to love me. Yes, I loved him.

'Yes,' I said.

'And do yer want it? A babby.'

A baby? A mewling, helpless creature? How would I look after that? No. But perhaps with a baby, I considered, he would love me more. I had a picture then, of the three of us as a family unit, something I had never had.

21

On the night before my wedding, I returned from Janey's cottage to find my room bare. There were no books, no hairbrush, no clothes, no bow and arrow and worst of all, there was no sign of the collection of treasures I'd kept on my windowsill. Perdie barked at the empty room, stripped of anything which had made it mine.

I ran back down the stairs, my heart thumping. Father was in his study, writing.

'What's happened to all my things? Where's my collection?'

He looked up at me, bemused, as if he was unsure what I was doing there. 'I asked Mrs Fairbrother to clear your room if you must know.'

'But why?'

'You're going to live at Old Hall of course. From tomorrow, you'll be married.'

'But my books! My collection!'

'I've sent your books and clothes to the Hall, although I'm sure they'll furnish you with finer things. And if by collection you mean the heap of rubbish and detritus you kept on the windowsill, it was unhealthy and best forgotten.'

The clock in the study ticked on as I stared at him, summoning the courage to speak without crying.

Finally, when he'd turned away from me, I spoke. 'Where is it?'

He didn't face me, but said to his desk, 'She threw it all out on my instructions. You're fortunate I didn't do it sooner. You're getting married, Rosemary. You cannot act like a heathen anymore. The past is gone, for goodness' sakes, it is pointless holding onto it.'

I stood in front of him, my shoulders shaking. I couldn't think how to explain to him what he'd done. How could I express to him the years I had spent collecting those objects that he called rubbish, the meaning they had which I could not even fathom myself?

On my finger the heavy gold ring Franklin had given me. It was inlaid with a sapphire that flashed blue every time it caught the light. I had been delighted with it at first – I couldn't believe someone like me could ever wear a thing of such beauty. I'd never seen anything like it. I don't know what happened to my mother's jewellery. But the ring was tight. My fingers were stumpier than the Laffertys', and underneath the metal, it rubbed against my skin. Now it felt too heavy, too tight, and the dazzling brilliance of the jewel felt out of place in the house. It belonged in Old Hall. I would have swapped the beautiful, blue ring for my bird's egg then.

I didn't even cry – I ran out, slamming the door, and lay on the floor of my room, spreadeagled to hold it in my body. Every part of me touched the floorboards: my fingertips, my groin, my knees, my forehead. I banged on the floorboards until my knuckles were raw and still the anger was coursing through me. I ran back outside and, stumbling up the Green Way, I went as far as it could go until I came to the creek. It was autumn and the marsh was turning and flocks of migrant warblers were arriving from the south. I took off my boots and stockings and waded, glad to feel the shock of the cool muddy water on my feet and around my ankles. Above, the great bowl of blue sky mocked me.

I splashed through the freezing creek, not stopping for the dripping grasses which lashed against my ankles, or the sticky mud which oozed through my toes. Hatless, I stomped on and on across the marsh, getting my hem wet and my face whipped by the wind. I came finally to the spit of sand dune where Franklin had taken me and collapsed onto the wet sand and cried. Thinking no one could hear me I let out all my horror at what I'd allowed to happen. I screamed at the open water and it shushed back at me, oblivious. Perdie had run after me and she put her wet nose against my face when I lay down, letting my tears soak into the sand.

I could not have said what I was crying for, only that it felt like the end. It was as if he'd taken my mother away from me again.

At some point I heard Janey calling to me over the marsh in her whooping call that sounded like an owl. She'd come to find me, and scooped me up and scolded me gently for my filthy, wet clothes and sodden boots. She coaxed me back to the house, told me I could make another collection, a different one, but I couldn't see how I could ever get back what I'd lost.

The following day, the day of the wedding, I didn't speak about it, but I wasn't the same anymore. A part of me had been lost with my treasures.

Let me paint you a picture, a portrait of a young girl. The sockets of her eyes are rimmed with grey, from sleepless nights and from the being which is eating up all her energy from the inside out. Her black hair has been washed, curled and pinned at the back. She is short – shorter than everyone else she knows bar Dolly, as if all the growing in her has been drawn into her belly. She's a little rounded on the hips and has small breasts. Yes, there is a bump, but it's barely there and no one would ever know if they didn't already that the child was with child. They've dressed her up like a wax doll in a crown of stitched white flowers and pearls that holds a fine tulle veil, embroidered at the edges with the finest lace blossoms. It is the most beautiful thing she has ever seen and belonged to her mother. There is no money for a new dress so her mother's old wedding gown has been expertly unstitched and re-stitched by a woman in the village, to hide the swelling in her stomach, and falls in a waterfall of creamy white to her silk-slipper-shod feet. When the veil is placed over her face, it looks like a shroud.

She's me, of course. In the image that stared back at me from the glass in my mother's room, I looked uncannily as she did in the photograph taken of her in front of the house. I felt a surge of pride that I had been chosen, but I was uneasy too. I did not look like myself.

I wish I could talk to that girl now, warn her somehow. But she was stubborn, that girl, and wouldn't have listened anyway.

The wedding itself was melancholy, although it's possible I'm making it more so in the memory. Dead leaves were falling in great numbers off the trees, turning the streets to a wet brown mulch. The marriage ceremony was held at St John the Baptist's and the new rector presided over it. Walking through the graveyard from the car on Father's arm, I took note of my favourite gravestones – the one with the two skulls and the cross-bones and the black marble headstone like a draped coffin. At the far edge of the graveyard was the ruined tower of Old Hall and, next to it, the tree I'd climbed. It felt like long ago.

As we walked out of the church and along the path to the car, George Bayfield was scowling at me from behind the wall. I kept my chin up and didn't look at him. Someone had organised the village girls to throw flowers at us, which is the local custom, but as it was autumn all they had were rose hips and dried rose petals which crunched underfoot. It reminded me of how we throw flowers into the graves of the dead – but when I caught the eyes of the girls throwing flowers they were glowing with jealous fire. On my finger, I wore the gold band and the sapphire. I raised my hand and flashed the rings, making sure they could all see. I turned back to George Bayfield then, and I smiled at him, triumphant.

I was a Lafferty now.

Hildy had looked her usual self at the wedding of course, tall and regal in a lilac silk dress that fell across her like waves and made her look like one of the film actresses in the magazines she read. She'd bent down to kiss me.

'Rosie, darling,' she said, 'welcome to the family.'

Then she did her usual thing and took hold of my arm, and held onto me until we were all the way back at the house. Their cook had put on a small reception in the drawing room and Hildy handed me a glass brimming with champagne.

'Mummy is awfully relieved,' she said.

'Relieved?'

'Oh, you know, after the incident with the girl in London, Frank is persona non grata with society. Thank God for you.'

I didn't tell her I had no idea what incident she was referring to or what she meant Frank was, but I kept it tucked up inside me, under my ribs.

I didn't eat anything that day as I felt sick.

By the time Franklin took me upstairs to bed, overlooked by the smiling, approving faces of the gathering – not including our own families who knew the act had already been done – I was light-headed. He was blithe, handsome and cavalier, no different to how he had always been. The champagne and lack of food relaxed me – I knew it had because I held his hand and didn't mind it and leaned on him as we mounted the stairs. I thought that he would leave me alone – he'd have no interest in me now that we were married – there was no conquest now, we were supposed to have 'conjugal relations'. And underneath my cleverly sewn dress, a small bump protruded, a clear sign of my pregnancy. Surely, I reasoned, he would be uninterested. All I wanted was to sleep.

But in the bedroom, he sat down on the bed and told me to take off all my clothes. I was bashful and hesitated. My body had changed. It was warped and swollen and it was no longer my own. And if I thought of him near me I could only remember the stone summer-house bench against the back of my thighs, his hand on my mouth and the roughness digging into me.

'Do I have to, Frank? I'm tired.'

'You have duties now, Rosie. It's your duty as my wife. And besides there's got to be some benefit to all the trouble you've caused me.'

I thought he was joking. His voice was light and I realised that he'd drunk a lot that afternoon as well. I hadn't approached the bed but stood by the door. The carpet between us, huge as that room was, felt too narrow, the bed a mere two paces away. I laughed. He smiled but didn't laugh in response.

'Come here,' he said, 'there's no need to be nervous. You've never been nervous before.'

He was beautiful sitting there, in his black morning suit and white waistcoat, the top hat tossed to the floor and his sandy hair swept back from his high forehead. He was leaning back on his arms, surveying me, daring me to come closer. I didn't move.

The look on his face changed as if a cloud had crossed the sun. For a second I thought he was going to rise and drag me to the bed, but instead he sighed and took out his cigarette case. He breathed out the smoke slowly, in elegant rings.

'At least sit down, Rosie. You're making me feel uncomfortable.'

I perched on the edge of the bed.

He pushed the veil away from my shoulders and ran his hands down the modest lines of the dress.

'You've got an advantage, my unchaste girl. Most girls learn the hard way about marital relations on their wedding night,' he said, rolling the words 'marital relations' around his tongue. 'Not you,' he said, 'you know how it works and, unlike most other girls, you know what a pleasure it can be.'

I winced. There was nothing pleasurable about this.

'Don't do that,' he said, and I bit my lip to stop from crying. He soon got bored of touching the silky cloth of the wedding dress and turned me around and undid the buttons one by one along my back, and rather than being disgusted by the sight of my rounded stomach he put his hands on me and kissed the swelling.

He didn't spend long on me that night. It was over quickly, which was one relief, and soon he was asleep next to me. I looked around the vast, high-ceilinged bedroom. This was my home now.

I cried then, quietly so I didn't wake him. I saw that it didn't matter what I wanted or what I liked. All that mattered was him. In allowing Franklin possession of my body I'd surrendered all of my freedom. It was the price I had to pay. But this is what I had wanted. I had wanted him desperately and I had got him. I felt the pinch of what Hildy had said about Frank in London, but I had to hide it away. Of all the girls he could have married, it was me he'd chosen. This was the important thing, I told myself, and wiped my tears. I was inside the fairytale now.

22

The Face in the Window

Malorie dropped the book. She felt as if she'd been under-water, submerged in the world of the notebook. She needed to breathe. Her head swam with questions about the girl. The mug shot from the newspaper cutting that Franny had found came back to her – that challenging gaze, straight into the camera. She swallowed a slug of wine. Her brain was fuzzy, thick with heavy clouds. She closed her eyes and curled up on the sofa. A sharp pain was growing at the back of her head. The light flickered at the corner of her eye. It must be the reflection of the moon on the wall behind her. She stiffened, became absolutely rigid. Someone was there in the room, behind her, by the window. *Don't look*. If she didn't look it would go away. But it was impossible not to – she felt her whole consciousness pulled towards whatever was watching her. She turned her head.

A face was looking at her through the front window. A pale oval in one of the leaded black squares. It was the face from the cutting, the same staring eyes, the dark hair close around her face. Dark green eyes. Eyes that saw her.

A choking sound came from her own mouth. The wine glass dropped and her hands flew to her eyes to cover them.

A groan came from somewhere above her. She opened her eyes and her fingers a crack. Her own face stared back at her, pale and black-eyed. Beyond, just the dark, empty glass and the silver glow of the moon. Shivers of relief ran over her skin. It had been her own face reflected in the window, the moon playing tricks. Just her reflection and the moon. A trick of the light. Her head was still cloudy and unclear – she needed to sleep. Shivering, she got up and pulled the old, frayed curtains across the window, as though from prying eyes, and slumped back onto the sofa. There was no one out there, no one at all, but she didn't want to be illuminated and neither did she want the dark to come inside. If she thought about the vast inky darkness out there, she wouldn't sleep.

Dribbles of wine had spilt onto the rug, little trickles running over the floorboards, but she did nothing about it. Her body wouldn't stop the prickles of cold, like tiny fragments of glass. In a jerking, lumbering movement, she got up again, picked up the still-intact wine glass and, with her foot, rubbed the spilt wine into the rug and smeared it over the floorboards. Still trembling, she stumbled up to her bedroom. She should stop reading the notebooks. She should stop thinking about the girl.

But as she curled up in the cold bed praying for sleep to come, the face was still there, the dark green eyes boring into her. It wasn't possible to sleep. She lay stiffly, with her face turned to the door, half expecting to see something. But her eyes grew heavy and the longer nothing happened, the more she thought she'd imagined it and felt foolish for how scared she'd been.

23

I've always been in the cottage since before the house was built. Long ago, before people came here for holidays and trips out in their motor cars, when there were only horses and walking, sometimes a carriage. I watched out for her mother and I watched out for her. She were my special one. That weren't no normal child. They all knew it but what they saw in her made them afraid, where I saw suffin precious, like a flower with a spot on it that marks it out as tainted, but makes it unique. She needed protecting, my girl, not plucking. Plucked, she withered. I'd do anything to protect her.

When I brought her squalling out of her poor mother, I saw right away she were a wild one, my Rose. And wild things are dangerous.

24

The Perfect Christmas
Christmas Eve

Malorie's mouth was parched and her throat hurt. She rolled over, away from the white morning light that made her eyes ache. At the back of her head, a girl's face, but as soon as she tried to fix on it, it spun to a pinprick and disappeared.

In the night she'd heard a cry, and in the morning she thought of the story of the girl stuck on the marsh, her mouth filling with seaweed, choking and shouting and no one hearing her.

She had absolutely no desire to get up. It was bloody *Christmas Eve*. She should be doing something festive: making mince pies or singing carols or whatever other people did. Last year, she'd taken Franny to a West End show and they'd eaten hot chestnuts out of a paper bag, scalded their fingers and stared up at the electric, coloured Christmas lights, deciding which ones they liked the best. She saw the two of them, their faces glittered with dots of neon. When Tony came home from work that evening, already half-cut, Franny had hung up her stocking by the gas fire and she and Tony had drunk snowballs.

She was making it idyllic in her memory and knew it hadn't been exactly like that. Franny had thought the show babyish and when they'd stumbled into bed at last, Malorie had pushed Tony away. He'd smelt of perfume that wasn't hers.

This year though, this year was supposed to be different. What had she done? Stop it. For God's sake, *stop it*. She was crying, maddening tears sliding down her nose and into her mouth. She made herself sniff them back in.

The house was quiet. Not silent, it was never completely silent: there was a constant undercurrent of creaks and whispers and rustles, as if it were being tossed about on the sea. But she could hardly hear anything from outside the walls. The snow must have come again.

She took out the two notebooks from under her pillow and turned them over in her hands, feeling along the smooth brass tacks and across the embossed gold-leaf writing. The deep red of the leather glowed up at her.

On the landing, Franny's bedroom door was open and the bed empty. Above the bed, she could just see the edge of the sampler. Curious, she entered the room. It was funny, now she saw it again, that there was no man in the image, nothing to indicate that the girl had a father; funny that the child had embroidered her absent mother and the strange neighbour with the enormous dog, whose name she now knew was Janey. It was uncanny how similar the likeness was to the woman she'd seen in the garden yesterday.

'When's Daddy coming?' was how Franny greeted her.

Malorie knew she should say, 'He's not coming.' But she couldn't. 'Look,' she said instead, 'why don't we take a trip to the nearest town? See the lights, pick up some treats for tomorrow. I'll buy you a hot chocolate.'

Franny furrowed her small forehead. 'Okay. But what if we miss Daddy?'

'We won't,' she said, and looked away before Franny could see her eyes.

She didn't want to think about driving along the hideously winding country roads. Snow had fallen through the night and was now coating the icy layers beneath in further whiteness.

'Larry wants to come too,' said Franny.

'No, Franny. He can't come. He wouldn't like it in a town.'

'He's from London. And he wants to come.'

Oh, damn it to hell, the day was going so badly already.

There was a tentative knock at the back door and it inched open, ushering in a draught of wintry air. Malorie started. A man's head appeared around the door.

'Scuse me, Miss. My daughter asked me to give this to you.'

He was togged up for the Arctic, in a cap and a scarf up to his ears, and without any flourish, he held up, by its scrawny neck, the great carcass of a bird. Malorie yelped.

'Christ!'

The man stepped back and peered at her oddly. He was a short man with a sharp nose and what must once have been a handsome face, like his daughter's, and was regarding her as if he was trying to place her.

'Sorry,' she said, 'I just wasn't expecting – such a large bird.'

'S'alright. I'll just leave it here then,' said the grocer, and placed the enormous beast in the sink. 'Got a drop of coal for you, too, Miss,' he added, plonking a small sack on the kitchen tiles.

'Thank you,' she said, ashamed of how rude she'd been. But there was an eagerness and wariness about him that was making her feel uncomfortable.

He put out a thick, rough hand and she took it lightly in hers.

'Noticed you don't have no holly up on your door, Miss.'

'We have holly up all around the house,' she said.

'I'd put some up in your doorway too, if I were you. And ivy. To warn against witches.'

It made her think of the superstitions running through the girl's account, all these little tokens sent up to the gods and goddesses of fate or dark magic. And his daughter telling her about the dead girl on the marsh.

'Surprised you're here on your own. Your husband coming, is he?'

'Yes,' she said quickly.

He regarded her with a sceptical frown. 'Right,' he said eventually. 'I'll be off then.'

'Thank you,' she said. 'Mr... ' She couldn't remember if he'd told her his name. But by then he was already nearly at the end of the drive.

Back in the house, she argued with Franny for a little longer then gave up. Franny could stay with the dog.

'I'll only be a while,' she said.

As she left, Franny was fixing the holly above the porch. 'You could hang up the ivy I found too,' she said.

The car wouldn't start at first and she had to shovel the snow on the drive, but it was just a few inches deep.

As she drove, she thought about the last time she'd been in a car with Tony, driving back from his parents' house across the city after a disastrous lunch, with Franny asleep in the back.

He'd tried to kiss her. 'What's the matter?' His voice was cold.

'Nothing.' She could feel tears coming and screamed inside for them not to come.

He fell back against the seat. 'Not this again.'

'I can't help it. I can't.'

'It's been weeks. You can't keep pushing me away like this. What's wrong with you? We can't make another baby if you won't let me touch you, can we?'

She was silent. How could they have another baby, the way they were?

'I don't know if I want another baby.' She'd never articulated it before, but now, there it was, out of her mouth.

'What?'

'Maybe if you didn't – I don't know –'

'Didn't what?'

'Nothing.'

He drove without speaking or touching her. She could feel the anger emanating from him. Warm, dry air filtered out of the heater, but she was still shivering. She wiped a finger under her eye to stop the mascara streaking down her face.

'Have you looked at the papers your mother left for you?' He said this like he already knew the answer. And he did, so why bother asking?

'No, not yet,' she said.

He sighed. 'I think you ought to.' Her neck was hurting with the strain of not responding. His lips were pressed tightly together and she could see the veins pulsing in his neck above his clean white collar. There was a long silence as they drove.

'My mother always said you were going to be difficult.' He didn't look at her but stared straight ahead and gripped the steering wheel. She wanted to say *Look at me, Tony. Say it to my face.*

'Your *mother*? How can you say such a thing? For God's sake, Tony, she can hardly judge. She's hardly a paragon, is she?'

'Don't ever say anything about my mother.'

'But she's a bloody alco—'

His hand met her cheek. Her head snapped back against the leather headrest. Her face stung but she clenched her teeth. The shock had stopped the tears.

'Oh baby, God. I didn't mean it.' He pulled the car to the side of the road. 'Come here. We're no good like this.' She leaned on him, accepting the warmth of his coat and his arms. Her cheek was still hot from his hand and her head was sore. He was kissing her hair. He didn't mean it, he never did. He was weak, that's what he said. Quick to anger, quick to love. It sounded like a song lyric he'd memorised.

As he turned the key in the ignition and drove on, he kept one eye on her and touched her face. Checking she was still there.

'Why did you ask about the papers?' It had always been a source of tension between them, the difference in their upbringings; her distance from hers, his closeness with his. He didn't trust her. What kind of person didn't love their family? *I did love my dad*, she ought to say to him, *but you drove him away.*

'I got the impression that your mother wanted you to read what was in there.'

Why? she thought. She made a noise of vague assent.

He wouldn't have understood if she'd tried to explain – that she didn't want to think about her mother. The fact that not once had her mother tried to say anything kind at the end. Not once had she told Malorie she loved her. She didn't want to be further burdened by the weight of her mother's guilt or remonstrance or whatever it was. Whatever she had to say, whatever it was, should have been said while she was alive. All this hiding, this secrecy, this lack of honesty. It sickened her. She didn't want her life to be tied to someone so cold, so remote, so entirely lacking in warmth. Her own responding coldness was a source of guilt and nothing she could do would expiate it now.

Wells-next-the-Sea was crowded with people, huddled in their coats, hats pulled low over their ears. It was strange to be there after days in isolation. As she walked along the bare streets with piles of old snow at the edges where shopkeepers had cleared the path, she felt as if she were an actor in a scene, not really there, not connected to the rest of the world. She received a few stares and realised that the fur coat and fur-lined leather boots must give her away as rather 'London'. She had a sudden unwelcome thought that these were the last fine clothes she'd be wearing for a while if Tony left for good. It scared her, that she would have to survive without him. It wasn't the clothes, it was all of it. The abandonment. The gaping emptiness and terrifying unknown of the future. She'd never lived independently. She didn't even know how. How would she pay the bills and feed them? She saw herself and Franny in a cold, dingy flat while Tony and his family showered their daughter with gifts and comfort and luxury. She wouldn't be able to compete with that and Franny would resent her, and she would grow bitter like her mother.

The pubs were open for the men escaping the Christmas preparations, the sound of singing coming from inside. She bought a few items, eking out the last of her housekeeping – a bottle of brandy, some crackers and cheese, some mince pies for Franny – but she didn't want to go back yet, to the house and her silently judging daughter. She wanted the sea and walked along the quayside until she was away from the shoppers and quite alone. Beyond the little boats in the harbour, there was the sea, a steel-grey churning vastness, whipped white by the wind. She sat on a bench. For the first time since she'd been in Norfolk she felt a sliver of peace. It was this she needed. Nothing else. Just nothing. A blank. A vast grey blank.

She fished around in her handbag for her cigarettes and smoked, staring out at the sea.

25

The Dog

It wasn't until she noticed that her fingers, clenched around the cigarette, were damp and her face was stinging that she realised she'd been crying again. It could have been the wind, all the way over the North Sea from the Soviet steppe, but it wasn't. Bizarrely, her watch told her it was twenty past three and she swallowed, wiped her eyes and gathered herself, put her gloves on and hurried back up the empty street. She had to tell Franny the truth about her father, get it over with.

The night fell as she drove. Soon the headlights created two small tunnels in the darkness. On either side of the road, hedges were fringed with snow which blazed white at her when the headlights swept over them. She would put Franny's presents under the tree; she would drink whisky, brandy, whatever she had to numb herself. It would be all right. But with each mile passed she had the sinking sense of what was to come. Of ruining her daughter's Christmas, of Franny hating her, of the empty flat in London.

The temperature in the car plummeted and she huddled inside her fur.

When the lane finally appeared, she murmured, 'Thank God.'

As she swung into the entrance to the Marsh House, the car slid from under her. The trees loomed at the start of the driveway.

'Christ,' she said, and tried to straighten up the wheel. She squeezed the muscles in her face tight in concentration and her arms strained to control the car. *Don't try to control it,* she heard Tony in her head. *Drive into it.*

It was too late. The branches were coming fast towards her. She was going to overshoot and hit them. But just at the last second, miraculously, the car missed the trees. It skidded and carried on skidding. She was going to crash. She gripped the wheel and braced for impact. Then ahead, something black. An animal, a shadow. A screech of the tyres. For a second she couldn't see. Blinded, she thought she heard a thump from somewhere, maybe a cry. It might have been her own. The car came to a sliding halt at the front of the house.

She had no idea what had happened.

For a minute she just sat, breathing heavily. Immediately, she was back a few days ago on the evening they'd arrived, when she'd swerved and crashed into the hedge. The same sense of disorientation overcame her now. The headlights were still on, shining up at the house. It was in darkness apart from a single vertical yellow line from between the curtains on the second floor and the faint glowing orbs from the candles on the tree in the living room. Something moved behind her and she snapped her head round. There was nothing but darkness. But there *had* been – something black and white.

Still shaking from the near miss, she emptied the boot of the supplies and carried them into the house.

Franny appeared in the hall. 'Larry got funny and ran into the garden but he hasn't come back –' Her face collapsed. 'Where's Daddy?'

Malorie's head hurt. 'I should have told you earlier. He's been held up in London, darling. He can't come.' Her voice sounded tired.

Franny's eyes were already brimful of tears. In a second they would drop, fall down her small face. She couldn't do this.

'I'm sorry, Franny. I'm really sorry.'

She stepped forward to put her arms around her daughter but Franny scrunched up her shoulders and recoiled, pushing herself against the wall.

'It's your fault,' she said, 'you made him not come.'

'No, Franny. It's not like that. It's not.'

'It is. It IS. You're a liar!' And she ran up the stairs. Malorie heard a door slam.

Malorie stood by the kitchen window with a glass of brandy. She was on her second glass and beginning to feel the unclenching of her muscles, the calming of her trembling hands. Her eyes fell on the little bottles above the stove. She picked one up. There were no labels. She opened one and sniffed it. Before, she remembered it had been unpleasant, as if something rotten had been distilled. But now when she smelt it, it was like going back in time. It smelt of herbs, oil and mould. But also of dark magic, the night and the marsh.

It could be the toad-bone oil, a tincture for an illness; it could be nothing. Holding the bottle in her hand, she turned around to the kitchen window, expecting – almost wanting – to see Rosemary or Janey. All she could see was darkness, and her own face staring back at her.

She glanced at the newspaper she'd brought. There was something about a nuclear missile, Europe hit by snowstorms and – Agatha Christie. The 'Queen of Crime' was confined to bed in Baghdad with flu. It reminded her of Rosemary and the notebooks.

She wanted to be somewhere else, other than in her own body, her own mind, her own life. Quickly, in a sudden burst of energy, she climbed the stairs to the bedroom to look again in the suitcase. It was only paper. Endless, endless sheaves of paper. More bloody fascist literature. Posters with titles like *FASCISM MEANS FREEDOM FOR BRITISH WOMEN*; *TOMORROW WE LIVE*, and the repulsive *MOSLEY CALLING – BRITAIN BEFORE JEWRY*.

'Mum.' Franny was calling from downstairs.

'Coming!' she called back. Sod it.

Underneath the papers, at the bottom of the case, was a soft cloth that felt like the plush of velvet. Opening it up, her fingers touched something else. Something smooth and cold, with a sharp, jagged edge. The smoothness of bone. With trepidation, she withdrew the velvet cloth from the case with its contents.

'Mum-my!' came Franny's voice from far below.

'In a minute,' she called.

The whiteness of bone shone in the gloom of the bedroom. They were skulls. Skulls of various sizes, some the size of a rat's head, another the size of a sheep, each with empty sockets where their eyes had been. She held them up to the pale slant of light from the window and the moonlight caught the bone. It was a strange, creepy collection for a girl, not like the things Rosemary had mentioned collecting, much more morbid. She bundled the whole bag back in the case and slammed it shut.

Franny was standing on the landing, holding her battered teddy, Frederick, and worrying at it. She looked forlorn, lost, and Malorie felt a jabbing pain in her chest.

'I'm worried about Larry. I whistled for him like Daddy taught me but he didn't come.'

'Don't worry, darling, we'll find him,' she said, then wished she hadn't.

The two of them went out into the garden in their boots, hats and coats. All she could see was the swing of the torchlight roaming the hedges, grass and trees restlessly, illuminating a circle of snow and making the rest of the darkness look thicker. 'Larry!' they called, but there was no responding bark, no scurrying of paws. Just the sound of a car from far away on the coastal road. She swung the torchlight around the garden but didn't penetrate the dark corners, afraid of what they'd find. She kept thinking about the way she'd skidded when she came into the drive. But Larry was a house dog, a pet, he was afraid of being far from Franny. Why had he run away from her in the first place? And if she'd hit him, they'd have found him by now.

'Let's leave it for now, Fran, it's time for tea.'

Back in the house, they had a supper cobbled together from the supplies she'd found in the town. Slices of ham and cheese – some Stilton for her and Cheddar for Franny – together with mince pies, washed down with tea for Franny and a bottle of red. They had a bowl of bright orange satsumas and it made her think of Rosemary with the juice dribbling down her chin. The two of them ate in front of the fire. Neither of them mentioned the dog. Franny sat her teddy on a chair by the fire and Malorie decided to say nothing. Strenuously, she tried to keep up a jollying conversation about what Father Christmas was doing up at the North Pole. A noise broke into the hushed quiet. A persistent, jarring ring. It took a second or two before she realised it was the telephone. She jumped up. Franny looked at her quizzically.

'What is it?'

'I'll get it,' she said.

'What?'

She held the earpiece to her ear in the hall. It crackled and whirred, a blizzard of white noise. Then it went dead, leaving just a thin whine. In the empty hallway the moon shone through the dirty glass in the door. She shivered, and was glad to return to the living room.

'The line's terrible,' she said. 'I couldn't hear anyone.'

'What are you talking about?' Franny was staring at her as if she was mad.

'The phone.'

'What phone? I didn't hear anything.'

'Oh,' she said, 'it must have been the wind.' But she really had thought she'd heard it.

Soon, Franny's eyes were drooping.

'Time for bed, darling,' she said, and tried scooping her up, but she was too heavy.

'What about Larry?' she yawned. 'He'll be cold out there in the snow.'

'I'll go and find him, Franny.'

'Promise?'

'I promise.'

When Malorie knelt by her bed, Franny said, 'Mummy,' staring up at her with her large dark eyes, 'why isn't Daddy coming?'

Malorie closed her eyes, pressed her knuckles into the sockets. 'Daddy is very busy in London, like I said.'

'But it's *Christmas*.'

'Yes I know. He's – he's really sorry. He wants to see you, he really does. He'll have lots of presents for you back in London.' Franny's stare didn't waver and Malorie wondered if her daughter would ever forgive her, if she would ever understand, if they were destined to be as distant with each other as she'd been with her own mother. 'He loves you very much,' she added, and kissed Franny's head, tucking in the sides of the blanket over her and her teddy. 'And I do too.'

There was no answer from the bed and she shut the door and leaned against it, exhausted.

Now that she'd promised, she had to mount a final search for the dog. This time she went out the front door. She crunched out along the ice-crusted drive, with her torch and the dim glow of the tree candles through the window, making fuzzy, golden circles on the ground to guide her.

At the edge of the drive, a few feet away from the car, was the shape of something curled up and half-covered in snow. She crouched down. A badger? A fox? It had to be. Please let it be. She knelt down and reached out her hand. *Don't touch it!*

'Oh no,' she said, 'Oh God.' It wasn't a badger or a fox. But her brain wouldn't fill in the gaps. Her torch shone on the dead animal. It was Larry, frozen and stiff, his creamy curly coat frosted over and encrusted, hard to the touch. Poking out from the snow, his eyes were glassy and black, open in shock, and his mouth was frozen in an ugly black grimace. Her knees buckled and she dropped to a crouch. What had she done?

But it can't have been her – the poor animal had obviously frozen. But why was he out here at all? It didn't matter, she needed to hide him before Franny found out. She began to take off her fur coat before she realised what she was doing and fetched a blanket from the car instead.

She wrapped the dog's small, stiff body in the blanket and carried it around the back of the house. She could bury it behind the shed, out of sight of the windows. Fumbling with the lock, she opened the shed and found a shovel. The ground was hard from ice and snow. She'd never even dug a hole before, certainly not a grave. The shovel hit the unyielding earth, but only small shards of ice chipped off as puffs of her breath floated up in the darkness. She would never be able to make a grave deep enough to bury him in. She had to hide the body, she couldn't let Franny see her dog, cold and lifeless. If it snowed again, that would cover him, but it might not snow. With her gloved hands, she picked up the stiff body again, trying not to look at the head, and laid him as far under the line of trees as she could. Then she began scooping up ice and snow to cover him. With it came bits of twigs and dirt but she kept piling it until there was an awkwardly-shaped mound in the shade of a hawthorn tree. If you didn't know it was there, you'd never notice it. As long as the snow didn't melt.

Her mind was slowly circling. The icy road, the skidding, the darkness, something black coming out of the trees. A shadow of something beastly crossed her mind. Had something wild killed him? She imagined the little dog, wounded and lost, dying of hypothermia. He would stay frozen, stuck in the moment of death until the thaw came, when his body would finally decay and eventually only his skeleton would remain. She thought of the skulls in the attic, the gravestone with the skulls and cross-bones, the woman she'd seen who did not speak. A slow ripple of cold went down her back.

Oh God, her poor girl. What on earth was she going to say? No father. No dog. Just a useless mother who had ruined Christmas.

In the front room, the lights from the tree were reflected in the crystal glass she'd found in a sideboard. Her fingers were red and frozen from the snow and ice, and as she rubbed them, they tingled and ached with the heat from the fire. She needed to hear something other than her own whirling thoughts. There was an old wind-up gramophone box and a few 78s in the corner of the living room, on a sideboard next to the tree. They hadn't tried to get it to work – it seemed too dusty and ancient to be functioning. Tony would be listening to jazz. She wound it up with the crank, lifted one of the heavy records out of its sleeve and put it on the turntable, then gently placed the stylus on the record. Static whirring burst out of the speakers. She allowed herself a small smile. Then some notes, the brassy blare of a trumpet, and a song filtered through the crackle, a soaring note upwards then a piano. It was an old song but it filled the room as if it belonged there. Malorie picked up her book, but it was hard to concentrate. She wasn't distracted enough, she couldn't stop thinking about what a mess she'd made of everything.

Giving up, she went back upstairs, clutching her drink, fumbled with the top drawer and took out the envelope with the pills. Just one. She needed to, otherwise she'd do something she'd regret. It was going wrong. Everything – tumbling out of her control. This had been a wild goose chase, a fool's errand. There was nothing about this house which linked to her father. And her vision of a family Christmas was spoiled. She shook the envelope and held the pills in the palm of her trembling hand. They were so small, so perfectly round. Such a pretty shade of green. Like sweets. Cochies. No. No, no, no. She couldn't. In the quiet room, her breath was shallow and loud. She screwed up her eyes, dropped the pills back into the envelope and shoved it to the back of the drawer, catching her still-cold hand on the wood. She winced and threw back the last of the brandy.

She wanted to say to the voice in her head – it wasn't me.

From downstairs she could still hear music. A loop of swirling, squeaking brass. Had she left the record on? Malorie held her breath, listened. Then a trumpet, low and mournful. A voice, old and deep that sounded like Louis Armstrong. But then it jumped and scratched. The voice was broken and stuck. It kept repeating the same word. *Soul*, it said, *soul*. She should go down and turn it off, but she was so tired. Finally it warped and stopped. The power generated by the crank must have run out.

Malorie lay awake, falling into a doze and then shuddering out of it, fizzing and restless. She was aware that she'd be woken by Franny early on Christmas morning, that she'd have to come up with something about poor Larry. Again, she ran through the sequence of events that led to her finding his stiff, frozen body. Why was he outside in the first place? Something must have scared the little dog. He'd been jumpy and whiny the whole time they'd been at the house. He must have been spooked, run out into the snowbound garden – he was a city dog after all, no sense of the country and its darkness, its strange sounds, its wild animals – and he'd become disorientated and lost and finally frozen. Just an accident, a horrible accident. This, logically, was what must have happened. Nonetheless, the car, the dog, the dark shadow she kept seeing – it made her uneasy, as if there was something out there that was malign, that wanted to hurt them.

26

Midnight on Christmas Eve. It were always a quiet time, when the world holds its breath, when the darkness keeps the evil at bay. But there were a sadness in that house. A sadness coming out in the girl and the child. It come out of the walls and the floorboards, the cracks in the ceiling. It were always there, this sorrow, right from the moment it was made. How can a house made from a wreck be anything else? It were never silent, the Marsh House. The bones of the house still remembered the storm from where it came. It forgot it weren't a ship. I could feel the sorrow when Miss Louisa got sick, when the babbies died, and when my Rose was born. It were always there, warping the beams, making the lights go off, bringing rats from the marsh into the rafters to gnaw on its bones.

27

Figgy Pudding
Christmas Day

'Mummy, it's Christmas Day, wake up.'

In the morning fog of half-sleep, Malorie saw a black dog chasing a white dog. Then Franny was pressing her in the side, dragging her out of the night-time into the day.

'What did Father Christmas bring for you?' Weeks before, Tony had come home with an extravagant doll's house for their daughter and Malorie had brought it with her, hiding it under the blanket in the boot.

'He didn't bring Larry back,' Franny said.

Oh Christ, the *dog*.

'Maybe he's gone to help Father Christmas with the rest of his deliveries,' she said, desperately.

'But he'd be back by now,' said Franny. She couldn't think of a suitable answer.

'I'll be down in a minute,' she said.

When Franny had gone she opened the chest of drawers. There, under her nylons and pants, was the envelope of pills.

It was fine. She hadn't taken one. She'd resisted. She'd had a difficult night, that was all. Under her ribcage, she could feel her heart beating like a fluttering bird trying to get out. Her hands wouldn't stay still. If she had one, it would calm her, but she remembered Tony's face back in London. The expression of disappointment in her, or rather that she'd once again met his expectations of failure. No, she mustn't give in to it. She pushed the envelope back under the clothes and shut the drawer.

After breakfast, Franny set off on a fruitless 'search for Larry' in the frozen garden, while Malorie set about the Christmas lunch. She had to tackle the bloated, repulsive white carcass of the turkey. She'd pulled the giblets out, rubbed over the pimply white skin with margarine and shoved it in the oven, and was now peeling and chopping mindlessly when shadows moved in the white square of the kitchen window and she shouted out, stabbing the knife into her finger.

A face had been there, definitely a face. An old woman in a brown hat. She was going mad, there couldn't have been anyone there. She wrapped her bleeding finger in a tea towel and chopped another carrot. But she *had* seen someone. It must have been the old woman from the cottage across the lane. A brown face, wrinkled and scrunched up, like a prune, swaddled in layers of cloth. She was gripped by an urge to look.

Heart pounding, Malorie went to the back door. There was no one there but, on the step, a round package. It was a cream pudding bowl, wrapped in muslin. The garden was white and empty. Spots of blood seeped through the tea-towel so she stuffed it in the bin and found a plaster in her washbag. She put on her boots and crunched out into the garden. They could be her footprints from last night, or Franny's.

'They are the old woman's,' she said aloud, to make it normal.

'Franny!' she called. Franny was at the other end of the garden by the drive, looking disconsolate.

'Did you see anyone come to the door?'

'No,' she said.

'Right.' But then, it was quite possible for her daughter to have missed someone quiet. She was always so caught up in her own world.

'What's that?' Franny was looking at the bundle in Malorie's arms.

'I think it's a pudding,' she said, 'for our lunch.' She put an arm around her daughter's bony shoulders. 'I think you should come in now. Why don't you play with your presents?'

The light fled the house and the garden so quickly that it seemed to be a day of only darkness. The lunch was passable. The turkey the grocer had brought was cooked through and the roast potatoes not too soft. Franny was quiet and withdrawn, and though she tried to cheer her up with cracker jokes from the expensive set she'd brought up from London, nothing worked. The figgy pudding was delicious and she made Franny smile when she doused it with brandy and lit it. The blue flame flickered across the glossy brown dome and the sprigs of holly gleamed green and red in the light.

Franny grimaced. She pulled a silver coin out of her mouth.

'Let me see,' said Malorie. On one side of the coin was the head of the King. Not the Queen, but her grandfather, George V. On the other side were oak leaves and acorns and the words SIX PENCE 1935. She held it in the palm of her hand, feeling the sticky crumbs and the weight of it. It was as if it had come from nowhere, an artefact from another world, appearing like a disconcerting magic trick.

'It's lucky,' she said finally and handed it back to Franny, although she wanted to hold onto it. 'Don't lose it.'

'Who's that?' said Franny, looking at the back.

'Just a dead king.'

When Franny went back to her doll's house, Malorie leaned back in her chair and lit a cigarette. The dishes were piled up in the cracked ceramic sink, but she couldn't face them. She sipped the brandy she'd taken from the cupboard and felt the warm sweetness coat her throat. Franny must have put one of the records on the gramophone because she could hear music. It sounded familiar, like the tune from yesterday, the same sad trumpet over the crackle of the old record. There was a creak from the upstairs floorboards. She downed the brandy and finished her cigarette, stubbing it out on the debris of leftover food on her plate. She could slip off now, while Franny wouldn't miss her. Franny *wouldn't* miss her. That was the truth.

In the bedroom, Malorie caught fragments of the same slow jazz. There was only the doll's house to distract Franny from the lack of her father and her dog. Earlier, she'd managed to find a weather forecast from the transistor but what it said hadn't been reassuring.

Norfolk has been cut off from the rest of England. All main roads leading westwards are impassable as far as the Cambridgeshire border. The RSPCA says it has received so many calls for help from farmers in the county it doesn't know which way to turn.

The suitcase where Franny had found the newspaper clipping and where she'd found the two notebooks and the bag of bones was under the windowsill, but she'd searched all through that, found everything there was to find. A sound above her – the scuttling of the rats – and she felt the pull of the attic. She was certain there was more up there. More writing, more artefacts. The attic was stuffed full of crates and boxes. There had to be more evidence of Rosemary's life in them.

Up in the attic, she felt she knew the spaces now – the shape of them, the map of their contents: the old cot, which she avoided looking at; the boxes of children's clothes, which she had glanced at but didn't take out. Right at the back, near where Franny had found the suitcase, was a space she thought she'd looked in but could no longer be sure. There, tucked under the furthest eave, were about half a dozen small boxes. Her hands felt for the contents and touched the thick layer of dust on the top. By now, her eyes had adjusted to the dark enough to see that they were about the size of a shoebox and in each was a clutch of papers. By the light of her torch, she hurriedly scanned each box and found family documents.

Deeds of sale for the land, receipts for furniture bought, a marriage certificate (Richard Wright to Louisa Mulcaney 1912); birth certificates (Philip Richard Wright 1913, Sebastian John Wright, 1914, Rosemary Louisa Wright,

1916). Rosemary must only be what – forty-six – about nineteen years older than she was. Settling into middle age. There was nothing that seemed to belong to Louisa, no record of her earlier life. There were death certificates (Philip Richard Wright, 1913, Sebastian John Wright 1914). They had only lived for a few days. These were Richard Wright's records, not his daughter's. But in the same group of papers was something that belonged to Rosemary herself. Someone must have mislaid it. It was another birth certificate for a child. Richard Charles Lafferty, born 21st January 1933. She'd had a son. Malorie had a sudden violent sensation that she shouldn't be seeing this – she'd jumped ahead in the girl's story and Rosemary hadn't told her directly. But that was ridiculous.

There was a bang from below, and Franny's disembodied voice cut in on her thoughts. 'Mummy? I finished the doll's house. I want to show you.'

'In a minute,' she shouted down.

She heard Franny sigh and the sound of her footsteps returning down the stairs.

There was a sheaf of other papers. And a death certificate. Her body shivered with cold as if a draught had swept through the room. It was the death certificate of her boy. Died 15th February 1934. He'd barely lived. Cause of death: Encephalitis. She didn't know what that was. The dim light in the attic shifted. She shrank back against the suitcase. Her skull was pressing down on her brain. She had to leave; to get out. 'Please,' she said, aloud, 'I need to go.'

Then, as quickly as it had come, the pressure was gone again. There were no ghosts watching her. It was just dust and paper and age and there was one last box with shapes like notebooks inside. Her heart beat fast. She took out two of the books. But they were the wrong shape. *Damn.* They were Agatha Christie novels. What if it was just a box of useless books? But this was *her* box at least. Rosemary's. Further down, underneath a knitted blanket, her fingers finally came to what must be the hard ridged edges of another notebook. She smiled, alone in the attic, and felt the air settle around her as if waiting. A faint sound like gnawing on wood came from near her ear and she jumped. The top of her head banged against a beam and she felt like Alice in Wonderland, too big for the house. Soon her head would pop out the top of the roof.

Malorie slid out of the attic without looking back, clutching the book, and went down to the sitting room and the finished doll's house to stoke the fire back to life. She was cold and she needed light and warmth and real things to feel and touch. Franny wasn't in the room and the gramophone was silent. The doll's house was lit by the firelight and the soft glow of the candles on the tree. In the sitting room of the house, a doll man and a doll girl were sitting on the sofa. The doll woman was in the kitchen, separate. Next to her, a doll baby in a doll cot, with a tiny painted yellow whorl in the centre of the forehead. The second child to make the family complete. She watched the flames rise and grow and held up her palms until they began to prickle with heat. She should take Franny back to London, she should leave her with her father. She'd become fixated on this girl from the past when she had a real girl, here, right now. There was no Rosemary.

And yet. She'd felt the girl's hopes and fears as she felt her own. The flames dipped and smoke drifted out. She *was* real. She *had* been real. If Malorie could only read the last notebook. That was all. Then they'd leave. Oh God, where *was* Franny? It was getting late, the darkness was coming down again.

In her fur, Malorie went out of the front door but there was no sign of her daughter on the drive. Instinctively, she looked over to where the strange little cottage was sunk, but there was no obvious sign of life.

'Franny!' she called, and held herself still to catch a response. There was only the wind in the trees. A well of panic flaring, she rushed around the side of the house and saw a gash of red from Franny's scarf in the grey half-light. She was standing at the back of the garden, looking down. Malorie's heart plummeted. It was the grave, the pathetic pile of snow where she'd hidden the dog. *Oh God, please don't let Franny find out.*

'Franny, it's getting dark, come in. I'll make tea and you can show me the doll's house.'

In answer, Franny turned and trudged back. She could see no sign on her daughter's face that she knew what was under the pile of snow.

In the bedroom that night, Malorie dug herself further under the covers to find a patch of warmth. She could see Rosemary, drinking champagne at her wedding; Rosemary walking towards Franklin, sprawled, waiting for her; Rosemary writhing with pain – on this very bed. Perhaps, she thought . . . perhaps. If Rosemary was only forty-six, maybe she could find her . . . she could give her back her journals. Talk to her.

She switched on the lamp and sat up. The door to the wardrobe was ajar. She'd not hung up any of her clothes, it hardly seemed worth bothering, but now she had a need to look inside it. She got up swiftly before she changed her mind and swung it open. There was nothing in it apart from a few blankets and bits of cloth at the bottom. Kneeling down, she picked them up, and gasped. In her hands she held a long, delicate piece of white lace that had been chewed by moths. She held it up to the lamp and the light shone through the holes, making it look like the pattern of a snowflake. It was her veil, she was certain. Rosemary's veil. She was communicating with her. All these clues: the shell, the stone, the bottles, and now this. She was telling her – *This was my life.*

Malorie snatched up the third notebook. As she did, a piece of paper fell out on to the bed. It was a page of thick, creamy writing paper with a letter written in an elegant sloping hand. It read:

Dear Rosemary,

I am so very sorry for what has happened to you. I have found it difficult to reconcile the sweet country girl I knew with what you did, and I feel some sense of responsibility for not seeing sooner that you were obviously deeply unwell.

Father and Mother are extremely distraught as you might imagine. They are selling Old Hall and never want to set foot in Norfolk again.

I leave for Rome tomorrow. It sounds as if there are exciting things occurring over there and I want to be where

the action is. The Italians are bringing modernism to Africa
and I feel Italy and to an extent, Germany, is where all the
really modern thinking is happening. Gerald is still trying
to pin me down to marriage but he's tied to his work for
the bank. I'm going to put him off for a bit longer. I crave
newness. Perhaps I shall meet an Italian instead.

I hate writing like this. I hardly know what to write. I
do hope you enjoyed the books.

Yours,
Hilda

'What you did.' But what *was it* that she'd done? The date
on the letter was 15th March 1935. 1935. She picked up the
first notebook and read again the first words. *March 1935.*
This letter was written *then.* But it said nothing about what
Rosemary had actually done, nor what had happened to
her. She had no choice but to read on.

Scanning down the first page of the notebook, Malorie
saw just a few short paragraphs about the pregnancy and
marriage. Flicking the pages, she looked for a reference
to the baby. Rosemary wrote of her enduring silence and
growing stomach. By the beginning of 1933, she wrote that
she had been just as abandoned and sequestered in Old Hall
as she had been in the Marsh House. And there was less
there for her than there was here. Malorie's eyes scanned
the pages looking for what she knew was coming and
found it. The handwriting sloped unevenly across the page,
splashes of ink spattering the paper, spreading sometimes in
dark stains. She began to read in earnest. *I am listening*, she
thought. *Tell me.*

28

I see the two of them in the garden where she'd played. The girl she'd made from snow was still there, frozen in time. I see the two of them, one at the door and one at the edge of the garden, not far from where the mother hid the dead dog. Both standing with the same hunched up shoulders as if they were ready to fight. I don't think either of them could see how alike they were.

THE THIRD NOTEBOOK

29

It took me nearly a week to write the last journal and now it's the second week of March and I don't know how much longer I have. So I must get on and come to my boy.

It wasn't long into the new year when the pain began. A New England was coming according to the guests gathered in their tuxedoes and silk dresses at Old Hall that New Year's Eve, but after my shape and expectant condition had been cooed over, I'd pleaded tiredness and gone to bed early. Much later, Franklin lay next to me blind drunk, but he didn't try to touch me. By then he was repelled and fascinated in equal measure by me and my shape. 'I can barely get at you,' he'd say, or, 'You remind me of one of the sows on Blacker's Farm.' Then other times he'd fondle my breasts, swollen as they were. He even put his mouth to one once and looked up at me with his pale blue eyes, daring me to pull it away. His teeth snagged on my tender nipple but I didn't move. I knew better than to rile him. He licked around the pinky-brown circle and I thought of how once, long ago, I would have been delighted with this, with the almost-painful sensation of his tongue and his teeth on the tenderest parts of me.

As if he knew what I was thinking, the fingers of his right hand pushed harder into my breast but I closed my eyes and thought of other things. Of Janey's garden running down to the marsh. Of me and my child (a girl, I hoped) picking herbs for her pot. Soon, he was finishing himself off with his other hand. He didn't ever want to be inside me. He didn't say why but I knew he thought it was somehow wrong and I was relieved for that reprieve at least. I kept hold of the thought that it would be different after my girl was born – Franklin and I could return to how we used to be.

When the real pain came, low down and deep, Franklin and the rest of the Laffertys were all residing at the Hall because the colonel had become interested in game shooting and it was the season then. They sent me to bed for most of January for my confinement. For my benefit they said, but I knew it was for the next Lafferty, not for me. My rings were cutting deep into the skin of my ring finger, but no one would let me cut them off. At first, the pain was welcome when it began grinding into me because I thought it would be over soon and I'd be released from the prison of the bedroom. But it was not soon.

They sent for a local midwife, a woman the doctor knew, but she wasn't Janey. She was a cold, unsmiling woman who told me off for standing up. In the eye of the agony, I called for my friend. I cried and screamed and told the doctor I didn't want a strange woman touching me. There were whispers outside the door and she came at last.

Janey held my hand, put cold compresses on my forehead and muttered charms under her breath. Everyone else stayed away. It got to be night and the baby hadn't come. The grandfather clock downstairs chimed midnight, then one, two. Sometime after it stopped chiming, the baby was drawn bawling out of my body, ripping me apart.

I can't remember now the raw feelings of the baby being pulled out of me, or the blood loss I was told I suffered, or even what he looked like, because all I remember feeling was a strange disconnect between the writhing, groaning animal who'd given birth to a boy (Oh, how they were pleased) and the rag of a being still lying in the bed. Janey held the baby up to the window and inspected him, saying, 'Thank the Lord for that. He's taken after the father.' I supposed she meant they would be pleased that he looked like a Lafferty. She paused. 'He'll not have the gift of seeing, not being born at the chime hours. But he's alive and crying.'

When they finally brought him to me – briefly, as it was clear I wasn't to be trusted with him – he was scrawny and angry and had a bright red face that reminded me of Franklin in a rage. The wet nurse they'd hired took him away quickly to the nursery and Janey had to leave. Janey stroked my hair and my face was wet with tears. When she left, I turned my body to the wall and wondered when love would come. I could see no connection between me and the squirming creature that had been taken out of me. My breasts were aching and sore and began to leak into the sheets. When the doctor came to examine me, I clenched my teeth and waited for his freezing fat fingers to get out of my soreness.

He covered me up and turned to speak to Lady Lafferty who was hovering in the doorway.

'She's damaged but she'll heal. She'll recover. Not straightaway though, mind. Give her a couple of weeks, my lady.'

A couple of weeks until what? I soon found out.

The Laffertys wanted to baptise him early so I was barely recovered when we had to troop with the baby to St John the Baptist's again. I still had little interest in him – the wet nurse fed him and they brought him to me swaddled in a blanket, his small head poking out, but he still looked like a miniature, pinched, red-faced version of Franklin to me. He had Franklin's fine nose, almond-shaped eyes and rosy lips. There was nothing of me in him that I could see. He cried whenever they gave him to me and I just wished they'd take him away. The nurse would fuss around and say 'he's just thirsty', or 'he must need changing', or 'the poor mite is hungry'. It was always something. I had no interest in anything – my baby son, the world carrying on outside the windows of the house, or even myself.

Finally, the day before the baptism, Hildy, up from London especially, said she was going to take me 'in hand'.

'Darling, it's time to buck up. You've done your duty.

You've given us Dickie and that's marvellous but there's no need to be morose. And look at the state of your hair.'

I was reading in the library – I often did, as no one else went in there – although I'd run out of mystery novels and had been forced into reading the dull books on their shelves. Luckily I'd found a Wilkie Collins, probably left by a visitor, and was pleased to discover it had an element of the mysterious about it too. Not that I was really reading. My mind kept drifting off and a servant would ask me if I wanted coffee in impatient tones as if they'd asked me more than once. Hildy dragged me upstairs to her room, which had an enormous window overlooking the disused farmland all the way to the woods. She sat me at her dressing table. It was true, I looked terrible. My face was sallow and queasy and my hair, still long, fine and black, was greasy and tarnished. She began brushing my hair, cleaning my face and applying rouge. At first I looked like a painted corpse – bright spots of rouge on my deathly pallor – but she kept working at me and by the end I did at least look alive, albeit an unnatural form of life.

They named him Richard Charles Lafferty, my father's name and the colonel's. I wasn't given any choice; at that time I didn't much care. He didn't cry at the baptism, which was strange. The new rector looked down at me and smiled kindly.

Franklin must have thought my revived appearance was a sign that relations were to be resumed. That night, he came to my room and lifted up my nightdress, feeling around under there. I clenched my legs together as if I could repel him, but he caressed the insides of my thighs and made me flinch.

'Don't you want me anymore?' he said in a little boy voice and looked up at me, supposedly hurt.

'Of course I do,' I said.

'Well you're not showing it,' he said.

I had no answer to that as it was quite true but I let him carry on and, although it was sore and I bit down so hard on my bottom lip it bled, I didn't cry out in pain because it would have annoyed him and I would suffer for it later.

It's funny, I don't remember a lot about the rest of that year. After all that's happened, it's receded and remains a series of scenes, like a set of still photographs. One of them is the time when Franklin turned up at the Hall in a Blackshirt uniform. I knew from Hildy that Mosley's first wife, Cimmie, had died suddenly in May and he'd gone off to Europe with another of his mistresses. It made me feel sick and uneasy, the way this role model of Franklin's treated his wife, who'd borne him three children. At the same time, I'd read in the newspapers what Mosley's party was up to. The press wasn't wholly complimentary, but I did see a copy of the Daily Mail which the colonel left, and they seemed to like them quite a lot. If I thought about it at all, I thought they looked rather silly in their new uniform, a bit like a pretend army, a version of the Blackshirts in Italy or the Brownshirts in Germany – or was it the other way round? But until that summer I hadn't thought about it much at all. And then Franklin arrived, dressed in the uniform. He picked up Richie and tousled his hair and all the time I had a niggling feeling of unpleasantness. He was attractive, as always – his golden skin and hair shone, and the uniform of black high-neck shirt and black breeches suited him, but it was not him. It was a costume, a show, and an ugly one.

I jumped up and took Richie from his arms.

'Why are you here dressed like that?' I asked.

'Dorothy's organised a rally over near Hillington. Trying to drum up support in the county. You and the boy could come. It'll be something to see.'

'But why do you need to be dressed like that? It's a political party, not an army.'

'Mosley thinks it instils a discipline in the ranks. The women's uniform is rather swish too, you know. You could get one. On second thoughts, no, it wouldn't suit you.' He bent down and pinched my cheek.

I pictured Franklin with a female Blackshirt. 'I don't think it would be good for the baby,' I said.

Throughout that summer he would come and go, to one rally or another, sometimes with the colonel, sometimes without. He seemed to be enthralled by it. At first, I think it was what his father wanted for him, but then, when he was singled out as a bright young hope for the party, he began to enjoy the admiration, the attention, the purpose. He would repeat odd things – 'A healthy and mighty race must have roots deep in the soil of a native land' – although his only concerns in the country were sport and the meetings. He knew very little about the country. There were rumours among the servants that he had a mistress at the party HQ but I tried not to listen.

I asked Hildy once about what she'd said to me, the night of the wedding.

'Oh, Rosie, you don't need to know.'

'Please,' I said.

Her mouth twitched. 'It was just a bit of a fuss kicked up by a girl's father, that's all. I think Frank threw her off – and she – oh, I don't know – she got herself into trouble and ...' She stopped and put her arm around my shoulders. 'Darling, don't. Don't be like that. He does adore you, you know. We all do. You're the only good egg in all of this blessed country as far as I'm concerned.'

Still I tried to ignore it, to tell myself that he loved me. I had to, for Richie's sake.

Another memory I have is of that Christmas. It was a picture-perfect, snow-covered, icily beautiful Christmas.

For a gift, Hildy – who had taken to wearing a brooch with the fascist symbol on it, a kind of lightning flash – had bought me two beautifully bound Agatha Christie mysteries that she'd found in London and I was so grateful I almost cried. They were The Sittaford Mystery and Peril at End House. I liked the title of the latter because it reminded me of the Marsh House, but the former was of particular interest because in that one, it snows on Dartmoor and a terrible murder is committed in a remote place. I thought what a perfect mystery plot it would be for all of us in this huge old mansion to be cut off from the rest of civilisation. But which of the awful characters surrounding me should be the murder victim?

I ate their food and drank their wine and slept in their house. I played with their heir, my son, on the rug before the fire and showed him the candles on the Christmas tree, watching the sparkle of them reflected in his big baby eyes. I listened to their tattle about Diana and Oswald and what a beautiful pair they were, although it was 'still desperately sad' about poor Cimmie, as Lady Lafferty said, and it was a 'terrible shame' about how he had treated her. I thought how small and lowborn and rural I was compared to such people.

Early in the new year, with snow still on the ground, we were out in the garden, the baby and I, he snug in his woollen hat and coat, and I in mine, when he wriggled in my arms and kicked his legs. Willingly, I put him down and there on the snow-covered lawn he began to walk, his short little legs waddling one after the other leaving pockmarks in the snow. I ran forward to catch him and, tottering, he fell at my feet. I picked him up and his beautiful eyes, shaped like his father's and yet so trusting, stared into mine. Up until then, Richie had been fussed around by the servants, ignored by the family and, shamefully, by me. I blamed him for making Franklin stop loving me. I blamed him for making me stop loving Franklin. But that day, with the look of trust he had in me, I thought then that I should love my baby.

I began to get used to the idea of Richie, to accept that I was a mother. I was *his* mother. He called for me, that was one thing. No one had ever done that before. No one had ever seemed to want or need me. I started to ask for him to be brought to me and I read to him from books that had been brought to the house at my request: Peter

Pan and Alice's Adventures in Wonderland and a whole set of Beatrix Potter. I think I enjoyed reading to him more than he enjoyed listening, but it soothed him when he cried and soon he began to look at the pictures and point at the silly animals dressed in hats and tailcoats. Franklin would sometimes appear while I was reading, Richie in my lap. I knew what was expected. I had to give Richie to the nurse and go upstairs. I shut my eyes and my ears to the rumours and tried not to picture him in the black costume.

30

I'll tell this part quickly because it still hurts. I've been putting it off but I have to do it. To put my hand in the fire.

In the late winter, I began to go to the Marsh House whenever Franklin was away. He was often in London on party business, and I spent more time by the marsh. It made life bearable and took away some of the loneliness. I could see Janey, walk with her along the creek. Richie would be carried on our backs or totter between our hands on the beach. She would tell Richie the stories – all the old folk tales she'd told me when I was a child – 'The Green Children', 'The Dauntless Girl' (that was my favourite) or 'Sea Tongue' – and I could be a girl again. Richie's favourite was the part in 'The Dead Moon' where the boggarts came out of the marsh. His eyes would light up with excitement whenever she said, 'The naughty boggarts scampered across the marsh', and we all laughed. 'Moon,' he said, pointing with his fat finger to the sky. It was his first word apart from 'Mama'.

It wasn't long after I moved us home to the Marsh House that he got a fever and a rash and he had to be quarantined in my old nursery for fear of contagion. I especially was not allowed near him, in case I contracted the disease. The doctor was brought but pronounced him over the worst and said he should be 'right as rain' soon enough with liquids and fresh air.

One day in February – a miserable day in my memory, though perhaps it was as bright as a summer's day, who knows? – he was playing at my feet in the nursery. The fever was past. I came to the nursery every day now because I could be with him rather than anyone else. I was reading and was immersed in the novel (it was The Woman in White, which I had stolen from the Laffertys' unused library) so I don't know how long he was like it, but something made me look up – a bird passed by the window, I think, and I heard Smutch howling at nothing from Janey's cottage – and I saw that he was asleep on the rug. It wasn't his nap time and he'd seemed well enough that morning. His cheek was pink and his blond curls stuck to his sweaty little forehead. I nearly cried out but then I noticed his chest swelling and falling.

'Richie,' I whispered, and felt his head. It was hot. His bud lips were slightly apart and his breath was wet. The fever must have returned. I picked him up and he was like a rag in my arms, his little arms flopping down at his sides. I remember he was heavy and it made me think of a 'dead weight'. I ran downstairs, past Fairbrother mopping the floor and out onto the front drive, covered in frost. Perdie began to bark as if she sensed my panic and ran along beside me across the lane to Janey's where I banged hard on the door.

'I was coming to see you and the babby, Rosie,' she said, but seeing him, and without another word, she took him off me. She cooled him down with a wet cloth and put something on his tongue. She lay him on a blanket in front of her hearth, attended to by Perdie who whimpered next to him. Old Smutch stood guard at the door. Richie opened his eyes finally but there was a filmy glaze over the surface and he didn't seem to see me. All I could see was the reflection of the fire flickering on the glaze of his eyes.

'What's wrong with him, Janey? He was better. He's been better for weeks.'

'Fever's got in him again,' she said. 'But it's stronger now.'

Over the next few hours we kept watch over him. He woke up at times and babbled but he never seemed to see me. One time I thought he'd be all right, but he slipped back into his thick sleep, his limbs heavy and his breath rasping. Have you ever heard a baby with a scratching breath? It is the most hideous sound. Unnatural. I don't know how long we sat in our vigil but the shadows lengthened over his sleeping body and it grew dark in the little cottage. Janey lit the oil lamps and the shadows guttered and waved, grew into hideous forms and shrunk to stuttering animals on the walls.

The pink light had faded to dark when Perdie began to whine and pressed her paw to his side. Smutch set up a mournful howl. I knew something was wrong with how Richie moved – he'd descended so far down into his sleep that Perdie's paw didn't rouse him at all. But I was paralysed by the horror of what it meant.

Janey stood up. 'Take him home,' she said. 'Best if I go fetch the doctor.' I had never heard her mention a doctor before.

I pleaded with her. But she lifted him up and put him in my arms, took hold of me and pushed me out of the door, into the night, with my baby. I crossed over to the Marsh House.

That's where he died. The rest of it spooled out before me and I could only watch, helpless. The doctor came, but it made no difference. It was too late.

'No,' I said. I kept repeating 'no'. It was the only word I had.

They took him away and put him in a box and buried him at the church on a bitter, grey day, but it was as if they'd buried something else – an animal, a doll. Maybe nothing at all. Not the beautiful creature I'd had torn out of me.

Janey said later that he was 'too good for this world'. And perhaps that was true because it wasn't his fault he looked so much like his father. None of it was his fault. All the anger I'd felt towards his small soul had evaporated like hot air. I'd allowed myself to love him and now he was gone.

31

'She lost her babbies too, she did. It's something else you've got in common with her,' Janey said.

'What happened to her, Janey? Why has no one ever told me?'

She frowned. 'I don't know what good it'd do you knowing. It ent a happy story, poor child.'

'I'm seventeen now, and I'm married and I'm a mother myself. I was –'

I was fingering the silver locket around my neck in which I kept a lock of his golden hair and tears came, choking the back of my throat, making me cough and splutter. Everything ran with liquid – my nose, my eyes, my mouth. She drew me to her and I sucked in the familiar smells of cloves and rosehips and soup broth until I came to a juddering stop.

'I want to know,' I said, and looked up into those small bright eyes with the fiercest glare I could muster.

She sighed. 'All I know is he sent her away not long after you were born. She were sick, you see, sick in the head. Wouldn't eat, would hardly look at you, would go off walking all the time. Got so bad your father sent for a quack. But I never knew where they took her, Rose, he'd turned against me by then, blamed me for her sickness, said I'd cursed her.'

'He'll never tell me,' I said. But I saw what I could do, what I should have done years before.

I waited until he was out on business and locked the door of his study from the inside. I rifled through his correspondence. He was not a meticulous man, and there were sheaves and sheaves of paper, mostly bills, unpaid. And one of them was a letter with the address marked St Andrew's Hospital. My heart jolted painfully. The anticipation was so great I could barely breathe. The letter said little. The condition of your wife remains stable. She enjoys walking in the grounds and painting. Platitudes – awful, meaningless platitudes. It was her, though, I was sure of it. And she was alive. But instead of a great feeling of consolation and joy, I found instead an immense sense of abandonment came over me. She had loved me so little that she'd left me here, alone with my father; she'd left me motherless. What kind of weak creature would allow herself to do that? Where was she, all those times I needed her? And another, terrifying thought hit me – that I was as weak as she was, that whatever it was in her was in me too. I could no more be a mother than she could. I took the little shell I'd thought was from her and flung it out of my bedroom window.

32

Malorie stopped reading and closed her heavy eyes. The temperature had dropped and she was cold all over. In the bedroom on the edge of the marsh, she lay on her front, with her face in the pillow, sucking in her own damp breath, her back to the room. She dropped the notebook to the floor. No shadows could get to her. It didn't matter anyway, all the shadows were inside her head.

Think of something else, think of something else she repeated but it was impossible. The dark blots in her mind swelled and grew and merged until they became all there was. She could feel herself being enveloped by them, their soft forms surrounding her. She fought against the well of darkness. It wasn't the same. Her grief was not an all-encompassing chasm like Rosemary's – the loss of a child, the desertion by a mother – just a great murky mass of darkness. There was nothing to get hold of.

Sound was coming from somewhere like waves in a storm. Her face was wet. She reached out for a handkerchief but when she lifted it to her face it was the old lace wedding veil. She wiped her eyes with it and stared up at the ceiling with red-sore eyeballs. She was too tired to think or to grieve. By the door, a shadow appeared.

A pressure of air, something solid but invisible pushed her back against the bed.

'Leave me alone,' she moaned.

She shrank back into the bed. There was a flicker of light at the edge of her eye. If she didn't look it would go away. But her head turned. Standing in the dark of the doorway where the shadow had been was a slight figure all in white. It was the same face she thought she'd seen at the sitting room window. Rosemary's face. She was wearing what looked like a wedding dress and a veil – the veil that Malorie was holding in her hand – and her small, translucent hands were on her belly. It stuck out, protruding, the swollen belly of a woman in the late stages of pregnancy.

Automatically, Malorie's hands went to her own, empty stomach. Her gaze rose as if pulled there, from the body to the face of the figure. Rosemary's eyes stared back at her, the inky-green-black of a bottomless sea. They seemed to see right into her and through her. Then a blank. There was nothing there. Just the door. She tried to keep her eyes open, she wanted to keep on seeing. She fought against it but sank deeper into the black sea of sleep. Sleep crept into her brain, drawing her into its soft darkness. Sleep was merciful and full, thickly black and deep.

33

Midwifery they call it now. I brought out so many babbies into this world, hauling them, dragging them into the light, screaming, squalling. And sometimes they're quiet and it's them you ought to worry about. He were a beautiful child, a blessed child. I wished he would bring her joy. And that he did for a short while.

After the child's death I didn't have much heart to go to the church on St Mark's Eve to see what was coming the next year. I were afraid of what'd appear to me. But I did go. I just didn't share what I saw with no one. Perhaps I ought to have done, now I think about it.

34

To the Sea
Boxing Day

The curtains were open and a watery yellow light filled the room. It was so cold the windows were rimed with frost inside. Malorie pulled herself out of bed, put on her dressing gown and breathed onto the windowpane, but her breath was white and made no impression on the ice. Her fingernails scraped letters onto the frosty pane. R – o – s – e. She stopped, confused for a second, and quickly wiped the window until the letters were gone. She shivered and thrust her hands into the pockets of her dressing gown. In the pocket was a scrunched-up piece of white lace. Her eyes swam. She saw the girl with the veil staring at her. A feeling like the wash of a cold sea flowed through her. She took the white lace and thrust it to the back of the top drawer. It could be anything, it might not be the veil the girl had worn. Her mind was confused between the notebook, the dreams and reality. She'd had a nightmare. Today. Today was reality.

The sky was a clear light blue and the ice-crusted snow shimmered. New snow had been covered with a thick frost. It was the first time the sun had shone since they'd arrived and it filled her with a fragile hope. They could finally go to the sea. She would tell Franny about Larry. No, she would tell her a white lie, a kind lie – that he'd run away. She'd promise to buy her a new dog. She would salvage what was left of Christmas.

She dressed quickly and hurried downstairs. The ground floor smelled of toast. Franny was munching in the sitting room in front of a fire.

'There's no tea,' said Franny, 'the water's off.' Oh God, the pipes must have frozen – it was a miracle they hadn't before. She had no idea where they could get water from. It was yet another thing that she couldn't cope with.

'Why didn't you wake me?' she said, then regretted it. She had to start again. 'You made breakfast by yourself?'

'Sorry,' said Franny, her face downcast. 'Are we going today?'

'Don't be sorry. Yes – but we haven't been to the sea yet.' It was too soon. The sea was so close – there at the end of the lane – she could see it from the bedroom. It couldn't be unreachable.

'After that?'

'Yes,' she said. 'We'll go after that.'

'But what if we haven't found Larry? We can't go home without him. We can't leave him here.'

'Darling.' Malorie knelt down by Franny and took her cold hands in hers. 'It's possible that Larry's been run – run away. He's probably very happy where he is, but we might not be able to find him.'

'But you said you'd find him.'

'Sometimes people say things that they want to be true but they can't make them be true.'

'You shouldn't have promised.' Franny's face was drawn tight in grief and anger. She tore her hands out of Malorie's and, grabbing her coat and boots, ran out of the house.

'Franny,' she called after her, but she'd gone. There was no sign of her daughter in the garden, but her hunched angry shape was trudging away towards the marsh.

The bitter wind made Malorie's eyes water and she wasn't sure if there were tears mixed in with it. As they headed away from the house, she felt as if someone was watching from one of the windows. She made herself face forward. The sky was heavy with the palest grey. Her feet crunched on the iced, packed snow on the path to the creek and, above her, birds – black terns she thought they were – wheeled, calling, squeaking. The whole world was a monotone; only the red of Franny's scarf provided any colour. At the end of the lane, they came to the creek running in a muddy gully to the right, alongside the line of trees on a slight rise, bare branches reaching for the sky. The two of them stopped. Franny's eyes were red-rimmed. She should say something to her, find some words of comfort. As they stood there, a formation of large birds like geese flew above them out towards the marsh, making a honking noise.

In a quick burst, without looking at her scowling girl, she said, 'Franny – I have to tell you – I found Larry. Darling, he – he must have got scared by something and I think he got very cold. So cold his heart stopped. I, I made a grave for him in the snow.' She looked down and her heart tore with pain. The anger on her daughter's face had been replaced by desolation and she looked so young suddenly that Malorie had no choice but to reach out for her, to wrap her with her arms. Franny was stiff, unyielding, but she leaned her head against her mother's fur coat, her small body wracked with tearless sobs.

'I should have told you earlier,' she said.

'Poor Larry,' said Franny finally, withdrawing from the fur. Then – 'I want to see him.'

'He's sleeping, darling. He's peaceful now.'

'He's not sleeping,' she said petulantly.

'No, not sleeping. You're right. But look, why don't we go to the sea since we're here? We're not very far away.'

'All right,' said Franny.

'It must be this way,' she said, relieved that the first cut was made. It was still far away on the horizon, but she could smell the salt in the air. Tentatively, she began picking her way along the thin scrubby path that seemed to lead through the marsh to the sea. She thought – one slip and you'd be ankle deep or worse in black, icy seawater. They crossed a small wooden bridge over another creek. The path seemed to disappear into nothing.

'What are we supposed to bloody do now?' The whine in her voice sounded like a child's. How ill-equipped she was, to be a parent.

'I'm tired,' said Franny.

'We can't be far,' she said, plunging forward along what could have been a path once – a smear of stone and mud between clumps of shrub and grass. She had to show Franny the sea. That was a normal thing for a parent to do. Closer now, she could see the tufts of the low dunes ahead and the pale-yellow gleam of the sand and the grey line of the sea. To the far left of them were the hulls of old boats, the blue and red paint, faded and mottled and peeling off. Now and again they came to another little creek with the stumps of rotting posts in the mud. Some of the creeks stopped dead; some were longer and wound across the marsh, but they were thin and lined with scrub that they could jump across. On either side of them were pools of black water like open sores. What nasty things lurked there? You wouldn't want to be lost out here at night, that much was true, like the poor cockler, stranded as the tide and the fog came in.

They tramped on until they came to a creek that was much wider, gaping and deep in front of them.

'How can we cross that?' said Franny. Perhaps they should turn back. It was filthy out here.

'Oh come on, we're nearly there,' she said. 'Listen.'

It was true. She could hear the faint shush of the waves above the sound of the wind brustling across the scrubby marsh.

Franny said, 'Look.' She was pointing below them. There, slightly hidden down in the gulch was a wooden board that served – could serve – as a bridge from one side to the other.

They lowered themselves down to the tiny bridge and scrambled back up the other side, slipping slightly in the slick mud. But now, after a few more steps, they were finally there and the beach opened out in front of them – a pale expanse of sand extending as far to the east and west as she could see, encrusted in patches of ice – and beyond, the white rim of the shoreline, the seal-coloured sea and a thin mist clinging to the water.

Wind from the sea whipped up the sand, and seaspray flicked over her face. She turned away to protect her eyes.

Further up the beach, Franny was picking up shells with her mittens off.

She left her and walked down to the sea and along the line of the shore. She watched the foam lick the sand and retreat, leaving a line of scum the way a snail leaves a trail of slime. There was something shining there. She leaned over, holding her hat down with one hand, and scooped it out of the wet sand. It was a shell, a shell with a pink interior, like the one Franklin had given Rosemary. She held the delicate, brittle object in the palm of her hand and it was funny how it made her feel closer to the girl in the notebooks, as if this very shell had existed in both her world and Malorie's.

Her parents used to take her to the coast when she was little – but somewhere else, she seemed to remember, where cliffs of great dunes fell tumbling to the beach, but otherwise it was the same long, wide sandy beaches and the same brown North Sea that turned grey-blue in the sun. It had been a thing of ritual, the trips to the beach: her mother with her headscarf tied tightly under her chin, and her basket stuffed with egg sandwiches carefully wrapped in paper, a bottle of pop for her and a flask of tea for the two of them. And best of all, a vanilla sponge. They would sit for hours on the sand, her mother reading one of her terrible romance novels (Malorie thought, as soon as she was old enough to be dismissive), her father dozing with his trouser-legs rolled up and his hat covering his freckly face. Alone, Malorie would dig huge holes, pick up creatures in the rock pools, gather a collection of shells. She watched the other children jumping off the dunes and splashing in the sea, but she never had the courage to do those things herself. She never made friends with the other children at the beach – she was wary of them. It pricked at her heart, the image of herself as a child, standing apart from the romping packs of other children, screaming with delight in the water. And here was her own daughter, accompanied only by her mother picking shells on a beach, alone. At the end of the long day, sandy-mouthed and salt-flecked, her dad would wipe her feet with a towel. She remembered looking down at the pinkness of his scalp through his bright wispy hair as he knelt at her feet, and the comforting largeness of his hand as he led her back to the car. Where had they been? She wasn't sure now. It could have been here. She remembered dunes, cold sea . . .

In the far right of her vision, something moved beyond the dune, back on the marsh. The dark figure looked familiar. A rounded shape with a creature the size of a tiger. It had to be the old woman and the enormous black dog. Malorie raised her hand and called, 'Hello!'

She thought that the figure – the old woman, she was sure of it – nodded in response but she wasn't sure. The mist rolled in from the sea and she seemed to melt into it.

'Hello!' she shouted, but the old woman had disappeared.

Slowly, Malorie walked back to Franny. 'Did you see an old woman, Fran?'

'Where?'

'At the other end of the beach. She was walking a black dog.'

Franny screwed up her forehead. 'Maybe,' she said. 'I saw someone but I didn't know who it was.'

It *had* been the old woman, thought Malorie. She remembered the girl in the shop telling her about the sea here. You could only go to the beach when the tide was out. She'd said that when the tide came in hard a spit of sand was often cut off from the rest of the land, stranding anyone stupid enough to be out there. Was the sea any closer than when they'd got here? They'd hardly been here any time at all. But when she thought about it, she had no idea of the times of the tide. Had the old woman been trying to warn them just now?

'I like the beach,' Franny said. 'Larry would have liked it here.'

'Franny, listen. I'm going to get you another dog. As soon as we get home.'

'I don't want another dog. I want Larry.'

Malorie watched the white wisps of her laboured breathing in the cold air. She didn't know how she could go on. Go on without Tony, without her parents. It was too much to bear.

'Mummy, what's the matter?'

Her cheeks were warm and wet with tears that stung. 'Nothing,' she said, wiping them with her glove. 'I know you want Larry, I'm sorry.' Franny looked down at her feet but she didn't say anything. Behind her, the sea felt close.

'Let's get back,' Malorie said, afraid of the tide coming in and cutting them off. She could imagine the mist thickening and the tide rolling in and not knowing which way was land and which way was the open sea. You could scream and scream and although they might hear you, no one would be able to find you. She picked up her pace, away from the sea-mist.

As they walked back the way they came, the mist merged with the thick cloud and snow began falling again, light flakes at first, then fatter and fatter. Franny's form was thin, her brown bobble hat moving up and down like a coconut on a shy, her red scarf flying out behind her, a streak of red on white. Rather than her usual slouch she was jumping and hopping across the creeks and clumps. She was quite agile, Malorie noticed with surprise, and she thought how little chance Franny had been given to be a proper child – to have adventures and to roam about free. How little she'd even noticed her own daughter. A wave of guilt came at her like a sudden gust of wind and she rocked back on her heels. She began to run, splashing and sliding in the mud.

When she caught up with Franny on the road, she laughed, 'Look at the state of these boots!' Both their pairs of boots were covered in a slick of shiny black mud, which was now overlaid with dots of snow. Underneath the slimy, pale-brown mud of the marsh lay another layer, an ooze of black. She imagined the bog creatures crawling out of the gullies and pools on the marsh, slick and dripping with black mud. She wouldn't let them get her. She took hold of Franny's small, mittened hand and squeezed it. Her daughter looked at her with surprise but didn't pull away.

By the time they came to the lane to the house, their coats and hats were covered with snow and their faces wet with it. She gripped Franny's hand tightly. The trees at the end of the lane were mere charcoal sticks in the whiteness.

Through the falling flakes, someone was walking towards them. Malorie could tell by the way the person moved that it was a man and that he was carrying something in a sack. Franny's hand slipped from hers.

'Hello!' the man called. 'I was just coming along with some –' He stopped. Malorie, walking ahead, realised it was the grocer. His weather-beaten face wore an expression of such shock a shivering pulse of cold ran through her and she stepped back away from him.

'What is it?' she said.

The man gaped at her for a further instant then, frowning, he put a hand to his forehead. 'T'aint nothing. I could have sworn – No, no. It was just the way you looked, coming along the lane. It's just this blessed snow getting in my eyes. Must have been.'

Her lips twitched in an approximation of a smile. She didn't like the way he'd looked at her. 'You were bringing something to us?'

'Yes, right you are. That I was.' But he remained staring at her. 'My daughter – she said you might be needing some coal. I brought you a drop of it with the turkey but what with all this weather, I reckoned you might need some more.'

It was Malorie's turn to frown now. 'Thank you,' she said. 'It's very kind of you, but we're going back to London today, so I'm afraid we won't be needing any more coal.'

The man looked up to the sky, frowning. 'You'd best be off then is my advice. Road's going to be impassable soon, way it's coming on.' She had a recollection of the man's voice on the radio: Do not travel unless it is strictly necessary.

'We certainly will,' she said, keen to get away. 'Thank you again.'

'I take it you're not from round here, then?'

'I'm from Norwich,' she said, 'but we live in London.'

'London,' he repeated, drawing out the syllables, making it sound like a different planet. 'Right,' he said. 'Right you are. It's just – I can't get over – No, it's nothing.'

She could feel the presence of Franny next to her, tugging on her hand. 'Mummy,' she was saying, 'come inside. I'm cold.'

'Best be off then, before it comes down worse. You be careful, now.'

'Yes, thank you, we will, Mr –?'

'Bayfield,' he said.

Bayfield. The name was familiar. It was the name above the shop of course. And, she realised, it was the name of the boy in the journal who'd bullied Rosemary. He was real. It was like seeing an apparition, or a fictional character come to life.

'Did you know a girl called Rosemary who used to live here?'

His face turned inward, frowning as if she'd said something terrible, and he began to back away. 'I did. Yes. Long time ago now. What do you want to know about her for then?'

But she didn't answer. She had a strong urge to keep the girl in the notebooks to herself.

'I did wonder if you might be a relative or something,' he said, peering at her curiously.

'A relative? No. But – actually – I'm here because of my father, Harry Skinner. Do you know him? He gave me a picture of this house. The Marsh House.'

He frowned again. 'That name don't ring a bell. Sorry, afraid I've got to get off on my rounds.'

She stood watching him go, deflated by the fact that no one knew who Harry Skinner was. But this man, Bayfield, had known Rosemary. He *was* the boy mentioned in the diaries. Though Rosemary had hated him and in some strange way she felt as if she was betraying her by talking to him.

In the house, they hung their wet coats in the kitchen and let them drip onto the flagstone floor. Malorie told Franny to get packed up. She took down the notebooks from above the wardrobe and sat on the bed, holding them in her lap. She couldn't take them with her – how could she? – they weren't hers. Yet what was the alternative? She couldn't bear the thought of leaving Rosemary and the unfinished notebooks. But that was weird. She'd become too attached to this girl. The whole story was far-fetched. She'd allowed herself to become obsessed with it and all along, the writer – whoever it was – had been manipulating her, making her believe in this preposterous world of Fascist sympathisers and witchy old women. And she'd allowed the eerie old house to make her feel unsettled. She'd confused the two things – her own real, actual grief and sadness, with that of a chimera, a made-up person. And even the funny old woman wasn't that strange when you thought about it. She was probably just an old busybody. In fact – Malorie's brain lit up – that was it! The old woman had been trying to put her off. She'd been trying to spook her the whole time, making the odd noises she'd heard and planting the notebooks so Malorie could find them. Maybe she even wrote them. God, she'd been such a fool – a credulous fool. There was a woman, yes, but it could be anyone. The woman was no doubt trying to spook her because she thought Malorie was going to buy it! She, Malorie, must have looked like a typical up-from-Londoner. They hated them up here in the sticks. Yes, the man had been friendly at first, but she didn't like the way he'd reacted to the name Rosemary. It made her feel uncomfortable, having read about him in the journal, which may or may not be true.

It was impossible now to verify the truth of anything in the notebooks. Either way, the sooner she and Franny got back to London, the better.

Not knowing what else to do, she stashed the books under the bed.

When all the cases were in the car and the two of them were too, their combined breath fogging the windows, she heard Franny's voice from behind her.

'We can't leave Larry here. He'll be lonely.'

She stopped herself saying *No he won't, he's dead* and swallowed. 'I'm sorry, Fran, we can't take him. We can . . . come back.' She didn't even believe herself. She turned the key in the ignition.

The tyres spun. The car didn't move. There was a spluttering, churning sound as the engine turned over.

'Franny, you're going to need to get out and push.'

'Mummy, I can't!'

But she did as she was told. The tyres spun again, she thought the damn thing would never get out, but then there was a sudden release and the car sprang forward along the drive, pulling onto the road, spraying white on both sides. A moment of suspension, of perfect emptiness, the snow coming down sideways onto the ice-encrusted oval of the front windscreen, the wind cursing through the trees and her, driving in her furs. Then the wind dropped, snow fell vertically rather than horizontally. She turned as if to say goodbye to the house but she could hardly see it for the thickness of the snow.

'Mum!' she heard, from far away outside the car.

Too late, she slammed on the brakes; the car slid. A wall of white came fast towards her. The car came to a thumping halt. It had skidded into a hard barrier of snow.

The drift was too high to see over. They left the car there and returned to the house with their cases, dragging their heavy feet back up the road. It was bad – she knew logically it was a bad thing – but her instinct was an uneasy, giddy relief. They had to stay. She would have no choice now but to finish the notebooks and, in that moment, she didn't care if they were made up or not; she had to read them.

As they entered the drive, Malorie could have sworn she saw smoke curling up from the chimney of the cottage.

35

Mother

That night, they ate leftovers from the Christmas Day lunch.
She melted snow for water and hoped it would be safe if
she boiled it for tea. While she made the tea, Franny had
gone and kneeled at the snowy mound where the dog was
buried, leaving bits of leaf and stone as an offering. When
she came in she was subdued and agreed to play cards but
hardly spoke. Malorie tried to find music on the radio, but
the white noise was too thick. When Franny went into the
sitting room to read, Malorie stayed in the kitchen drinking
wine. The third notebook was waiting for her back in the
bedroom where it belonged. She could feel the pull of it but
she was holding off, too. She wasn't exactly sure why, but
she both wanted to be back in Rosemary's world and was
wary of it. She was thinking about the little boy who'd died
in the house and the girl's mother, rotting in an asylum. Her
mind moved to her own child.

The birth had been a breeze. Everyone said she'd done
very well, she had a lovely, healthy girl and look, isn't she

dinky? Such a dainty little thing. But she, the mother, was afraid of the baby. It was a tiny, scrawny animal that relied on her. When they tried to get the baby to latch onto her breast, Malorie had felt repulsed at the sucking of the baby's mouth, the violent yank on her nipple. The baby wouldn't stay still and spat out the milk. It dribbled down onto her dressing gown. Eventually, the health visitor said words like 'failure to thrive' and 'bedrest'. They took both of them away to a maternity hospital. When the baby was taken to the hospital nursery, Malorie felt only gratitude. Every time they brought her back, the baby's screwed up face broke into a yowling wail and Malorie had no idea what to do to stop the crying. They gave her baby formula and she tried to use the bottle, or a dummy, or her finger. She tried rocking, stroking, jiggling the baby up and down on her still-tender belly, saying soothing, cooing sounds. None of it seemed to work. Each time, she would gladly hand the baby over to a capable-looking nurse and they would take her back to the nursery, judgement in their eyes.

Tony said they had to give the baby a name. Did she want to give the baby her name, Mary? No, she said, Mary was her given name and she'd taken her middle name, Malorie, as soon as she'd left Norwich for London. What about her mother's name? She made a face. No. She couldn't fix her mind on a name for this baby. In the end, Tony suggested Frances, after his grandmother. His mother would like that. Fine, she said, and fell back into longed-for sleep. She couldn't seem to keep awake after they gave her the Luminal. But something would inevitably wake her, dragging her out of the quiet – the clattering of a trolley, the cheery good morning of a nurse, the yanking open of the curtains, the wailing of the baby, or someone else's baby. Once, in the middle of the night, she was woken by the sound of crying. It was soft crying, not a baby, a woman's sob. She lay there thinking that if only she had the energy she could call out to the woman, to say *I'm here. I know what it's like. You're not alone.* But she was afraid. Eventually the woman sniffed and stopped and the ward returned to its temporary hush.

The days stretched to weeks and the weeks to months. A nurse at the mother and baby unit told her that her time was up. By the time they left, she couldn't imagine how she was supposed to look after the baby on her own. Every day and night in the flat with the baby while Tony was out at the club was a trial. Malorie didn't like thinking about those years now. Once, she was in the park when Franny was a toddler – she must have been walking because she wouldn't go in her pushchair. She'd stiffen her legs and cry if Malorie tried so they'd walked to the park, a scrubby rectangle of dirty grass and a few swings on a concrete patch near the flat. In the park was another mother with her daughter, who was about the same age. She couldn't actually remember how old Franny had been then – why couldn't she remember? This other mother was neat and smartly dressed, with a daffodil-coloured spring coat and sensible shoes. The woman wasn't as pretty as Malorie; she was probably older than her too. Malorie had only been about twenty-one then. But the woman looked happy. Radiant – that was a word they used about new mothers. And the baby looked happy, chubby and healthy. She remembered thinking *How have they done it?* How did the mother know what to do? She picked up Franny and shoved her roughly into the pushchair. The baby had set up a forlorn cry instantly and Malorie had marched out of the park, tears welling in her eyes, full of rage at the perfect mother and her perfect baby, at her imperfect, hateful child and her own inadequate, terrible self.

Her mother visited and tidied, washed up, prepared the bottles and complained about how dirty London was. Malorie was grateful to her, but her mother had no words of advice to give her on how to bond with her child and returned to Norwich without any promise to return. She tried hard not to think about how much her father would have loved being a grandfather; he'd only missed her birth by months.

Mostly she avoided the other mothers in the area. Their friends, Clemency and the others, didn't have babies. Malorie would take Franny with her to the parties and put her on a pile of clothes. Or she'd hear Franny crying while she was trying to dance and stones of guilt and hate would fall heavily into her gut. Once, she was stumbling out the door of a party when Tony held up a squalling baby.

'I think you've forgotten something.' His face was full of disgust.

On the way home in the taxi, she said, 'She's yours too.'

'What kind of mother are you?' he said.

What kind of mother was she? It was a question she asked herself.

Franny turned from a difficult baby to an isolated child. And here she was, eight years old and sullen, friendless – only at ease, it seemed to Malorie, with her feckless, insubstantial father, who seemed to prefer being in his bloody club to being with his daughter. She could hear her own whining in her head. *It isn't fair*. But it *was* fair, that was the cruel truth. A lonely person had bred another one. That was all. And why wouldn't their daughter prefer her father's company? He was more *fun*. Her disgusting self-pity was feeding on itself. She was sick of her own sadness, growing and growing inside her like a choking weed, clogging up her every waking thought, until she loathed everything and everyone.

Tottering slightly, she picked up the half-empty wine bottle and her red-smeared glass and took them upstairs to the bedroom. The house creaked and a thin wind cried in the chimney. It was late and she should sleep but she wasn't tired, she was buzzing with nervous energy.

What kind of mother was she? One who had never known her own mother, even at the end, when she'd been dying. She remembered the papers her mother had given Tony, the last time in the hospice. She'd avoided thinking about anything left behind, unwilling to acknowledge the emptiness left by her parents' deaths. It seemed easier to ignore it than to engage with it. Theirs was a history she didn't want. But – what if it told her the connection to this house? She thought of all this tangled mess of inadequacy and rage and blame. Of secrets carrying on and on from one generation to the next, and accepted that finally, she should just look at these papers. He'd said they were in the suitcase. She had it with her now, the same one she'd taken to the hospice, which she'd hardly bothered to unpack. It must be there.

Her fingers were stiff and cold as she rifled through the piles of jumpers and vests, and found it, still there, tucked at the bottom. She fumbled with the large brown manila folder. She flicked through the sheaf of documents, letters from the bank, that sort of thing, the detritus of small lives that no one wanted to deal with. And an envelope with the words *To be opened after I'm gone* written on the front. For God's sake, Mother, that was an unnecessarily emotive way of putting it. Why only then, for goodness' sake? Why not while she was alive? Inside it were official-looking documents. But there was no letter, no explanation.

Her face and neck flushed suddenly with heat. A strange sensation of falling. Adoption papers.

A baby, named Mary Skinner. Parents Mr and Mrs Skinner. Nothing else. No place of birth. It was her. She could hardly breathe. The date of adoption, 3rd August 1935. Her birthday.

There was a photograph attached by a paper clip to the certificate. A swaddled, dark-eyed baby and a smiling woman in a nurse's uniform. On the back it said *Mary, three months, with Mrs Babbage.*

She understood it was her, that the baby in the photograph was her, in the way she understood the moon circled the earth. But she did not *understand*. And then very quickly, in a rush of knowledge, she did. Her mother's drawn face in the hospice. The way she'd looked at something out of the window rather than directly at her. The room began to spin. She made some kind of guttural groan, staggered two paces to the window and opened it to the night.

She thrust her head through the window. Snow fell lightly on her hair and her upturned face.

Her head was teeming. Who was this Mrs Babbage? Maybe she could find her. Who were her real parents and why had they abandoned her? Her mother. Her *mother*. The word itself had changed. She felt like laughing.

She thought of all the years when they could have told her. Her parents. Her mother. Her father. Her *dad*. Her heart seemed to physically ache with the pain of it like a knife wound, plunging again and again. Her mother's words filtered into her head. *I can't tell you. It's too late.* She was the shameful secret. *She* was.

A musical note floated up from the living room downstairs. A single low, mournful trumpet. She must be imagining it. It was the song again, the song she kept hearing. She put her hands over her ears but the song was still there, faint but audible.

She ran down the stairs and into the living room where the gramophone sat innocuously on the sideboard. No sound came from it.

Suddenly exhausted, she flopped onto the sofa. You've suffered a terrible shock, she said to herself, the way someone would to a victim of a crime. It was a terrible shock. But also, what she felt was a small sense of relief that she'd belonged to another mother once, and a dull sadness that she'd been so horribly ungrateful that they'd chosen her, looked after her as their own. And a gnawing, aching feeling that she would never be able to say to her father that she'd loved him. Why hadn't they told her? Why hadn't they let her know she was chosen? And the question which bothered her the most: *Why* had they chosen her when they obviously found her so bemusing? Why had her mother never let her know she was loved? And the impossible realisation that it was because she wasn't.

36

It began in thirty-four. Around the summertime. A hot one it was.

She were eighteen then, still a mere sprite of a thing, hardly grown. Bit like the young one in the house now, only angrier. She could get a right mard on, that Rose, when she wanted to. Both got them narrow greenish eyes, like cats. It were a funny time, cos in one way she were glad, back at home with me and her father. But she'd lost that baby of hers and she began to act like an animal building its nest. She'd always done it, the nesting. When she was younger, she used to pick bits of rubbish off the shore and bring them back to her room – bits of tidewrack what had no place in a home – dried seaweed, tree roots, old bits of blue fishing line, that kind of thing. I don't know why she did it, 'cept she had a liking for the sea. Then her father got rid of it all when she was married. But it were different this time I'm talking about. She'd walk down to the marsh every day, and right across it, to the sand and the sea, picking up gruesome things, strange things. Bones, mostly. Then that boy came and got her and he started taking her back to the hall. I knew what he were playing at. He ought to have left the poor child alone, but he were always sighing at her and whispering sweetness and buying her fancies. And she didn't have her baby no more and I reckon she didn't know what else to do. I tried to tell her, course I did, but you can't tell nothing to a dreamy girl like that, she'd gone away from me, or that's what I thought.

Anyway, she were bound to him. There weren't much I could say about that. I know in some places people hop about in and out of each other's beds and there were those what did that then, I can assure you. But there weren't options for her like that, left out here in Norfolk. She might as well not have existed. It were a hop-pole marriage after all – cos she'd been with child.

Every time he went off to London she came back here to the Marsh House, but I didn't like the look of her. She were getting thinner if anything and that don't make no sense when you think about all the fancy food they had at that hall. Bones sticking out, hollow cheeks, like she were sucking cochies. It weren't right.

'Are you eating?' I say to her.

'Of course I am,' she says, but she don't look at me straight. 'I'm just tired, that's all.'

By then she never talked about him no more. All the shine had rubbed off him, revealing a cheap, empty pot underneath.

We were in my garden. That were alive with my bees and so hot the birds had gone quiet. We were sitting on the back step – her legs sticking out, brown as nuts they were, but *her face had a sick look about it like she weren't getting no nourishment.*

'You'll always be able to come here,' I say.

But my words didn't seem to make much impression on her. She barely nodded, as if she didn't believe what I was saying and I wondered what was going on with that husband of hers to make her so sad. And it reminded me of Louisa after the babbies died, and again when Rose was born. Like some sickness had got into her and was poisoning all that was good and true. I should have seen it coming, the way she was then.

37

Snowdrift
27th December

It was dark and Malorie didn't know where she was. Blearily, she hauled herself up onto her elbows. She was in the living room. There was the tree she'd cut down, there was the fireplace, the mirror above it. She couldn't remember why she was there. A cold draught was coming from the door. Her head ached and her mouth was dry.

An icicle of light jutted out into the hallway. The front door was open a crack and through it, she glimpsed white outside. There was a sprinkling of snow on the hallway wood floor. She had thick socks on and her dressing gown but the cold from the door was icy and penetrating.

Like a sleepwalker, she moved towards the open door. Outside, snow was falling in thick flakes. It was already in high drifts, stacked against the boundary hedges, heavy on the branches. It was so unreal. She stood, bewitched by its cold magnificence, until she noticed a sudden movement from the darkness in the opposite trees. A swaying, a fall of snow brushed off the tree. Staring at the white garden, she remembered the dull shock of the papers, the sense of disorientation. As she stood there, she wasn't at all sure whose body she inhabited. Was she Mary Skinner? Malorie Cavendish? Or someone else?

She went up to the bedroom. No sound came from behind Franny's door so she went back down to the kitchen to make a pot of tea and cut the leftover bread for toast. They were soothing, these automatic, small movements. She twiddled with the knobs on the radio and eventually managed to find a local station. The words drifted through the familiar dense wave of white noise.

. . . railway line between Sheringham and Holt is closed due to the overnight snowfall but British Rail assure us that it will be up and running soon . . . Snow drifts up to three feet high on parts of the coast . . . the Wensum in Norwich is iced over . . .

It went on like this, in and out of range, giving up little snippets of the icy conditions around the county. Malorie tried to imagine skating on the river. It sounded magical, like something from Narnia. They'd gone boating on the Wensum once, taken a pleasure boat from Pull's Ferry to Thorpe St Andrew, she aged about ten and her parents (her *adoptive* parents) already old in her eyes. It was not like the trip on the Broads on the *Dancing Light* that Rosemary had written about, she'd been a child with her parents, but in some ways, it was not so very different. There was something about being on the water that took you out of time. The boat had been called – she strained to remember – it hadn't been given a name. Her father fussed about the stern, while her mother sat clutching her handbag and refused to look over the side at the flowing river, or look up at the birds in the branches of the trees they passed. Malorie had loved it, but it had only been that one time. She asked herself again with a flare of resentment, why had they chosen her? Had she been a terrible disappointment to them? In the pub at Thorpe, they'd sat on the grass with bottles of pop. Her father had a beer and did tricks with his hands to make her laugh. It had been wonderful, time away from themselves. The fizzing of the pop up her nose, the hum of other people, glittering water just a few feet away. But swans had come up from the river and her mother had shouted at her to get away from them, so they'd gone back up to the pub tables. It was always that way. There had always been something that irritated her mother. Something that *she'd* done.

The lights in the kitchen kept flickering and humming. It seemed incredible that they were still working given yesterday's blizzard. She'd run out of the milk she'd brought on Christmas Eve and even if the house received deliveries, which she doubted, they wouldn't have been able to get through. She reboiled the melted snow for water, drank the brackish tea black again and nibbled at the toast. She tried to see herself as a child, eating toast with her parents, a normal childhood, a typical breakfast scene. But she was always picking at something. Eat up, her mother would say. She was always trying to get her to eat. A rush of anger and pity ran through her – for her mother and for herself.

Something her mother used to say came to her. *You were such a slight baby. There was nothing to you.* She'd said it as an accusation, as if it was Malorie's fault. Now she thought of it, it made sense. Her parents were short, stocky people. Her slightness, her insubstantiality, must have seemed like an affront – a constant reminder that she wasn't theirs. And she didn't have the blonde hair and blue eyes that all the other girls seemed to have. She was a dark, dull mouse with pond-coloured eyes. The other girls plaited each other's hair. No one touched hers. It was only when she went to London that she'd had an awareness of herself as desirable.

She ought to move, to go and look at the car, see if there was any way out. There was no need for the two of them to be marooned out here for another day. Christmas was over. There was no point staying any longer. Her body felt heavy, as if the weight of her mood was dragging it down. A thought, slow but sure, like a slug, slipped into her brain. Her daughter.

Upstairs, it smelt strange. She turned right instead of left at the top of the stairs and went into her empty bedroom. As if it had been a dream, she saw herself opening the window to the night air and thrusting her head outside. The window was now closed, but through it she could hear the groaning of the trees in the wind. It was nothing but whiteness and white noise. Ice patterned the inside of the window and outside, wind picked up the snow and sent it in whirlpools and tornadoes as far as she could see. The room faced north, out to the sea. Something, down in the garden where the trees must be, was moving. Shivering, she wiped the window and – yes, she was sure now – someone *was* on the edge of the garden. It was like déjà vu – a memory flared of seeing someone like that in the night, a white figure. It was probably one of the dreams she'd been having while she'd been here. She was about to prise open the window when she heard a cough behind her, and she returned to the light of the day. Franny.

The funny smell came from her daughter's room. It smelt of sweat and liquorice. It made her gag and she put a hand to her mouth. Franny was lying on the bed, the covers half thrown off. The bed was small and high but in it she looked shrunken, younger. For a second Malorie was reminded of her daughter as a baby, a fragile form of skin and bones that had shocked her with its vulnerability. Where Franny's skin was visible – her lower arm, her neck and face – it was pale and blotchy pink in patches and covered all over in a sheen of grease.

'Franny, what's wrong, are you ill?'

The girl's eyes were rimmed with grey and large and sunken in her small head. She nodded and tried to speak. 'Really tired,' she said.

'Don't speak, don't move,' she said, and rushed back downstairs to fetch a glass of water and then back up to her bedroom for the pills. Had she forgotten to give her dose to her last night? She tipped the tiny pills out onto her palm and picked one up in her fingers. It was tempting to swallow one herself. One swallow. Gone.

She tried to lift Franny up but she was limp and heavy. She held the glass to her daughter's parched lips but Franny only took a tiny sip and jerked her head away as if a fly was sucking on her blood.

'Have a bit more, sweetheart, you need it.'

But Franny shook her head. 'Don't want it, Mummy.'

'No, darling. You have to take the pill. Open just a tiny bit. Come on now.' She slipped the little pill in between her lips and held the water glass to her mouth again. Franny swallowed then shuddered, coughing.

They were for her own good. It had been Tony's idea at first. Franny had always been a worrier – shy, withdrawn – and he wanted her to be more confident, less moody. He thought the Luminal would help. Malorie had gone along with it. And really, what was the difference between giving her those pills and the herbal remedies that people like Janey gave out? But in her heart she knew she hadn't been paying enough attention to her daughter. She'd been too wrapped up in her own pain.

'It's all right, darling. It'll be all right.' She held her palm to her daughter's head and it burned.

Franny convulsed and vomited over the bedspread – a vivid pink pool spread over the wooden floor and the sour, noxious smell of vomit overrode the stale odour of illness.

'Oh Franny,' she said. Franny had tears in her eyes. 'It's all right love, it's all right.' She stroked her daughter's damp cheek, fetched a bucket and a bowl of water and wiped her mouth and chin.

Above the bed, the sampler looked down on her. She felt that she knew the figures depicted in it as well as she knew herself. They were more real to her than anyone else. Staring at it, she noticed something she hadn't seen before. The tiny images in each of the four corners weren't patterns as she'd thought before, but pictures. A shell, a tuft of grass, a wave and, disturbingly, a skull. She had to get Franny out of this room. It was the room itself that was making her sick. She knew this didn't make any sense but lifted her gently out of the bed anyway. The boy had died here. She saw it suddenly, as clearly as if she'd been there: the baby dead in the bed and the dark-haired girl kneeling, rocking, keening. She shut the door on the pink room.

The girl's body was light in her arms as she carried her across the landing. There was so little of her. Malorie laid her down on the bed in her own room and stayed with her until she fell into a fevered sleep.

'Mummy's here,' she murmured, over and over again.

38

That morning, the day it happened, there were a last blaze of summer heat before the autumn came. I walked Smutch along the marshes and beach and it were so hot he sought out any shade he could. Slunk off to lie under the wreck of the old mussel flat run up on the dune. Normally he's out there pestering the oystercatchers and sanderlings. Not on that day though. We weren't out there long, the poor animal was too thirsty. I were at the cottage in the afternoon with the drapes shut to keep out the burning. I remember I had the back door open to the garden and it were buzzing with bees and jaspers and crickets. Smutch was slumped right out on the floor and he'd snap his jaws now and again at some fly teasing him. When I went out in the garden to snip the herbs for the pot, the sky was still blazing blue and nothing in it. The sun was high up, glaring down on us. The cuckoo clock someone gave me for helping cure an old boy's warts chimed and cuckooed two, three, four. It got hotter and hotter. I fell into a doze on the sofa and was woken by a banging on the door.

I rubbed my eyes, stretched and cranked up my old bones to open the door, but before I could, she came flying in. Door weren't locked, never is. It were my Rose, in a right old puckaterry. She were all red-faced and fly-blown, hair in a tangle, jabbering away at me, all duddering. She were talking so jumbled I couldn't make out what she were saying. I sat her down and gave her a glass of water and made her catch her breath. At last she started to make sense.

She said he was sick. Vomiting all over the drawing room and he's lying on the floor, not moving. She couldn't get him to move. Said something about the marsh fever.

She stared at me then with those glass-green cat eyes and for a second there I doubted what she was saying, so fixed and hard they were.

But she pleaded with me to come so I followed her across the lane to the house. I had a horrible doom feeling.

39

Poisons

Malorie peered out of the bedroom window but the blizzard wasn't abating. Tony would blame her for this. He already blamed her for all their misfortune. But they couldn't travel now, not with Franny feverish, even if she could get the car out of the snow, and she didn't believe she could. She could go to the village to get help. Ask the man. George Bayfield. She couldn't go the way she and Franny had gone the first day because of the snowdrift. It felt like many weeks ago although it was only – what? – a week? No, it was five days ago. Only five days. She'd hardly seen a soul since then. She stood staring at the window, rocking back and forth on her socked feet. All this pretence, this effort to be a proper family. She didn't know how to do it. She had failed at everything. She took out the white envelope with the pills. It was nestled in the white lace veil. Just one. She would take just one. She needed to calm the racing of her heart. It was easier to be numb, to take all the feeling away. She had tried to not need the pills but she wasn't strong enough. Could she take two? She put the envelope in her pocket for later.

She swallowed it down with water.

Nothing happened. She sat on the floor of the bedroom with her back against the door. Her mind was a blank. Good. It was better to be a blank than have that weird electric intensity coursing through her.

A moaning sound came from the bed. She sat up straight. At first she thought there were two figures in the room. Someone else sitting on the end of the bed. A white dress. She fell against the doorframe, and looked again. It was just the old dressing gown in a pile. The window banged against its frame but Franny didn't wake. She had no idea how much time had passed. She had a vague recollection of eating breakfast and then confusion. A blank.

The wind outside seemed to rise up. Snow battered against the window. Shadows from the low lamplight in the room waved and then the light went out completely. Malorie cowered in the corner of the room. It's the wind, it's the wind, she said in her head.

She tried to switch on the lamp but it didn't work. Downstairs, she tried the hallway lights, the kitchen. Nothing. The power was off.

Snow was still falling and it was hard to tell, but what light there'd been outside seemed to be fading away. Her watch said nearly two o'clock but it seemed incredible, as if time itself was being twisted by the house. How could it be so dark this early? How had the time disappeared? There was no sound outside except the pattering of the snow against the window and the agonising creaking of trees being battered by the blizzard.

Malorie pulled her scarf tighter around her neck. She was alone again, no Tony, no Franny, no dog. What had happened to the dog? She struggled to remember. Light was fading and she thought *I must get out there now* – before it goes completely.

The draught from under the front door sliced across the room and she shrank from it. She was supposed to do something, but what it was she couldn't remember. Above her, she heard the faint scraping of the rats as they moved around. She shuddered. She felt her eyes move up to the ceiling, her body pulled towards the book. The third notebook. In all the confusion of the snowdrift and the papers and now Franny being ill she hadn't finished it. It seemed imperative that she do this.

After fetching the book from her case, she returned to the warmth of the living room. The tree sat in the corner, dark again, the candles unlit. She lit a candle and stuck it to a plate and it made dark, dancing shadows on the ceiling. She poured herself a glass of brandy and made up the fire. Matchstick on matchstick, struck with trembling fingers, flamed then went out, until finally, one of them caught and the fire came to life. The gramophone and the records were there but she didn't put one on, there was enough noise in her own brain, a whirring that would not rest. The slow heat of the fire spread across her upper body and the brandy burned inside. She was shattered, but her heart was racing. The drugs weren't working. In her hands she had the third notebook. The firelight flickered and cast a stuttering light over Rosemary's handwriting. It was like looking at an old friend. There was comfort here, in these pages, someone to listen to, someone to talk to her, someone whose life was infinitely worse than her own, someone who made her feel less alone. She looked at the words greedily. She wanted to suck them up and swallow them, like food. And she thought, if her father had wanted her to have the photograph of the Marsh House, perhaps it had something to do with *her*, rather than him. There was nothing in the notebooks that would suggest that. But it didn't matter anymore. She just wanted Rosemary to keep talking to her.

There were a few pages of writing about the rest of the summer of 1934 when Rosemary wandered the marsh, collecting things, including a strange, elongated skull of an unknown animal with its teeth intact, and taking them back to her childhood room. The ink was darker and spots flew across the page when she wrote about Franklin's visits, as if the pen had been pressed hard on the paper.

But then after a few lines of this, the handwriting changed and became scrawled and sloping and almost indecipherable.

THE THIRD NOTEBOOK

continued

40

After Richie's death I hardly went to Old Hall. Franklin was rarely there – he was often away travelling on behalf of his father at rallies and meetings around the country. Whenever he wrote, he was quite sure there was a great support building in the country, the Daily Mail was right behind them and victory in next year's election was assured. I asked to go home and the Laffertys and my father agreed that it was for the best, at least for a time. The high-ceilinged, bright rooms of Old Hall reminded me of Richie's babyhood and the winter I'd begun to love him. There was no comfort there. The Laffertys were not the sort of people to discuss what had been lost and he wasn't spoken of. Now Richie was gone, there was little to bind me to that place – the marriage so hastily arranged seemed to have been dropped as quickly as it had begun.

There was little comfort at the Marsh House either, but its gloomy rooms and lopsided, low walls suited me. It was my fault he'd died – I hadn't loved him enough. I wanted to punish everyone and everything that wasn't my baby; this darkness, this damp dreariness was all I deserved. I walked every day out onto the marsh at low tide, and trudged on and on until I reached the sea. I hardly saw a soul but Janey. Father was busy with his work and didn't notice the time I spent away from the house. The only person who offered any solace to me was Janey. She was the only one who'd known my mother, who knew me. I wrote a dozen letters to Louisa, my mother, never sent. I burned all of them, unable to find the right words to speak to her. I could barely forgive myself, let alone her.

I look at the person I was then and I want to shake her, to shout in her ear that she is letting life go by, wallowing in the pit rather than crawling out of it. There was still time then, to have found her, to have made it better. But I didn't know how little time I had left.

The seasons turned and although I didn't think I would, I began to notice the changes. Spring came and the black terns flew over on their way to breed. The marsh evolved from brown to green. I was hardly thinking, or feeling, just being part of the earth. I began to collect remnants of the dead: the perfect white, delicate skull of a bird I found stripped clean; a broken bone that reminded me of Richie's ear; the scaly skin of a dead eel; the skeleton of one of the rats caught by Rogers' traps; a black mermaid's purse with the translucent foetus of a baby skate still visible within it. In time, my bedroom, the room where I'd been a girl and where my son died, became a kind of mausoleum of the marsh. I gathered up the fragments around me. Day after day I walked, my only companion the curlews overhead and the changing sky. The landscape was as flat, as low, as bleak as I was, but it was mine. My mud, my coarse grass, my murky water. In the summer, the sea lavender turned my marsh purple and I felt the sun on my back. My fingers had withered and the rings fell off but the locket was always around my neck, a constant reminder of my short-lived son.

If they could have left me like that, none of this would have happened. But it couldn't last.

It was a warm airless day in late May. I'd walked all along the tidal creek to the beach as I did every day. I was bent over, knees in the sand, stroking a smooth stone when I felt the shadow of something behind me. There was a clutching at my waist and I screamed, buckled and collapsed forward onto the sand. My teeth crunched, I choked. I sat up, spat sand out of my mouth. The spring noon sun was high in the sky behind my assailant, creating a burning halo of light.

After an initial second of terror, I knew it was Franklin. There was no one else in the world who would dare to touch me like that. No one else who – and for this I was grateful – who wasn't hushed and awkward towards me, after Richie.

'I've missed my sweet girl,' he said, crouching beside me.

'I'm not sweet,' I said.

He laughed. 'No, but you are mine.'

I didn't answer. I put the stone into my pocket.

Franklin held out a handful of brightly wrapped sweets. 'Bonbons,' he said, 'from Paris.'

I shook my head, although my mouth was salivating.

He laughed again. 'Don't be silly,' he said. 'I bought them for you.'

I always had a sweet tooth. I took a bonbon from his hand and unwrapped the shiny paper. They were little balls coated in a white powder. When I bit into one it was sugary-sweet and hard like caramel toffee and the white powder tasted of lemon sherbet. It fizzed on my lips. I was taken back to long ago when I was a young girl and my kind governess, Miss Cannadine, would bring me sweets on a Friday and I would devour them all, each one more delicious for being completely contraband. 'You mustn't ever tell your father,' she would say, smiling at me indulgently. And I never did. It's funny but the only other person who ever bought me sweets was Franklin. He was clever like that.

We ate his bonbons and he told me of Paris, Rome and Berlin. It sounded so foreign, so exotic – it had nothing to do with me and my dead boy. But he took my plait in his hand and stroked it as if I were a pet and I fell into a sugar dream, lulled by the soft crash of the waves, the hot sand under my feet and the rhythmic touch of Franklin's strokes.

He kissed me on the top of my head and murmured 'Rosie,' into my hair, and where his lips touched my hair stood on end, electrified at the roots. Eventually, he pulled me up and we walked, me still half in slumber, along the beach. The sand was wet and hard-rippled from the outgoing tide and there was nothing all around us apart from the mudflats and creeks to the left and behind, and the sand stretching out ahead of us until it faded into the glittering sea. As Cabbage Creek came into view, dissecting the beach, a dark shape appeared beyond it on the sand. Coming closer, I could see it was a grey seal. Close up, you could smell the sweetness of rot. I thought of the sperm whale I'd seen once when I was a child, a huge grey beast beached at Titchwell that we'd all gone to gawp at. I'd touched the side of the poor half-dead animal before Fairbrother had shouted at me to come away. But I remembered its skin was cut with lines like an etching and I'd looked into its eye, the size of my own head, and seen the distress there. Some of the other children were mucking about throwing sand at it but their mothers shooed them away. The men tried to keep the beast wet before the tide came in to take it away again. It died before the tide came and rotted out on the beach for weeks and weeks. The bones of that whale are still there now, like a great shipwreck.

I thought of the tiny toad's bones floating away under the Rose Moon.

I thought of Richie's small bones buried under the earth in the graveyard.

Franklin pulled me away from the dead seal and we retraced our steps along the beach to the creeks of Stiffkey and the Marsh House. He had to go back to London soon, he said. There was an important rally in Olympia. At the gate to the house he took hold of my shoulders and said, 'It's all over now.' I didn't know what he meant. Did he mean he and I? I had a moment of terror that he was releasing me. 'You mustn't be morbid anymore and hole yourself up here with only an old witch for company. Come back to the Hall with me.'

He meant Richie. My allotted mourning time was over and he intended to keep me.

'It's not over for me,' I said.

'There's no point moping about it,' he said, his beautiful pink mouth twisted in distaste, and I had never felt so far from him then. How could he not feel the pain I felt?

'How can you be so cruel?' I said.

'It's not cruel to say you're doing yourself no good wallowing like this,' he said. 'And it's no good for me, either.' His face softened. 'I miss you. I miss my sweet Rose.' He stroked my hair. He held my hand in his, rubbing the skin on my fingers. 'Where are the rings?'

'They were too big, they fell off.'

I had an unexpected, wild idea. 'Can I come to London with you? And to Paris and Rome and Vienna and all those other places?'

He looked amazed. 'You wouldn't like that to-ing and fro-ing, Rosie. You're too good for the city.'

'How am I too good?'

'You wouldn't understand,' he said, and touched his fingers lightly along my temple and jawline, making me shiver.

So that was it then. He wanted me as a country plaything and no more. I went back to Old Hall when he was there at weekends and returned to the marsh when he went back to London. The rings were resized and I had to wear them again. I noticed Franklin didn't wear his but apparently the Lafferty men didn't wear them. I submitted to him, and sometimes, when he was gentle with me, as he mostly was, I was reminded of the kisses he gave me years before when I was fifteen, before I was married and had borne and lost a child, and all of that had taken away the simple delight I'd once felt in him. There were times when I wanted him again; I allowed his touches to block my mind, I even craved them. But each time he went away, I returned to my marsh.

I found out soon after he came back to me that the rally in Olympia was a disaster. There had been protests, the Blackshirts had acted like thugs and the entire thing had descended into violence. In The Times, a witness described what he'd seen: 'Five or six Fascists carried out an interrupter by arms and legs, several other Blackshirts were engaged in hitting and kicking his lifeless body.' I haven't forgotten this. It stuck in my mind. 'It's just a nasty element,' said my father when I asked him about it. And Franklin used Mosley's words to me in a letter. 'We never start fights, we only finish them.' But all I could think of was my husband in his black uniform and shining black jackboots and how pleased with himself he'd been, and what kept repeating in my head was a picture of one of those smart, black boots smashing into someone's skull. It was not him, I told myself.

Later that month, I read in Father's newspaper of Germany's purge. 'Herr Adolf Hitler, the German Chancellor, has saved his country', the paper reported, but I read that over a hundred political opponents had been killed. All the papers seemed to think this was a necessary 'clean-up', but how is killing people cleaning up? The Führer himself called it 'The Night of the Long Knives', which did nothing to quell my growing unease.

I waited until the dead seal's flesh had completely rotted and went back to collect its skull. I washed off the sand in the kitchen sink and placed it on my windowsill. Every night when I was at the Marsh House, I'd look at its gaping eye sockets and ask it what to do. How I could find a way to recover my love for Franklin.

41

That summer there were boat trips on the Broads and beach visits, but when he came to see me in the country, we were not the same. I knew there were other women in the city, though how many, I didn't know. He continued to be preoccupied with the party, which he said was tearing itself apart about 'the Jew problem'. He'd complain sometimes about the thugs, certain elements of the Blackshirts, as Father did, but when I said wasn't he part of all that? he would fob me off as if I was being stupid, tell me I wouldn't understand. He treated me like a child, but I wasn't a child anymore.

Hildy was mostly absent as well. I think she was wary of my grief, and perhaps she was bored of it too. I wasn't the pet they used to play with.

Something else was different in me too. I was nauseous in the morning and my breasts were tender. I knew I must be pregnant again. I should have been glad – it was what everyone wanted. Surely it was what I wanted too. A boy to love, a child to dote on. But this sickness felt like a sickness throughout my entire body – rejecting the very idea of a baby. I couldn't see how I could do it. How could I give birth to a child after what had happened to Richie? How could I love another child? My belly, which had been his so recently, still belonged to him. And – unarticulated then but I think now – I was afraid that a baby would upset the precarious balance of my relationship with Franklin.

There were no outward signs, no protruding belly. If I acted quickly, no one would ever know.

'I can't have it,' I told Janey. 'It'll destroy me.'

'Don't be all dramatic,' she said, 'normal as anything, having babbies. Women do it all the time.'

'My mother couldn't do it,' I said.

She frowned, making all the lines on her face scrunch up. 'That weren't her fault.'

'What if I'm the same? What if I'm not meant to have babies?'

'Don't do nothing stupid now,' she said.

'Then help me,' I said.

Down even lower than the cottage and closer to the marsh, Janey had a small garden that she called her 'medicine cabinet'. It had lavender, thyme, costmary, arnica and lemon balm, rue, valerian, cowslip and yarrow. And many more but I can't remember all their names. Certainly in the summer, as it was then, the air was full of the competing scents of these herbs and plants. Under the twittering cacophony of the birds, the pinks and purples of the echinacea, foxgloves and the dusky nodding heads of the poppies stuck out above the greener, prettier plants. There were even the shining dark leaves of a mandrake bush which Janey dug up once a year to use for invigorating potions. We were here for none of those though; we'd come for the pennyroyal.

Janey picked some of the small, bright green pennyroyal leaves and crushed them between her fingers and the most wonderful peppermint fragrance was released. We gathered up handfuls of the puffy lilac flowers and returned to the kitchen for Janey to make the tea.

I'd taken many of these herbs before, like my cold remedy/love potion, and wasn't worried. It tasted fine too, just like peppermint. She said that to have any effect I'd have to drink a few cups of it and by the end of the third cup I was sick of it and my stomach had begun to gurgle.

'You take care of yerself, my girl,' she said, with her hand warm on my head, when I said I better go home or Father would be wondering about me. 'Come back straightaway if you're taken bad. Now all it should do is bring on the bleeding, but if there's too much of it, or anything else rum, you come straight back, you hear?'

I promised I would but I was feeling nauseous by then and just wanted to lie down. At the Marsh House, I told Father I was unwell and went directly to bed.

I plumped up the cushions and bolsters and tried to read one of my precious novels, but the print was too small and began to move across the page like a procession of drunk ants. The pain in my stomach came in waves, and when the wave crashed I was pinned back in the bed, unable to see or breathe. I told myself I didn't mind;

I wanted the tea to do its work. Let the blood come. Let the blood gush out of me, taking the poor creature with it. But the worse the pain ground into me, the more I was afraid. What if it didn't work? Or if it did and took me with it?

Once I felt a warm rushing between my legs and thought it must be coming. Helter-skelter I ran to the water closet along the hall. Through the little high window, I could see the pale blue of the sky but it felt like nothing to do with me. My stomach contracted. I bent over, clutching my belly. Nothing else. Nothing came flowing out of me. I had a strong urge to lie down again.

'What's ailing you?' said Fairbrother, with no hint of sympathy, as I hurried past her on the landing, but I just shook my head at her and rushed back to bed.

In the small mirror on my dressing table, I caught sight of myself. It was as if someone had drained all the life out of me. My pupils were so tiny in my irises, I looked like a staring ghoul. Crawling back into the bed, the pains in my abdomen increased in severity and frequency and I curled into them. I began to feel as if I was being punished. My face and neck were clammy, but my hands were cold and I couldn't get warm. I must have groaned, because there was a knock at the door. Someone was there, then they went away. I lost time and consciousness. At one point, I thought Janey's big black dog, Old Smutch, was licking my face. I cried out and buried myself in his fur.

The pain was even worse than labour – I felt as if someone had dug a knife inside me and they kept twisting and twisting. I thought I would die of it. It was a cruel reminder of what I had gone through to give birth to my lost boy. Each time it eased, I felt the sweat roll down my face and I was aware of light and movement, but when the pain came again it was worse for the relief. I forgot what was supposed to be happening and I forgot who I was.

They must have called the doctor because someone or something was pressed into me and I screamed so loudly, Janey told me later that she heard it in her cottage and she thought my time had come. She knocked hard on the door until her knuckles were bruised, but Father hissed at her to 'Take your black magic away from my door, you've caused enough trouble already.' I don't think he was referring to the tea I'd drunk but something to do with Mother.

'He always had me wrong,' said Janey when she told me later, very quietly as she never liked to draw attention to what she did, but I knew she was frustrated by the way people like my father misunderstood her. All my life, people had been visiting her damp little cottage for remedies, or future-telling, or to ward against some terrible misfortune. Few people thought of her as a witch, but my father did. He barred the door to her, so she was forced to return to the cottage.

'I watched out for you, child,' she told me, and perhaps she did because sometime on the day following, I woke from a dream in which Smutch was carrying me on his back and my uncontrollable shaking had stopped. The pain had eased to a normal stomach-ache and I drank some hot water. It was Dolly who gave it to me, Fairbrother having given up nursing duties. 'She said you were cursed,' Dolly said.

I thought that Fairbrother, for once, was right. I'd been wrenched back from the edge of death but the bed wasn't drenched in blood; no menstruation had been brought on. Not even a drop. It was still possible that the tea had killed the growing form, but I didn't believe it. It was stronger than I was, this thing inside me.

It is hard to recall now, the curdled emotions of that time. I worry that what I've told you is shocking, but I can only tell you how alone I was. I could not conceive at that point, in my dazed state, that anything good could come of it.

Within a week I was up again and in Janey's all-in-one room with my head in my hands. Father had issued orders that I wasn't allowed out, but I woke early one morning with the dawn chorus. I thought if I slipped out then, before anyone else was up, I could see her.

'You didn't give me enough,' I said. But I couldn't really blame her, I knew the herbs were notoriously tricksy and imprecise.

'And let you leave us? You nearly did as it was,' she said, stroking my hair.

I didn't try to persuade her to help me again. I think I knew that what was growing would cling on no matter what I did. And I couldn't stop it now; I wasn't even sure I wanted to. I'm glad now, that it didn't work. It's important you know this.

42

Some time in late July, on one of his visits, he took me out in his new motor car. He wanted to show it off, to parade it to gawping villagers. It was a Silver Eagle, in what he called 'racing green'. He was in summer whites that day, rather than black, and wore a white cap like the one he'd worn on the boat trip two years before. Despite all that had happened between us, the sight of him still gave me prickles of heat.

I hadn't seen him for a while. I think Father had conspired to spin some tale of illness. They must have told the colonel, Lady Lafferty and Franklin and any other nosey parkers that I was contagious. In my darkest moments, I think that the sad thing is that if I had died from the pennyroyal tea, it would have been a relief to them all.

But when he drove up to the house and honked the horn, sending Perdie into spasms of barking, I looked down from Father's room and saw him with his arm slung over the car door, his pristine white suit shining in the sun. He'd taken off his driving gloves and the sunlight glowed on his tanned wrists and hands. It bounced off the white linen and the shiny polish of the car and shone back up to me in the dark house, a beacon of beauty. A chink of light in the darkness.

So I called down that I was coming, dressed in one of Hildy's old dresses with a fashionable low waist which hid the fact that my waist had expanded, and emerged onto the sunlit driveway.

'I'm taking you out,' he said. 'Mother said you could do with a jaunt.' His mother had suggested it then. But he smiled at me and squeezed my knee. 'You do look a bit unwell.'

'I'm fine,' I said.

We drove along the coast road towards Cromer, the same route we'd taken years before on that first day out. I didn't feel as if I was the same girl who'd been in the back seat with Franklin then, the girl who was thrilled by the touch of his hand on my bare leg. It was almost the same scene – the yellow of the wheat in the fields, the blue-grey sea, glimpsed in snatches of brilliance, the red dots of poppies – but he was driving now and I – I was changed.

We stopped for a picnic of wine and crackers in a field just after Cromer. I could only take a mouthful of the wine. It tasted sour and thick, like drinking blood, and it made me nauseous. The sun beat remorselessly on us and I wished I could lie down and sleep. And although he was still beautiful, when he laid me down in the wheat, and pulled my skirts up, I had to stop myself from crying. The crushed, spiked heads of the plant scratched at my underside, and the ground was dry and hard beneath me.

There was the smell of the hot earth and the sharpness of his cologne. I turned my head away from his silhouetted form in the tall spikes above me and the violent red of the poppies, and concentrated on watching a beetle crawl slowly over the cracked soil. I closed my eyes, the light struck my eyelids and all I could see was a vivid orange, like the colour of a blazing sun bleeding into the sea.

43

I haven't got much time left to write this so I'll tell you what you really want to know. You'll be able to judge for yourself whether or not I am guilty of the crimes they say I am. I feel I owe you an explanation. Not so you can forgive me, that's too much to hope for.

There was a day, late in the summer. We were eating strawberries and drinking lemonade in the garden of Old Hall. Franklin made me open my mouth and put a strawberry in between my lips. I felt like a stuck pig with an apple in its mouth. Ready to be eaten. He reached forward and touched my ankle, making circling motions on the bone. It tickled and I shivered.

The summer was almost over and you could feel the change in the air. The wind was cooler from the east and the colours were turning on the marsh – the purple fading to a pale blue violet. My body continued to alter as well. Under my dress, the faintest hint of a protrusion. At first I did nothing. I carried on as before, collecting my bones from the marsh, until at the end of August, Franklin summoned me to Old Hall.

'You're looking healthier, Rosie. Almost back to how you used to be. The little girl I corrupted.'

I looked across the long lawn down to the river Stiffkey, the pasture on the other side, and the trees on the slight rise above it. I saw the glade where the summer house was hidden and remembered how he'd forced me a long time ago, before we were married. And I knew he would carry on doing this, again and again, while I grew fat with children who would die or thrive. It didn't matter – either way, there would be nothing else for me. I wasn't expected to do anything apart from breed for him, for them. He would go to London, to Paris, to Egypt, it didn't matter where, and keep his mistresses and his prostitutes. Even Hildy would go to London for the season and marry someone interesting – or even not marry – and she would travel too. But not me. I would stay here with my swollen legs and my ruined womb and no love for me from anyone except Janey. All I'd wanted, I see now, was someone to love me as I imagined my mother had. But no one had.

I pulled my shawl around my shoulders, but there was no breeze that day. The trees were still.

'You'll stay here tonight,' he said. 'And the day after tomorrow, your father and I have business in Cromer.'

'What kind of business?' I asked, but he gave me a sharp look.

'I'm not sure that concerns you, my strawberry pudding.'

I frowned at him. 'I'm not a little girl,' I said.

'Oh, I beg to differ,' he said. 'That's exactly what you are and how I want you to be. And if you ever become anything else I won't like it at all.'

'Are the girls in London young?' I said, some worm of boldness wriggling in me. 'The ones you have?'

He pinched my thigh, quite hard, leaving a pink mark. 'Some of them,' he said, biting the head off a strawberry. 'None as sweet as you.' He spat out the green top of the fruit into the silver dish on the table. 'Some of them are rather grand, you know. Real ladies. Bored of their dull old husbands. And some of them are as common as anything.' He winked at me. 'Does it bother you?'

Stupid tears sprung to my eyes. 'But I thought you loved me. I thought I was special.'

'You are special. There's no one in the world like you, Rosie.'

'You ruined me,' I said quietly.

He laughed. 'That's rather melodramatic. And anyway, I do love you in my own way, if that's what you want to hear. It's just . . .' He opened his arms out and gave me a helpless smile. 'I can't help it. Come on,' he said, tired of the conversation, 'you can't mind that much. It's normal for men. Even your father needs . . . distractions.'

'Why did you marry me, Franklin?' I said.

He stared at me for a bit, his lip twitching as if he felt like striking me. 'You know why, don't torture yourself.'

'Because of our baby?'

'Yes, that. And because I'd been naughty in London and Mummy wanted me out of harm's way.'

'What did you do?' But I didn't want to know the details. I got up so quickly that I spilt lemonade down my dress but I didn't stop. I ran down the lawn to the river. It was warm and still, hardly a breeze rustling in the trees, and the river trickled invitingly, dots of light dancing along it. I took off my stockings, held up my dress and got in. The water was pleasantly cool on my feet and ankles. I remembered what Hildy had said about some incident in London and it made sense.

A shadow behind me and Franklin's voice. 'They warned me you were like your mother. Mad as a hatter.' I stayed looking down at the water running over my feet, green and soothing. I heard him laughing and then a splash. 'But that's why I like you, you're my wild girl,' he said, and I turned around. He was in the river. Completely naked. It was impossible not to gasp, for my hand not to fly to my mouth. He opened his eyes wide and cocked his head to one side, as if daring me to be shocked. I took my hand away from my mouth and tried to stare at him coolly, but my eyes were pricking with tears. His body was golden from the summer sun, from beaches on the Côte d'Azur and sun loungers in hotels. The dappled river light fell over it, creating a filigree of green and dark leaves. He came towards me and drew me to his naked body.

'What would your mother—'

'My mother gave you to me. I can do anything I like, remember,' he said, and planted his lips on mine.

I could feel him pressing against me, his bare flesh through the thin material of my summer dress. We were shielded from the eyes of the Hall down there in the river and Franklin knew it. He pulled up my dress and half-lifting, half-shoving me, he put me up against the muddy bank of the river and pressed down on my hips again and again until it was done. I gritted my teeth and thought about the roots of the trees I was up against, imagined the roots growing up into me and through me, sprouting out through my ears and nose and mouth. At the end, when his body shuddered against mine, I looked up to see his neck arched back like a swan's and his face glowing, lit up by sunlight, his expression one of exquisite torture.

'I've muddied your dress,' he said after, pulling his clothes back on. 'You look like a kitchen maid who's been dallying with a gardener's boy. I rather like it.' He ruffled my hair. 'Don't be a misery, Rosie. For God's sake. You used to be fun.' I began to cry then and his face darkened. 'Not that,' he said. He stalked off to the house and I was left to follow behind.

That night he was rough with me and pinched me again. He whispered into my ear that I was his. I owed him this. I belonged to him. The more I turned away, the harder he pinched and thrust.

In the morning there was a pattern of purpling bruises blooming on my skin.

I didn't breakfast with the rest of the family that morning. Instead, I got up early, leaving Franklin sprawled across the bed. The sun was already warming the grass, and I ran back along the vale to Hollow Lane and to the Marsh House, a confusion boiling in me so explosive, I thought I would vomit a lava flow of rage.

'I can do anything I like,' he'd said, and I thought *But I can do nothing I want. Nothing at all.*

In my room, I tried to read but I could hardly concentrate. It was a hot, still, silent day, too hot for the birds. Perdie lay whimpering, afraid of my mood, at the foot of the bed. I tried to close my eyes, I tried to drift away somewhere else. I would feel calmer if I slept. But I couldn't stop my limbs from twitching, my mind from flailing around for something, anything to do. I hurled myself off the bed, flung open the window to stagnant, warm air. Perdie barked, expecting a walk. How could he hurt me like that? How could he do it knowing I'd given birth to and buried our son? How could he sleep with other girls, other women, when I could do nothing? The unfairness of it was a bitter taste in my mouth.

I wanted to hurt him back, but I was powerless.

Down below my window, the great black form of Smutch moved slowly in the shade of Janey's garden.

Janey. The poison. An idea was forming. It did not have to be drastic, but I could damage him, as he'd damaged me. Make him ill, give him pain as he had given me pain. My breath came faster and my pulse quickened.

I'd already got the arsenic from Janey before he'd come back – I lied to her about Rogers needing it for the rats – but until then I hadn't considered anything other than taking it for the pregnancy. I don't even know if I was really going to use it for that. It was under the sink in the kitchen, forgotten about.

I could just put a drop in the sugar. It would be easy, I had read about it in the Agatha Christie books. No one would ever know. Only I would know. I would know I held something over him, some power over him. I gripped the windowsill as the sun blazed down on my face. It could be done. Yes, sugar in his coffee. The tiniest drop, just to make him suffer. Perhaps he would be sorry, then. He thought of me as a child, but I was not a child. Not anymore.

So on that day, the morning after the river, when I saw the bruises on my legs, and the red marks of his fingers on my upper arms where he'd held me down, I remembered the poison and it seemed as if it was waiting for me.

44

The following morning, the day of the journey to Cromer, I brewed a pot of coffee for the travellers. I put out a cup for myself as well. Normally, Dolly or Fairbrother would have done it but Dolly was busy with laundry and Fairbrother was away visiting a sister in Sheringham. So no one bothered about me making coffee and Dolly was grateful if anything. I brought the tray into the living room myself. The morning light was coming in through the windows and the whole room was alight. The two of them were smoking and talking in the pair of leather chairs either side of the fireplace. I placed the tray on the coffee table in front of them and knelt down to stir the pot. The spoon clattered loudly against the edge and I hoped they didn't notice that my hands were shaking.

'Thank you, Rosie. What a lovely wife I have, don't I, sir?'

'When she behaves herself,' said my father.

I poured the coffee, concentrating hard to make sure I didn't spill any, and they resumed their conversation about their plans for the day. Franklin was going to drive the Silver Eagle to Cromer and they'd have a meeting at the printers where they'd thrash out a copy of the new manifesto. (This was for the great Oswald.) Then they'd repair to the Newhaven Court Hotel for lunch.

Into Franklin's cup, I poured cream and stirred in a spoonful of sugar but it dissolved immediately. I added another. I put just the cream into my father's. I stirred and stirred until all the sugar must have dissolved. I sat back on the sofa opposite the fire, enjoying the sun on my face and drank the coffee I'd poured myself. No sugar. It was too hot and I scalded the roof of my mouth. I waited. They chatted on, not including me in any way. But this was preferable as I'm not sure how much I could have spoken. I could feel my heart banging against my ribs. Finally, I watched Franklin drink the coffee in two long gulps. I waited.

'No cakes this morning, Rosie? I'm disappointed.'

'I haven't had time,' I said.

'Surely you have something tasty for the road for us men of business?'

I watched his face for signs of distaste or sickness but there were none. He was brushing his trousers, a sign that he was about to get up, but just then my father made a face and said, 'This coffee is rather bitter, Rosemary. I'll have to have a spoonful of sugar.'

I sprang up. 'Let me,' I said, and gave him the tiniest amount into his cup. I sat back, my heart pounding.

Franklin was standing up now. 'Good God, do you really have nothing for us to eat, Rosie? I'm famished.'

'I'm fine, Franklin,' Father said, raising a hand. It had almost been a bark, which he'd softened right at the end.

I could see he was irritated by this young, flamboyant layabout, but he was bound to him as much as I was. It was the colonel's money that was funding the fascist propaganda and without it, my father's business would have floundered.

'All right then, I'll make some biscuits quickly, before you go.'

'That's my girl,' said Franklin, grinning at me. I'm sure he would have whacked me on the backside like a horse if my father hadn't been sitting right next to him.

In the kitchen, I hurriedly mixed sugar, flour and butter, egg and vanilla seeds and patted them into rounds and laid them on a greased tray for the oven. It took less than ten minutes. By the time they were standing by the car in their coats and driving caps, and Franklin in his leather driving gloves, I handed him a batch of still-warm biscuits wrapped in a cloth. He kissed me on the lips and waved from the car, as if he was the perfect gentleman, a loving husband.

For the rest of the day, I lived in my head. I walked down to the marsh with my dreams. I cannot remember what I thought about, if it was anything at all. I took a pork pie and a cheese sandwich wrapped in cloth and ate them out there on the dried-out marsh grass, in the full glare of the sun. I walked and walked, along the path that ran along the bottom of the marsh, away from the village, towards Wells, enjoying the solitude, revelling in it, and only came back because I realised the sun was now quite low in the sky. Dolly had left for the day and Perdie started up a high-pitched whine when we got back to the house but I gave her a bone and she was quiet.

It was worse, much worse than I'd expected. Now, I don't know what I'd expected. I didn't even know if it would have much effect on him at all. Since then, I've read about poisonings from last century and the terrible effects it has on the victims, but I didn't know all that then. It was, perhaps, something fantastical. One of my presents from Hildy two years ago had been Mrs Christie's The Thirteen Problems. In one of the stories, a man dies from arsenic poisoning. It's possible I got the idea from that. Then again, she uses lots of other poisons in her novels. In her first novel, The Mysterious Affair at Styles, it's strychnine. And in Peril at End House, it's cocaine in a box of chocolates. But I didn't have either of those. Arsenic was just what I had.

In acute poisoning, what arsenic does to a body is this:

It makes the victim experience 'extreme nausea, vomiting, abdominal pain, and profuse diarrhoea'. I'm quoting here, from the coroner's report. This is what happened to Franklin.

He arrived back at the house, brought there by a man who'd found him at the hotel. There was no sign of my father. Franklin was sickly pale and could hardly walk and was clutching his stomach, doubled over in pain. I knew it was the poison, that it had worked far too well. I held him, together with the man, and we took him into the house, and laid him down on the sofa. The man was desperate to leave – afraid, I think, of the appalling state of Franklin, and of catching it from him. I was seized by a sickening fear of what I'd done and a dizzying feeling that it could not really be happening.

For a moment, I looked down at my young husband, at his wretched, writhing body that had so recently been proudly displayed to me. A knot in my stomach twisted and I felt faint. He grasped hold of me in his sweaty hand. I knelt down and could smell the garlic on his breath. He was trying to say something to me. It might have been 'biscuits', but I put a hand to his hot forehead and extricated my other hand from his clutching grip and said, loudly –

'I've got to get help, darling.'

I trotted to Janey's. I didn't run. I wasn't thinking. I was in a daze, like a ghost.

'What happened to him?' she asked.

'I don't know,' I said, the words coming slowly, painfully, 'he came back from Cromer clutching his stomach and he could hardly stand. He collapsed in a hotel according to the man who brought him back. I don't know what would have happened if he hadn't—'

'Start from the beginning,' she said.

'I'm afraid, Janey,' I said, and I was. 'I'm afraid he's going to die.'

'He's probably got a bad stomach upset. You called the quacks yet?'

'No, I didn't think it was that bad. I'll try now.'

I ran to the telephone in the Marsh House but the line was busy. Janey appeared behind me in the hallway.

'Tell me the whole story now, Rosie,' she said to me. 'And where is he?'

I indicated the living room, but I didn't dare go in. 'He – he came here to see Father this morning before going on business to Cromer. He was going to Father's printers to see about getting some leaflets printed for the BUF and he had a cup of coffee then, but I don't know what he ate for breakfast or for lunch – he could have got anything at Cromer. I don't know! He could have had a bad crab or whelk, couldn't he?'

She nodded, walked past me into the living room. I stayed in the hallway. 'I suppose he could. Who brought him here then?'

'A man from the hotel. He said Frank had come in looking green and holding his stomach, then he'd tottered and fallen. The man brought him here as there's no one at the Hall.'

'So he can't have eaten or drunk anything at the hotel, can he? And you don't know about nothing else, do you?'

'No!' My voice high and loud. On the sofa, Franklin's breath had become rasping and the smell was so bad I knew it was coming out of him.

She took over then. I'd known she would.

'I'll see to him now, Rosie. You run to the village and call for the doctor from the public phone if yours ent working. Tell him to come quick.'

As I was running out, she asked me, 'Where's your father?'

Then I remembered my father hadn't come back with Franklin. It was odd – I'd seen him leave, but not seen him return. But I'd been on the marsh all day.

I heard Franklin moaning in the living room and a rank smell wafted through the door. I turned away, afraid, and opened my father's study door. He looked like he was sleeping. On his desk, surrounded by papers, his head was sunk. A thick, bitter odour of faeces filled the room. I gagged and covered my nose and mouth. There was no movement from my father's body. I didn't want to get any closer to the reek but I had to. I lifted the hair on his head and saw that his eyes were open, staring, unseeing, completely cold. I let the hair fall back down. Then I noticed that on the desk next to his hand were crumbs. They were biscuit crumbs, the biscuits I'd made and given to Franklin. My father must have taken them from the kitchen when he'd returned. He must have had lots of them. I must have mixed the tainted sugar into the biscuits.

All this was going through my head in a quick succession as I stood there in the quiet, dark study, the setting sun casting orange daggers across the wooden floor. Flies were buzzing around my father and I wondered how long he'd been like this. Then slowly, oozing out of me like pus, a realisation: I had to make a sound.

The bodies were taken away and the Laffertys were summoned and it was a nightmarish whirligig of a night. I couldn't cry. When they were gone – I'd said I wouldn't go back to Old Hall, I didn't have to anymore, I decided – I stayed at Janey's cottage. Much later, that night, she asked me straight out if I'd used the arsenic and I told her the truth.

I just wanted to make him ill. I hadn't intended to kill him at all. At that time, in the molten heat of grief and horror, I wanted to make him suffer so badly he wouldn't be the same person. I'm sorry.

45

So I were there when he died. I knew then it would lead to no good.

It were all quiet in the Marsh House. All hushed and dark out of the hot day. That miserable mawther, ol' Fairbrother must've been off cos there didn't seem to be anyone there at all. Smelt funny though. In the sitting room it were all bright from the sun setting and I couldn't see him at first cos it were in my eyes. But I heard a moaning from the sofa and I bent over to get a better look. It were the Lafferty boy all right and he were in a terrible state. Barely moving apart from now and then he'd go into a kind of spasm, like a fish what couldn't breathe. His pretty face was greenish-grey and he were all a muckwash, sweat rolling off him like an old cheese. I leaned over him and his breath were rank with puke and stank of suffin sweet and rotten.

I loosened the boy's collar and he looked up at me with his milky eyes and I knew he'd not got long. The doctor would never get here in time. The nearest quack was old Harrison *in Wells but no one from Stiffkey ever went to him. They all preferred Dr Lacey in Blakeney who was more lax in collecting his debts. Personally I never had much truck with either of them, but I knew she needed to do something with herself so I sent her off. Whatever she thought about the boy, I didn't think she ought to see him like that. He were snatching at the air by the time she went and it were awful to watch. They all thought I was a witch, but I weren't ever a bloody magician – I couldn't do nothing for him, he were too far gone. It were coming out both ends and all I could do was make it a little more comfortable. I got a pan to put under him and took off his soiled trousers, wiped the mess from his mouth and cooled his forehead. But then he went into a series of fits so severe, he gripped onto me with his young, hard fingers and I saw the fear in his eyes. Whatever he'd done – and I knew some of what he'd done – he didn't deserve that end.*

I heard the front door opening and I shouted at her to not come in, but to find her father. He had to be somewhere nearby. Then I heard her scream. It was a shocking thing to hear. I had the boy fitting and gasping for his last breaths in my arms, and I hear this blood-curdling scream.

I couldn't do nothing. The boy was dying. I called out, 'Rosie?' And all I hear is sobbing, a sort of choking-crying. Finally the boy shuddered out his last gasp and fell quiet. I laid him gently on the sofa and put a blanket over his body. I heard her blarring from across the hall and she were standing in her father's room.

46

On the marsh

The notebook went on for a few more pages, still in the same rushed scrawl until it came to an abrupt stop, followed only by a few short, scrappy lines at the end of the book. But Malorie couldn't finish. She felt sick, dizzy. The smell of Rosemary's father's dead body stung her nostrils and she could see the dead man's gaping mouth, hanging open, a black pit, like the frozen dog's. Her soul was sick. Sick to your soul. She understood what that meant. There was something rotten that had been hiding in front of her and here it was revealing itself. And it was inside her, it had infected her.

She dropped the notebook and fell back in her seat, drained. Her lip trembled and she realised she was about to cry. She let it come.

Against the window, the soft thuds of snow, and in the chimney the howl of the blizzard. It had started up again, stronger than before. Her candle was still lit and it shone a low light onto the ceiling. The cracks on the ceiling became the branches of a tree that grew and grew, twisting across the plaster. Her eyes followed them, crawling across the ceiling. She needed to sleep. With an intense relief, she remembered that she'd put the envelope with the pills in the pocket of her blouse. How many had she taken? What did it matter now? She washed a couple down with the last of the wine.

A scream woke her, jerking up into the darkness, staring. An orange glow. Eyes. No, there was no scream, no eyes. It must have been the wind or the screaming cockler calling for help. Dark outside. Light coming from the fire. Slowly, her vision adjusted and she saw that there was no light coming through the thin curtains. Her candle had been extinguished and was a low white stump deformed by globules of wax. The embers of the fire burnt dull orange in the grate. No heat came from it now and the room was as cold as if the snow had come inside.

On the worn red rug on the floor next to the sofa, the notebook lay where it'd been dropped. Arsenic poisoning and the agonising deaths of two men. It was unreal – a piece of fiction. The girl, Rosemary, was living out an Agatha Christie fantasy. The more she thought about it, the more she thought that must be the case. It couldn't be real. The 'account' was made up. None of it had happened. It was just the scribbling of a bored girl who'd been denied an education. She clutched at this idea and smiled uneasily in the dark, empty room. She was Malorie. She was real. The other girl was fiction.

Next to the notebook lay a white mass of lace. The veil. She lifted it to her head and stood up, curious to see what she would look like. In the mirror was the wan face of a girl with a snowy waterfall cascading behind her, cold as if snow was actually falling on her hair. Tentacles of ice on her skin. She dropped the veil.

In the notebook, Franklin had died right here where she'd lain, a horrible, ugly death, everything pouring out of him, dying in a pool of his own effluence. She shuddered.

There was no human presence here. It was how you feel when you are entirely alone. The rooms stretching out in their space. But there was *something* here, something else, a memory. A shadow memory of the people who used to live here. That was all it was.

'You're not real!' she shouted.

As if in response, the radio in the kitchen crackled into life and she heard a voice – *Vehicles have been abandoned on roads as the drifts are now up to fifteen feet in* –

I'll gladly surrender – a mournful voice. *My life* –

That sound wasn't coming from the radio, but the record player. The slow, sweet trumpet got louder and louder. She put her hands over her ears but could still hear it in her head. She ran back into the living room. The gramophone was blaring with the trumpet and the voice. How could it? She hadn't even wound it up. She grabbed the record clumsily off the turntable and it broke. Jagged pieces of black shellac fell to the floor.

In the hallway, she could hear the hiss of the out-of-tune radio and the cry of the blizzard in the trees.

She rushed up the stairs. In the bedroom, Franny was asleep, curled up in a foetal position that grasped at Malorie's heart. Across her daughter's face the blizzard created wildly moving shadow-fingers that seemed to be clawing at her. She put a hand on Franny's forehead. It was clammy and warm. The girl's breath was shallow, hot and moist against her palm. What if Franny was really ill? What if she had a dangerous fever? She had to get to the village to get help, fetch a doctor. She thought of the baby that had died here, in this house. The little boy with the blond curls. If anything happened to Franny – it was too awful to contemplate. Tony didn't trust her with their daughter. He would take her away from her if he could. In a burst of anger and fear, she picked up the envelope and swallowed another pill.

Down in the kitchen, the back door was open and hanging on its hinges, banging and letting in the chill air. Malorie stood staring at the snowy gap. Had it been open just now? She was sure she'd shut it. A door slammed behind her. She spun around. The front door must have been open as well. In the shadows of the twilight, the yellow flowers on the walls were the colour of nicotine; the tar-coloured vines twisted up the walls and towards the door as if they were reaching for the outside, and the light. In the dead time of the night, the house was telling her to leave. The ceiling was pressing down on her. She needed to get out. She had to get help for Franny. The walls were very close. Her head was pulsing. Out. She must get out.

Malorie snatched her fur coat from the banister, pulled on the boots she found by the back door and scrabbled around for the torch in the kitchen drawer.

Outside, snow spun. Ahead of her in the beam of torchlight, a great clump of snow dropped from a tree, spraying white, as if someone had brushed past it. She ran, stumbling in her silly, city boots. When she got to the gate, no one was there, but footprints led to the cottage across the lane where smoke rose from the chimney. There was no sign of any other footprints. She looked left and right. To her right was the snowdrift, the stuck car, the way to the village. To her left, only the marsh. At the end of the lane, where it met the marsh, there was a stumpy line of trees, warped and stunted by the salt and wind. There was a path at the end of the lane that led east. A memory surfaced. She'd gone that way before, when she went to the church. Now, as she peered along the torch beam towards the sea, a shadow moved in the trees. It might have been an animal. A flash of white. A bird? A fall of snow? She stumble-ran towards it.

Reaching the snow-laden trees, she heard a crackle in the icy undergrowth and at the same time, a crow swooped up, calling *cree-aa, cree-aa* into the swirling snow. Her eyes and the torch were drawn upward with its soot-black wings in a grey-black sky.

She stood now, unsure of which was north, south, east or west. There was no sound of the sea, no sound apart from the rush of the snow and the shriek of the wind across the marsh. At least she presumed it was the marsh because she couldn't see. The world was reduced to a whirl of whiteness circling her head.

She heard ice cracking in the creek then another crack from close by. A thin figure was standing in the woods. It was her again, the dark-haired girl. Malorie's throat clamped in fear. She would see her. She turned off the torch and the swirling white night closed in, as the bird screamed above her.

She turned to run but there was nothing beneath her feet and she fell, her arms flailing, unable to grab hold of anything, wheeling through the air. She tumbled down the bank into the creek, sprawling awkwardly, her leg twisting to the side. An urge to scream gurgled up in her throat. Her mind was closed.

Someone was calling. She tried to shut her ears, to listen only to the soft patting of snow on her face. An icy wetness seeped into her back. She didn't know why she was there. She'd been trying to do something. Something important.

Who was making the noise?

Someone was close by, breathing on her, hands under armpits, lifting her.

'Franny?'

It was the dark-haired girl, it was Rosemary. She tried to speak again but her throat was closed.

She had to see. The torch. Her fingers searched until she touched it, where it had fallen. She shone the torch back the way she'd come to the dark stacks of the chimneys of the house, poking above the hedge. But there was no girl. Frantically, she swung the torch around her, throwing a band of light into the darkness, but she could see no strange girl.

Franny. She had to get back. Her daughter was ill. She remembered now. Her daughter was ill.

She tried to stand but a shock of pain ran up through her right leg. She couldn't stand on it. Wincing, she put all her weight on her left leg, leant forwards to the muddy edge of the creek and with effort lifted herself forward and hauled herself onto the lane. She kept sliding and slipping down. The pain in her ankle was intense. She must have twisted it, falling. Halfway down the lane, she stood stock still in the dark, bent over, feeling her own laboured breath pushing against her ribcage. An owl hooted. The back of her head jabbed with pain. She looked around to where she'd been and there was something there, some mass of darkness moving towards her.

Hobbling, stumbling, panting, she slowly dragged her sore ankle along the lane. She felt the presence of the girl behind her. A shape appeared at the entrance to the house. A stout woman dressed in brown.

The woman moved towards her through the shadows. She didn't say anything but Malorie felt a force, like a strong wind, pull her to the house. Inch by inch the chimneys of the house got closer until finally she reached the drive. She stopped and got her breath, turned to look back, but it was completely black, no girl, no woman. She hurled herself to the porch and, lurching, fell across the threshold to the hallway, slamming the front door shut.

A doctor. She must get help. The phone. She picked up the black earpiece of the old candlestick phone and held it to her ear. She strained to hear the dialling tone.

'Hello?' she said, into the mouthpiece. '*Hello?*' There was nothing, no tone. The line was dead.

47

Breaking glass

A voice was coming from somewhere. It sounded familiar. It was someone she knew. Shakily, she stood up and saw a shadowy form in the old mirror on the living room wall. Limping towards it, she saw it was a young woman with dark hair, very straight, and small features and pale, olive skin. She knew her. The large eyes staring back at her were the eyes of the girl in the photograph. It was Rosemary. Herself.

Something came out of her mouth, some lost sound.

She was on the floor of the room.

Darkness. Someone above her. She opened her eyes.

A face was above her. It was the old woman, the one she'd seen so many times. The wrinkled face was close to hers. Close up, Malorie could see that her eyes, small and sunk into her head, were dark brown and shining, like a rodent's. Her hair, poking out from under a brown felt hat, was fluffy, like animal fur. Her skin looked soft, as if lit from the inside, and her small snub nose seemed to be twitching. Her neck was enclosed in a brown woollen scarf, tightly wound. Malorie thought of the voles her father used to catch and kill in the garden in Norwich, because they spoiled his lawn – their soft, brown fur, tiny black, bright eyes and short stubby tails.

She remembered now – the woman had been there on the lane. So had the dark-haired girl.

Watch out there, girl, sound fit to wake the dead.

This sound seemed to come from the old lady but it sounded far away, not in the room at all.

She struggled to stand up. Someone had lit the candles on the tree. The room was a vision of the cosy-glow family Christmas that she'd been yearning for, but the shapes the candlelight created on the walls were like the shadow puppets of ghouls and bog creatures and sprites. On the glass-topped coffee table were cups and saucers – the remains of a tea she didn't remember having. The gramophone was playing a soothing song, a jazz trumpet.

Round the walls the blizzard roared. The front door banged repeatedly and then the back door in the kitchen began to do the same. The candle flames guttered; the shapes became monstrous on the walls. The music began to jump and trip. The night was turning against her.

Watch out there, girl, you're shaking like a jelly. Janey's voice was talking to her. It was muffled now, overlaid with an excited chattering that she thought was coming from her own brain.

There it was again. The young woman's face in the window. A shadowy pale head with eyes like stagnant pools staring at her. Above the hearth in the old, rust-stained mirror, the same face, wavering. Rosemary's face.

Come on now, girl, don't take on so. That's your face in the glass. Just your face.

The old woman was saying something else because her mouth was moving but it was just a distant hum. Another voice was in her head , a younger one –

Purple bruises blooming like pus. Asked for it. Drinking blood.

Opening her eyes, the face – her face – Rosemary's face – had multiplied. She was in the coffee table glass. She was on the old woman's face. The pale oval reflected back at her from the window, from the mirror, flickering in the candlelight, a snow girl with eyes of coal. Malorie put her hands to her eyes. The face was still there behind them.

She picked up the nearest thing – one of the notebooks – and threw it at the mirror. It hit the glass and bounced off, falling at her feet. The face was still there. She picked up a china cup and threw that. The mirror cracked and splintered and the face became hundreds of tiny shards of white and black. The face was still there in the window, a whole moon-face with black-green eyes, staring. She pulled back her arm and threw another cup at the glass. The window shattered, the cup shattered, and hundreds of pieces of glass and china fell to the wooden floor as droplets of tea rained across the room. Now through the hole in the window there was only the darkness of the night and the white of the snow. Finally, she picked up the notebook again and smashed it down into the glass-topped coffee table. A hairline crack appeared and spread into tiny lines and fragments, like a spreading tree. A moaning was coming from somewhere, a keening like the high notes of a trumpet.

On her knees, glass all around her. Glass in her hair. Someone put their hands on her shoulders to steady her as she trembled. All the time the bulk of a body – the old woman – kept hold of her, intoning words over and over in a low breath.

My girl. My girl. S'aright now.

She wanted to say *What is it?* But she couldn't speak. Her jaw was locked.

Calm yourself girl. I'm not leaving you.

– Let her go, Rose. Leave her be. It's time to go.

I won't let go of you.

Again, her brain was filled with the girl's voice.

> *Purple bruises blooming like pus*
> *Asked for it*
> *The coffee is bitter*
> *Poppies like spots of blood*

Her body rocked with a force streaming, coursing through her bones. The ends of her hair static with electricity. The old woman held her so hard she felt her bones would break.

Rosemary screamed in her head, stronger and louder.

> *Cream and sugar biscuit crumbs*
> *Just for you*
> *Flies buzzing*
> *Orange daggers*
> *Blood, blood, blood*

The old woman's hands around her head, earthing the current, subduing it, sending it back into the ground.

Her skull was going to explode.

As if a valve had been opened, she felt a pop in her ears

and the pressure released. There was a high, thin screech like a screaming child.

Silence.

Snow fell softly against the window.

She's gone. It's just you now.

All feeling left. She collapsed onto the floor. The antique red rug was littered with broken glass next to her eye and the dark red cover of the notebook lying where it had fallen.

From the floor, she felt Janey's lips, like a dry leaf scratching on her cheek. A swash of brown fabric as she disappeared out of the door.

And someone's small arms around her, tugging her back to herself.

'Mummy.'

Just before she fell into the darkness, she saw green eyes close to her own.

48

Witch, Old Witch
28th December

A ceiling, buckled and mottled, undulations like the sea. Watery light across it. Morning. Cold. A bitter winter morning. Where was she? The house on the marsh. The Marsh House. Images came rushing in – a tumult of fragmented memories – the sampler with the girl in plaits, a snow-girl with coal for eyes, pebbles on the beach, a frozen dog, an Edwardian photograph, a cot in the attic, an axe, Franny vomiting. An old woman with shining brown eyes. Black wings in the snow. It seemed like something she'd dreamt. A too-vivid dream that wouldn't recede and kept lapping at her brain. She was still staring at the patterns of mould on the ceiling. She had a weird sense of abandonment, a tugging empty feeling, like the vacuum that had been left behind inside her when her mother died.

Malorie pulled a blanket around her shoulders and sat up. Her ankle twinged. The sight that greeted her was hard to understand. She was in the sitting room, hazy in the weak winter morning light. Wax had dripped down the side of the extinguished candles on the tree and dropped in white pools to the branches of the fir so it looked like it was covered in a glutinous snow. The curtains were drawn across but they were gently rising and falling and from behind them came a chill air as if the window was open. The mirror was cracked. Bad luck. In her head the lines from the poem appeared – *The mirror crack'd from side to side;/ 'The curse is come upon me,' cried/ The Lady of Shalott.* Shards of glass were scattered across the rug and the floor. Something had happened. She strained to remember. The blizzard. Outside in the dark. It was too strange, too surreal to be true.

And Franny? Franny was ill.

A noise. It came again. It was a knocking, a knock on the front door. Then the sound of feet crunching on deep, frozen snow. A shadow passed behind the thin, gauzy curtains of the living room window and Malorie pushed herself against the back of the sofa. A tap on the window and a gasp, a mutter and an eye appeared in the gap between the curtains. The eye caught hers. Malorie froze as if the eye had pinned her.

But then the head drew back and a hand waved.

It was a woman, Malorie saw, an older woman with a preposterous furry hat, like a brown cat sitting on her head, an unflattering, squashy version of her own black Russian hat, and a large coat with fur around the collar. The woman was waving a leather-gloved hand towards the door. Malorie realised she wanted her to open it.

Unfolding her aching body, Malorie stood up shakily. An icicle of pain pierced from her ankle up her right leg. What had she done to it? She still had on the same clothes she'd been wearing yesterday. Her sweater smelt stale. The smell of stress and distress rose from her skin. Her left foot fell on something sharp. Bending down, she picked up a bead of glass from her sole. She tried to smooth down her crumpled skirt and knotted, sticking-up hair.

At the door, it wasn't the woman she saw, it was Franny, poking out from behind the woman's bulk, dressed in her coat and hat.

'Mummy?' she said, small and hesitant.

'Why are you in your coat? Where've you been?'

'I was scared. I went to get help.'

'But you were ill,' she said, 'you were in bed.' She pulled Franny to her and grasped her daughter close to her chest.

'It's gone now, Mummy,' said Franny, breathing into her chest.

Over Franny's head, the woman beamed at her. 'Mrs Cavendish? I can't tell you how wonderful it is to find you alive and well. It's been so frustrating not being able to get hold of you for all this time. What on earth happened to the window? Was it the branch of a tree in the storm? I'm sure you've been wondering where on earth you've ended up. Can you believe this weather? Isn't it remarkable? It's not been like this since forty-seven. You would've been a child then, that would have been a lot more fun. I imagine you've been having a fine time of it, haven't you, dear?'

The last was addressed to Franny, who was tucked under Malorie's arm. Malorie blinked at the woman. The sun was rising directly behind her outline but its weak rays reflected off the blanket of snow and directly into Malorie's eyes. She raised her hand to shield her sight and tried to understand what the stranger was saying.

'Sorry,' she said, giving up. 'I don't understand. Who are you? Have you come about the house?'

'Yes, dear. Although I wouldn't have made it through if it wasn't for the wonderful men, they've been working marvels, bless them.' She gestured behind her, at the drive. 'Now, do you mind if I come in? I was supposed to have done an inventory days ago.'

'Pardon?'

'For the house. Check all is present and correct. I know it's a bit late, but better late than never is what I say.' She'd shouldered her way in by then and was standing in the hallway looking around her, already totting it all up. 'We'll have to see to that window right away. Can't have the snow coming in.'

'Please. You haven't told me who you are.'

'So sorry, I let my words run away with me, dear. My name's Mrs Pollock. Like the fish. Mr Poke of the agency sent me to meet you when you arrived, but our dates must have got mixed up because I thought you were coming on Christmas Eve and he told me it was the twenty-second, and anyway, I couldn't get here on account of the snow. I called a few times but the line kept getting cut off. Probably because of the storm. So I must say on behalf of the agency, we're very sorry to have left you stuck out here, and Mr Poke is quite annoyed with me but it was quite impossible. The road from Salthouse has been completely closed for days. I said to him, I said I'm sure you'd understand. Decent people would understand. I was on my way over here, when your daughter came flying down the lane, with an alarming message about you, my dear.'

Malorie's head was aching, just above her right eyebrow, a vicious stabbing pain, increasing in intensity.

'Yes,' she said, not understanding anything.

'You seem, if I may say so, somewhat disorientated. Can I get you anything?'

Malorie swayed slightly. The woman's hat really did look like a cat.

'I'm fine,' she said.

'I am intrigued though, dear, how you got into the property without the key. Was there a spare under a pot? Though goodness knows why there should be. The agency would never do that. Terrible practice.'

A key? Yes, there had been a key. Now it seemed odd, but she'd not thought about it. She'd assumed it was what people did in the countryside. Trying to ignore the pain above her eye, she thought back to when they'd arrived at the house. The bloody car had skidded and she'd arrived flustered and fed up. She remembered that clearly.

'Excuse me?' said Malorie. 'Do you mind just waiting here for a minute? I need to just check on something.' She looked past the woman to the lane.

The woman in the hat was looking at her askance. 'Madam, I really think that you ought to wait here. The men are coming. You should probably sit down. You look terribly pale.'

'I'm fine. Fine.'

With the blanket still wrapped around her shoulders, Malorie crunched down the snow-covered drive to the lane. The night rime covered the trees with a sparkling coating of frost. The sky was a pale, luminous blue and wherever sunlight fell on the white encrustations of snow and ice it was a flash of pure brilliance. All was deathly quiet except the distant sound of shovels on snow and the hum of men's voices. She crossed the lane with a sense of foreboding as if – and she couldn't explain to herself why this came to mind – as if she would find the old woman who looked like a vole, dead in her cottage.

Above the cottage the sky was clear. No smoke came from the chimney. She stood outside the door for a full minute before knocking. Something was stopping her. It wasn't exactly fear, daylight had robbed her of the horror of last night. Franny had recovered. For herself, there remained the overwhelming sensation of emptiness.

Little flickers of memory were coming back from the night – the old woman holding her, her papery hand, the voice saying the same thing over and over. Her own ghostly face in the mirror, but she wasn't sure what any of it meant.

She knocked on the door. It was important to say goodbye at least. The old woman had been there last night. She had touched her.

No one answered and she knocked again.

Still no one answered. Her bare head was cold and no warmth came from the morning sun.

She raised her hand to knock again when she heard the crunch of heavy feet behind her and a man's voice at the same time –

'Ent no point knocking on that door, Miss. That's empty that is. Far as I know.'

She whipped round, heart thudding. It was the man from the shop, George Bayfield.

'But . . . the woman who lived here . . .' She couldn't finish.

He touched his cap as if he was about to tug it in an old-fashioned sign of respect. 'I thought you were supposed to be leaving, last time I saw you, 'fore the snow come down.'

'We got stuck.'

'I can see that.'

She didn't like the way he looked at her, sizing her up, examining her. She didn't know what he wanted from her but she had to know at least one thing.

'Mr Bayfield, would you mind telling me who used to live in this cottage? I'm just curious.'

He squinted up at the old cottage. 'For as long as I can remember there was a spinster living there. A cunning woman some of the old folk called her. Name of Jane Gidney. Folk always called her Janey. I was afeared of her as a kid. All us kids had a rhyme about her.'

He began to chant under his breath:

> *'Witch, old witch, what do you eat?*
> *Little green toads and children's feet.*
>
> *Witch, old witch, what do you drink?*
> *Poison moonshine and night blood ink.*
>
> *Witch, old witch, what do you do?*
> *I make potions and curses and I'm cursing you!'*

'Funny,' he said, 'I've never forgotten that. It was a chasing rhyme and whoever was "it" sung the rhyme, and when you shouted the "you", you had to catch someone. It were brutal.' He had a faraway, dreamy look in his eyes and said it with relish as if those days were the best of his life. He saw her staring at him and looked guilty. 'We were horrible cruel back then. Kids are though, ent they?'

Malorie's organs were being slowly flooded with cold. 'What happened to her?'

'Awful scandal it were. She were hanged. I remember it well. Not many women were hanged then so it were something special. Quite famous.'

It wasn't possible. But it was true.

Words came out of her mouth without her thinking them. 'Why? What had she done?'

He paused. 'You're telling me you never knew none of this before you came? All what occurred in that house?'

She shook her head.

He tutted, muttered something under his breath like 'Shouldn't be allowed.'

When he answered she felt the crushing, cold horror of something already known.

'She killed two men in thirty-four, that's what. Poisoned them with arsenic. I was the one what found out about it first. The other one though, the young one – it was her what was really behind it. A strange one, she was. More like a sprite than a real girl. Could be vicious, mind, but I felt sorry for her in the end. I always liked her, though she never knew it. It was sad, how it turned out. I never thought – I don't know.' His eyes had clouded as if he was lost in the past.

'Rosemary?' she said, faintly.

The man peered at her. 'That's right. So do you know about her?'

'I need to sit down,' she said. The man in front of her seemed to fold and wave and turn upside down. The sky rushed down on her. Her knees buckled and she felt the path rise and thud into her body.

49

I saw her fall and I knew it'd be that Bayfield. Same as he was when he was a boy, sticking his nose in what ent his business. Still had his beak out of joint 'cos my Rose went off with the Lafferty boy. Still feeling sorry for hisself. That's what it all comes down to in the end: lust and all the foolishness what comes with it. And I thought to myself, Janey, she ought to know now. She ought to know all of it, nothing left out, all the truth of it, what happened. It were time.

50

Cromer

Before she opened her eyes she could hear a gurgling and clanking that sounded like nothing at the Marsh House, and her muscles relaxed into the hard mattress below her. She didn't know where she was, but it smelled metallic and bitter like cleaning fluid and vomit and faintly of burnt dust. She tried to turn over, to stretch, but her legs were bound and seemed fixed to the bed. A dull ache was coming from her right side. It was dark and hot. From what she could tell she was in a small room with nothing on the walls. The only light was a tiny red pinprick but that seemed far away.

Was she in an asylum? Tony had sent her there. He hated her, he was sleeping with that tart at the club. She was mad. He had called her mad. Her throat closed and her teeth ground together and she fought against whatever was binding her to the bed. But she couldn't move. Her arms and legs were fixed tight against her body. She shut her eyes again and lay still, trying to breathe little exhalations through her nostrils, trying not to panic.

Slowly, she remembered certain things. There had been a man dragging her, a voice she recognised. A cup of warm water. A burning taste in her throat. The bright lights in the grey dawn, an ambulance, men's voices, joking. A child. Franny. Oh Franny, where was she? What had happened to them all?

Where *was* she? She wanted to wake up now. It was time. But they must have given her something because there was a weight on her body and in her head that was dragging her back into the drug of sleep. No, she had to know where she was. *Wake up.* In front of her a square of light switched on and she realised that it was in the door of the room. A face appeared. A young woman with a round face and a nurse's hat.

The door opened and the nurse said, 'Are we awake now, Mrs Cavendish? Excellent, I've brought your breakfast.' She turned on the light switch and the strip light flickered on, flooding the bare little room with a fluorescent glare. Malorie screwed up her eyes against the light. Her body was still firmly tied to the bed. The nurse wheeled a little trolley towards her.

'Where am I?' she said, and the nurse gave her a funny look, like you would to a child who had said something incredibly stupid.

'Cromer hospital, Madam.'

'Is it a mental hospital?'

The nurse laughed. 'No, Madam. I should think not!'

Her neck was aching for craning to speak to the nurse. 'In that case,' she said, light-headed with relief, 'please – please can you release me from this bed? I can barely move.'

'Of course,' said the nurse, and dug her fingers in under the tightly-bound blankets and sheets and with a wrench drew them back. Malorie was suddenly exposed to the chest, only wearing a thin hospital gown. She struggled to sit up and pain jarred at her hip. Her head felt fuzzy like it was stuffed with felt and there was an ache in her right ankle.

The nurse fussed about, smoothing corners and putting the tray of unlikely-looking food in front of her.

'Nurse, I wonder, could you tell me about my daughter, Frances Cavendish? Is she here?' Her voice sounded awkward.

'I'll check for you. It doesn't say on the notes.' She gave them a cursory glance.

'I'd be very grateful.' She wanted to shout at the silly cow but she mustn't. They would suspect something was wrong with her. She was safe. She wasn't at the Marsh House. This was a sanitised place with white walls and cleanliness and warmth. Neither was she locked up in an asylum. The strange trickles of memory from the last few days were just bad memories, bits of nightmares. She'd got herself worked up.

The food on the tray was unappetising, but she was suddenly starving. She ate the piece of limp toast, took a mouthful of overcooked beans and then another and another until they were all gone. The egg remained congealing on the plastic tray. She picked up the cold rasher of bacon and nibbled the edge and took a sip of the milky tea they'd made for her. Her eye caught a deep red colour on the bedside table, next to a cardboard bowl. She recognised the bowl from the maternity hospital in London, the kind used for patients' vomit and urine. She focused on the red object.

It was the notebook. How had it got here? She had no memory of taking it with her. Why would she have done? She couldn't have.

For a full minute, maybe longer, she looked at the notebook lying innocuously on the utilitarian hospital table and tried to weigh up whether or not to open it. Rosemary. Janey. The story and the people in it pulsed in her mind, in and out, like a kaleidoscope, achingly clear and blurring to nonsense. Certain words and phrases popped up and disappeared again –

arsenic

flies buzzing vomit

orangemoonshinepurplebruises

These words did not belong in this place. If she left the notebook alone it could fade away and she could live here and now. She could go back to London, find a way to make it better with Tony.

But the red notebook radiated, like a neon sign saying *READ ME*. Rosemary's story hadn't let go of her; it hadn't finished with her. There were more words and she had to read them. She reached over and picked it up and it seemed to glow a brighter, bolder red than it had before. But at the same moment she opened the red leather cover of the book, the door to the room swung open and another nurse came in. She was an older woman in a darker blue uniform, with a pinched, hard face, not like the doe-faced girl who'd come in with the breakfast.

'Mrs Cavendish? Have you eaten your breakfast? Good. Nurse Mackie told me you were awake. Well, I've good news for you. Your daughter is absolutely fine and will make a full recovery. She's weak but there's no trace of fever or lasting damage.' There was a pause. Malorie brightened and she lifted herself up in the bed. The nurse frowned. 'The doctor did say he was going to do blood tests, but he'll let you know about that.' Blood tests? What for?

'When can I see my daughter?'

'She's on the children's ward. It will have to wait until visiting hours. And, I might add, until we're certain you yourself are not contagious in any way.'

'And if I'm not?'

'Then this evening between five and seven p.m. I'll get the nurse to take your tray away. The doctor will be doing his rounds shortly.' And with that, she turned and left, shutting the door firmly.

Now Malorie understood why she was in this room on her own. They'd thought she had something infectious, like measles or flu. Measles. It made her think of the baby boy, Richie. And from there to the last thing she'd read in the notebooks, the anguished, prolonged death of the young man, Franklin, and the girl discovering she'd killed her father. She had a vague recollection of being so horrified by what she'd read that she'd thought it must be made up, a pseudo-Agatha Christie, or a false confession of a disturbed mind. It didn't matter. She and Franny were fine, truly fine. Safe. Now she was no longer at the Marsh House, she might as well finish them. She'd still not read those last few lines in the third notebook. Just out of curiosity. It couldn't do any harm to read them now.

51

That's it then, the end of the story. I hope you've enjoyed it. I enjoyed writing it. I don't know if that's true, I think rather it has come out of me but it's what writers always say, isn't it? I wonder now if I could have been a writer like Mrs Christie. But I don't think I could construct the plots the way she does, full of red herrings and twists and turns. I don't think I have the cunning.

If I had, I'd have got away with it, don't you think? But I was caught. And Janey too, I'm sorry to say, the only person I'd ever loved until now, apart from my son and my mother, but I lost one and never found the other. I'm going too fast, but time is really short now. I feel it every night I look at the sun setting from my cell window. Another day gone.

I'm quite a cause célèbre. I learnt that from the newspapers. It does strike me as strange, that I, an odd girl from a very odd family on the far edge of Norfolk, have attracted the press from all over the world. They call me the Stiffkey Poisoner. Many of the papers have made the link between me and the Laffertys' Fascist politics but I don't think any of this has had a positive effect on the BUF because from what I read, their numbers have declined since that terrible rally in London last year and Mosley's support of Hitler. I'm not sorry.

I can only imagine what this has done to the Lafferty family, because none of them has come to see me, not even Hildy. I thought she would, is that naïve? A package did arrive though. It was postmarked Highgate. Even though they'd opened it (to check for bombs or knives?), the paper wrapping was still partly attached. The Laffertys' London house is in Highgate. I feel it's a clue. Perhaps I'm turning into Mrs Christie after all. The package contained two books. And yes, they were Mrs Christie's latest: Murder on the Orient Express and Three Act Tragedy. I devoured the first one. It was a relief that it was not about poisonings, as it turns out I have no taste for made-up tales of poisons anymore. I read halfway through the second book before I realised what was happening and had to stop. I remember relishing the poisonings in The Mysterious Affair at Styles, but that was a different person, from a different time.

I don't seem to be able to be my real self anymore. I'm not sure I even know who she is.

I didn't have long as a criminal. The police came knocking on the door the day after. They found the arsenic under the sink. I found out much later, at the trial, that the man who'd brought Franklin back from Cromer had told a boy in the village. From the silence of the

Laffertys, I suspect the boy told them and they called the police. They never liked me, the colonel and the lady. I thought Hildy did and maybe I was right. After all, I do believe she sent me the books. I still hope she comes.

I didn't try to lie, I'm a bad liar anyway. I remember getting in the police car and seeing Janey watching from the window of her cottage. I raised a hand to wave but she shook her head and I let it fall. I hoped they'd leave her alone. Dolly came running out of the house with Perdie in her arms yapping away like a mad dog, and they let me kiss her through the window of the police car before they drove off. The police assured me that she'd be looked after but I don't trust them. My hopes of Janey being kept out of it were dashed because at the trial they called her as a witness. It was horrible to see her, away from Stiffkey. She didn't look right with her raggedy old clothes and weather-beaten skin in the pomp and ceremony of the court. I was worried about Old Smutch and who was looking after him. No one would dare to look after that great beast in the village. They were all afraid of him, as they were of her. I started to cry then for all of us: Father and Janey, Old Smutch and Perdie, and Franklin. My lawyer told me to carry on, the jury would have sympathy for me, but they didn't. I was probably too haughty, even with the tears. That's what the village children always said about me, that I was stuck-up. I wasn't, you know, just lonely and shy and angry because no one liked me.

They were cruel to Janey. They called her wicked, a practitioner of black magic and purveyor of poison, and made out that she'd encouraged me to kill Franklin and my father. And when she answered their questions, she was too clear, too sure in what she said.

'Yes, I knew Miss Rosemary as a child,' she said. 'And her mother before her. I was called on to help her, and I did what I could.' But Janey is an innocent in all this. I don't believe she would have ever wanted to harm them.

It worked against her. I think some of the jury turned on her then. They were afraid too, like the villagers. They were afraid she would curse them or something stupid. I wanted to tell the court that Janey had been midwife to countless babies in the village and the hamlets around – myself and my baby included, that she'd healed fractures, soothed fevers and laid out the dead. But no one asked me. Instead they said, 'Did you, Miss Gidney, give Rosemary Wright the arsenic she used for the murder?'

I had insisted on being called Rosemary Wright. I wanted to be who I used to be, not what they made me.

'Not exactly,' she said.

'Please be precise, Miss Gidney. Can you tell the court whether or not you gave arsenic to the defendant, Mrs Rosemary Lafferty née Wright?'

'Well, I did give her some, of course I did. I done it before, plenty of times to others too. For the killing of rats.'

'Was it for vermin in this case, Miss Gidney?'

'I thought so, but –' She paused and the whole court held its breath. 'It might have been for the stopping of a baby.' She looked at me then and I saw she knew.

After that, the court was adjourned and I had to be seen by a group of women to find out if I was pregnant or not. They prodded me as much as the doctor had done years ago, with Richie. Tears ran down my face and I summoned Janey in my head for comfort. I felt her with me, holding my hand, and I stopped crying. And of course, I was pregnant. With you. So that's why I'm here now, writing all this down with you growing your fingers, toes, eyes and ears inside me as I write. It is to you I've been writing all this time, although I've only lately realised it.

I'm the subject of even more press now. Some of them have campaigns for a reprieve. They can't bear the idea of a poor girl being hanged just after I've given birth. In these accounts, I'm a wronged woman, a child who was led astray by an evil witch. There are other accounts though, from different newspapers. Especially the Daily Mail, who've been digging into the Laffertys and their connection with Mosley. In that paper, it's the Laffertys who are wronged, and I have taken their innocent son from them. Mosley is quoted as saying that Franklin was a promising young man, the kind of man this country needs. It actually made me laugh. I do wonder if the Laffertys themselves are turning against Mosley now he's declared himself for Hitler. He's shown himself to be quite a fanatic. The papers say that Diana's sister Unity is a follower of the 'Führer'. I think some women are attracted to men like that – the sort who seem absolutely certain about everything, the cruel sort. I can't quite see Franklin like that, he was too much a pleasure-seeker and I don't even know if he believed in any of Mosley's politics; I don't know if he cared enough.

In these newspaper reports I'm portrayed as a lunatic, the daughter of a madwoman, a madwoman herself, in thrall to black magic and a follower of satanic rituals. People in the village are quoted too, saying how I had no friends and was strange and spent all my time with the weird woman, Janey Gidney.

My pregnancy couldn't save Janey. They didn't wait long to hang her. One of the warders came in to tell me but I knew already. The warder was quite sympathetic. Some of them have been nice to me since it came out that I'm pregnant. Before, when I was awaiting trial, there was none of that. They were cold and hard then. But here, one of them even brought me the newspaper report with an article about it. It said she was suspected of being a witch but really she preyed on innocent minds and corrupted them. Poor Janey, no one had ever understood her like I did. I couldn't save her.

At least I saved you, my baby.

I sat here and wrote this because it was the only thing I could do. I've read my books and I only have this account left. But I don't know what else to tell you because it's nearly over. In my cell there's a small, high window and I watch the sun rise and fall through the bars. I think that whatever happens to me, you'll be here to see the sun rise and set every day, long after I'm gone. But I'm sounding maudlin now. I started writing this account to set it all straight, to show what kind of person he was – not to feel sorry for myself, because there's not a lot of point in that now – but so you would know. Not what I did, but who I was.

I miss Hildy. I wish she'd come.

I miss Franklin too, and the summer I first met him. The Broads, his white suit reflected in the water, him running down to the sea, the first time he kissed me. I touch the sapphire on my finger and remember the blueness of his eyes when he looked up at me, perching in the tree.

20th March 1935

Hildy has written to me. You can read the whole letter, such as it is, as I've kept it. I've read it and re-read it over and over but I still can't tell if she's forgiven me or not. I wonder what you think. 'I am sorry for what has happened to you,' she writes, as if it happened to me not to him, and that gives me comfort, but perhaps I am reading too much into her words and it is just a formality. 'I hate writing like this', she writes, and how I too hate the way she writes. There is no warmth, no friendship, none of our old intimacy. And yet, what can I expect? Her brother is dead and I am here.

29th March

It's not long now. I can feel you kicking at night when I lie on the mattress. I don't know what will happen to me when I give birth. I can't imagine Janey not being there. Sometimes, when I lie on my back with this bump rising up above me, I think I should have taken the arsenic and got rid of you.

4th April

I didn't mean that about taking the arsenic to stop you. I'm trying to think of all the things you would want to ask me if you could, but I'm not sure why I'm writing this now. They'll never tell you who I was. I'm afraid the Laffertys will try and claim you, bring you up as their own, deny me. I'm going to ask if someone else can have you. A kind family who can't have children.

I think now that it was you that Janey was trying to save. It wasn't me at all.

5th April

The campaign is trying to get my sentence commuted to life imprisonment. But that isn't <u>life</u>, is it? It's like an endless death, a purgatory. I read in one of the papers that our old rector is on display, alive but packed in ice, in a glass coffin on the Golden Mile in Blackpool, as if to suggest that he is a curiosity. Which of course, he is. I hate the parasites who feed on such notoriety. Even if they don't hang me, I don't want to take a longer time to die in prison, like an exhibit in a glass case. I don't want to give them that.

Sorry, I'm low again today.

6th April

I think you would want to know that I did love Franklin, and that even in the worst of it, he had some fondness for me too. I didn't mean to kill him, just to hurt him, very much. And I didn't mean to kill my father either. That is the truth. But I <u>am</u> sorry about Janey. She never deserved this. I wish I could – but it's too late to wish for anything now, except for you. You are all I care about now. I love you, what I imagine of you.

The labour pains have started and I need to stop.

Oh Janey, if only you were here. Please come.

I am sorry, Janey. <u>Please forgive me. Please help me.</u>

Oh Janey. Oh my mother.

I'm afraid. Not of dying but of not being able to see you. I want to see you first. I <u>must</u> see you.

52

A Feverish Madness

The rest of the page was blank. Malorie looked up from the book. The fluorescent light above her was pulsing. A hum of voices came from through her door. She needed to get up, to see people, to breathe real fresh air, not torpid hospital air. She needed to see Franny. She needed to read the notebook – but when she turned the pages, they were all blank. There was nothing else to read.

A wave of something like terror flowed through her. How could there be nothing left? She wanted to shout – *Rosemary*. It was true. Or it seemed to be true. She tried to release the tension from her shoulders. Perhaps it was so cleverly done that it seemed real. She didn't know. Her hands were shaking, her heart was racing too fast. It was like something she loved had been taken away from her.

Don't leave, Rosemary. Don't leave me.

*

Later, when she had gathered herself, she heard the door to the hospital room open. A new nurse walked in, smiling, with a doctor behind her.

'The doctor has a few questions for you, Mrs Cavendish.'

'But I'm fine, really. I just want to see my daughter.'

The doctor was young, about her age, smooth-haired, smooth-faced and with a red tie under his gown. He sat at the end of the bed and peered at her kindly.

'Mrs Cavendish, we're concerned about your state of mind.'

'My state of mind?'

'You've been talking in your sleep, saying some – uh – some rather odd things. For example, that there was an old lady who helped you at the house and a young girl in a white dress. From what I can understand, these are figments of a fevered imagination. Now –' He held out his unlined hand and seemed to be about to stroke her arm in reassurance, but rather held it hovering in the air. 'You mustn't worry, these things sometimes happen in young women. A kind of feverish madness. An excess of feeling.' He lowered his voice. 'We know that you had an experience of some disturbance at the house, Mrs Cavendish.'

'No –' she started, but he carried on.

'We wanted to reassure you, there are treatments that can be offered to help with these kinds of neuroses.' He paused, rearranged himself on the bed and focused more closely on her. 'You've had a recent bereavement, I understand. Again, it is not uncommon in such cases for a woman's mind to become – destabilised, even temporarily unhinged. This period of mental fever might indeed pass away of its own accord. But just in case, we thought it best if you were monitored – just for a short while, you understand. I know you live in London?'

She nodded, mute.

'That's excellent. There are marvellous psychiatric practitioners in London. We'll set you both up with a visit when you return home.'

She opened her mouth to speak but it was dry.

'One more thing,' said the doctor as he got up to leave. 'Have you been taking any prescription medication for your nerves?'

Malorie bit her lip. He didn't know. It would be on her records, but of course they were impossible to get hold of at short notice. And certainly not now, with the freeze.

'No,' she said. 'Nothing.'

When the doctor had gone, Malorie took out the Luminal from her washbag and held the envelope in her hand. They reminded her of Tony, of how he saw her. Malorie, who couldn't cope. Perhaps she needed something, but not these. She didn't trust them. First she put them all in the metal bin in the corner of the room. Then, thinking someone might find them, she fished them out again and, one by one, flushed them down the toilet until they had all gone.

53

London
March 1963

The kitchen clock said 9.45. It was already a full hour since Franny had left for school and Malorie was still in her nightdress and dressing gown. She'd made Franny's breakfast – a bowl of cornflakes – and watched her eat while she drank a cup of tea, kissed her daughter goodbye at the front door and stayed there until she walked to the bus stop through the slush and puddles to get the bus to school. Every morning, she'd wait for Franny to turn around and look at her. Every morning since they'd got back to London, she'd return up the narrow stairs to their flat and get back into bed, pulling the covers high up around her neck. She couldn't go back to sleep. Instead, she lay there, trying to ignore the thoughts that came crowding in.

It was just her and Franny for the time being. She'd told Franny that Daddy would be back soon and kept up a show of strength for her daughter, but she didn't know when, or if, he would be back. It had taken forever to get back to

London. They'd had to wait for a slight thaw to open up the roads in the middle of January, before the chill swept around the country again and closed off Norfolk. There had been an awful phone call with Tony. She thought he might have said he'd missed her, that it had all been a mistake, but he was too angry. He'd snarled at her, threatened court. She held the phone away from her ear while he ranted. She realised that too much had happened in Norfolk for them to return to how they were. Her leaving like that had been a way out for him. He lived in the flat above the club in Soho and she took Franny up to his parents' villa in North London on the bus and dropped her off. He'd bought a dog – a fluffy replacement for Larry – but it stayed at the house in St John's Wood. She told her daughter that she had errands to run but mostly all she did was take the tube to Highgate and walk around the snow-covered cemetery looking at the graves. She also knew, because Franny had told her, that sometimes another 'lady' was there, a pretty brunette whom Tony called Babs. She found she didn't mind as much as she thought she would. She had the flat in Pimlico, for the moment at least. He'd not been cruel about that. It was in his name though, it was he who had bought it with help from his parents. They had not yet gone to court to decide what would happen but she thought, she hoped, he would let her stay in it with Franny, at least until she'd set herself up. Once, his mother had telephoned the flat suggesting Marriage Guidance. Malorie, biting down her retort that she herself may need it, said that she didn't think Tony was interested in saving the marriage.

'You don't know if you don't try,' said his mother. 'There are ways of making a marriage work, that look beyond – a man's indiscretions. It would surely be better for Frances if her parents remained together. At least in name.'

What would be the best for her daughter? This was what occupied her every day. The doctor in Cromer had been true to his word and had referred them both to see a psychiatrist. Neither of them had gone to the appointments. She told herself that she wasn't ready, but in truth she was afraid. And she'd said to Franny she didn't have to go to her referral either. She didn't think the hospital in Cromer would follow it up. Not after the chaos of the winter.

They had a silent agreement, she and Franny, that they wouldn't talk about it. She hadn't given Franny any of the Luminal since the night they'd left the house. It had been Tony's idea in the first place, and he was no longer here. Since they'd left Norfolk neither of them had taken another one. She was hardly sleeping and woke each morning with a headache.

The Big Freeze, as the broadcasters called it, carried on until the end of February, fresh snow replacing the old, grubby mounds and covering the city over and over again, until it seemed there would only ever be a winter and it would never be warm again. She hadn't expected it in London for some reason, but when she and Franny returned home, the pipes had frozen and burst and there was no running water. Somehow, though, London still functioned: the roads were cleared by local men with shovels and the milk got through. It was only now, as March began, that the thaw had finally come. But when it came, it was all of a sudden. What had been packed snow and ice mixed with grit and gravel began to melt, causing a torrent of dirty water down the streets. Franny carried on going to school in her wellington boots, sloshing through the puddles.

After ignoring it for weeks, at the end of February, she'd gone to the library, alone, when Franny was at school. At first, she'd put off searching for information on Rosemary Wright and instead looked up what had happened to the BUF. There'd been the famous rally in Cable Street, she knew about that. She read about the king's abdication and the BUF support for him and for the Italian invasion. She read about Mosley and his next wife, Diana Mitford, being interned; most of the BUF disbanding, the failure of it all. He seemed ridiculous now, a bogeyman, a pathetic version of Hitler. But there were plenty who'd believed they were right. They still did.

Finally, she looked up the old newspapers from 1934 and 1935 and read the accounts of the murders in Stiffkey and the trial. Under the yellow light of the machine, she read about the hanging of Jane Gidney, midwife, by Albert Pierrepoint, the famous executioner. Her heart began thumping hard and fast under her ribs. She turned the knob of the microfiche, her legs twitching uncontrollably underneath the heavy desk. Then there it was.

Woman on 'death row' gives birth. – A baby girl. – Healthy. – Whereabouts now unknown.

With shaking hands, she turned the knob.

Stiffkey Poisoner reprieve denied.

She turned again. Then later –

Girl Murderer Dies. Cause of death unknown.

She'd walked away from the library and nearly under a bus she was so disorientated. The rest of the article seemed to hint that the death might have been due to blood loss in giving birth to the baby girl. She thought of Rosemary giving birth alone, no Janey to look after her.

While she was finally dressing, Malorie heard birdsong outside, the first for weeks. Then a clatter and a thud. The post had been delivered.

On the mat was a thick brown envelope addressed to her. The postmark said Cromer. Perhaps it was a bill for the Marsh House. She'd tried not to think about the house since she'd got back to London. She'd focused on Franny. She'd gone straight to the Midland bank and written a cheque, praying that there was money in the account and that Tony hadn't put some kind of freeze on it. She didn't know for how much longer she'd be able to access the account so had withdrawn slightly more than usual, but not so much as to be noticeable. They'd been on visits to the library, tobogganing, even to the centre of town where they'd had hot chocolate in an expensive café off Covent Garden and gone skating together on the frozen Serpentine. Part of the Thames itself had frozen and once they'd watched a man skating on it. She kept a close watch on her daughter for signs of the after-effects of withdrawal, or of damage from the trauma of what had happened to them, but there seemed to be none. She was withdrawn, yes, but no more so than before. And sometimes, in an occasional glance they'd shared, she caught a glimpse of an understanding between them that was new. This morning, for the first time since they'd returned, Franny had turned at the corner of the road and a small smile had crossed her face. It had to be a new beginning. She'd thought, for the first time, that she could survive on her own, that one day Franny would forgive her.

In February, she'd read of the suicide of a young American poet on the other side of London. She'd put her head in the oven, leaving two tiny children behind. Malorie understood. The black forms in her head still came and grew. But she was not going to die – not yet. Franny needed her if she was not going to grow up like her father.

Quickly, Malorie ripped open the envelope, as if she were tearing off a plaster from a wound.

Bulwer, Frankling and Reynolds
15 Prince of Wales Road
Norwich
Norfolk NR1 1EF

Dear Mrs Cavendish,
I trust this letter finds you well.

She scanned the rest of the page and had to steady herself with a hand on the wall to stop collapsing.

With the letter crumpled in her fist, she got herself to the kitchen where Franny's bowl still sat on the table, the mushed cornflakes encrusting the edges. She dropped the letter on the table and made herself a cup of tea. She was slow and deliberate in her movements, trying to remain calm. Leaving the house on the marsh had been the end of it, she'd thought. In the hospital, it had felt like a bad dream. Here in London, it had seemed like something to be put away like Pandora's box and kept shut up. Had it opened itself? Christ, that didn't make any sense. She was acting like she had at that house again. Just read it. Perhaps she'd misread it the first time. She read.

> *In my capacity as lawyer for the estate of Mrs Louisa Mulcaney-Wright, I write to inform you of her death on 28th December 1962 at St Andrew's Hospital (Norfolk County Asylum) of a heart attack.*
>
> *Mrs Wright died intestate and we are therefore writing to inform you that, as her only heir, you are now the rightful owner of Swalfield House (known locally as the Marsh House), Stiffkey, Norfolk.*
>
> *We apologise for the delay in corresponding. This is due to a series of probate issues and problems tracing the family line.*
>
> *Please find enclosed the deeds to the property and the appropriate keys.*
>
> *Please do contact me or my associates on the telephone number or address supplied above to discuss this matter further.*
>
> *Yours faithfully,*
> *Mr Leonard Bulwer-Thorne*

Malorie sat staring at the stack of papers in front of her, the letter still in her hand. 28th December. She had been in the house. It was the day . . . Oh. She dropped the letter onto the table. Something fell out. It was a silver locket. She opened the clasp, certain of what was inside. It was still there, a lock of tawny human hair with a touch of gold.

Hardly knowing what she was doing, and still holding the locket tight in her hand, Malorie went up the stairs to her bedroom and opened her underwear drawer. She took out the velvet cloth and the stack of red leather notebooks and, with them bundled in her arms, she returned downstairs. She laid them out on the kitchen table. There was the bone shaped like an ear; there was the tiny skull of a bird; there the scaly skin of a dead eel; the entire skeleton of a rat; the skull of a seal with the huge dark eye sockets, the size of a child's head; there was the long skull of what looked like a boar, complete with yellow teeth.

On the kitchen table, she laid them all out. A song began to play in her ears, a low, sad jazz trumpet. She wondered if she would ever stop hearing it.

Next, she lay out all the documents she'd found or been given. The photograph, still in the old book, the envelope with the adoption documents and now this. There was a birth certificate for Louisa Mulwany. Not Mulcaney like the letter said. Oh. Daughter of – oh. And she thought back. When Rosemary was born she did not look English. Louisa had been – what did they call them – half-caste? – *Anglo-Indian*. She looked at herself in the hallway mirror, trying to see it, this strain of foreign blood that had caused so many problems for Louisa and her daughter. She came up close, put the locket around her neck. It was a shame her hair and eyes were such a nondescript colour. But then she smiled. She thought of Franny's black hair and green eyes. It was still there, even if no one knew; a secret on view.

Behind her shoulder in the mirror she tried to see her mother – her adoptive mother – a young woman picking up a small dark baby, trying to love it. The image wouldn't cohere. She could only see her as she'd been at her death, shrunken and soured by years of hiding the truth. But all that was over now. All they'd been doing was trying to protect her from the stigma of who she was.

Standing in the hallway, she imagined pulling her suitcase out from under her bed, the one she still had from years ago when she'd come to London from Norwich. In it she would place the velvet bag, all of the documents, and her own things. She'd pack a bag for Franny too, go down to the street and open the boot of the awful orange car. It would begin to rain and the rain would putter onto the pavement and the roofs, and the people on the street would look up and open their umbrellas. Her father would step from behind the streetlamp and wave his hat. (Not the other father, she could not think of him as that.) The windscreen wipers on the car would swish from side to side as she drove to Franny's school to pick her up. They'd drive out of London, leaving the tightly packed, grubby buildings, and up on the A11 to the big houses of the suburbs and then beyond – where the rain would stop, and the sun would set behind them as they drove past fields and fields and the road just going on and on. They'd arrive in Norwich late but they wouldn't stop there. They'd be back later. They'd carry on driving as it became night, the headlights two bright beams on the straight, dark road, Franny asleep on the back seat, she smoking with the window down, until the road became smaller and the dark grew bigger. In the car with them would appear an old woman wrapped up for the cold, a sad woman in an Edwardian dress and a small girl with long, dark plaits and green eyes.

And then they would be there.

The house and its ghosts.

Malorie smiled at her reflection in the mirror. She went back to the kitchen and placed the notebooks on the edge of the table. Franny might want to read them one day. They were her birthright. Franny's grandmother's journal. Her mother, Rosemary Wright. Murderer.

54

Up our lane, there's still lumps of old snow, dirty, grey mounds shrinking as each day passes. The trees're dripping with rain and the marsh looks half flooded with the meltwater. Life's coming back. We're still here, me and the dog, clinging on. We're waiting – us and the house – waiting like we was before, back when they come the first time. I don't think it'll be long. I ent sure I'll last much beyond the spring. I'm cold all the time now, despite the thaw, cold and bone weary. I just need to be here long enough to feel the sun and see them back here where they belong.

Smutch starts barking to the sky. Couple of marsh harriers swoop in low over the garden on their way to the marsh. Ke-ke-ke they call, announcing the change in the weather. It won't be long now, Louisa, my love, it won't be long.

Author's Note

This novel had a number of inspirations: the first was the children's book *When Marnie Was There*, by Joan G. Robinson. This was a childhood favourite and I still own my original copy. More recently, it's been made into an animated film by Studio Ghibli. It is the story of a lonely girl who goes to stay with an old couple in a cottage on the Norfolk coast and discovers a deserted house and a mysterious girl who lives there, called Marnie. The novel is a beautiful story of ghosts and friendship and finding out about oneself, and conjures the Norfolk coast vividly. It also gave me the name for my house and the title of the novel: *The Marsh House*.

Another inspiration was the true story of an arsenic murder and hanging from the 1830s. In the real story, one hundred years before my invented one, a local wise woman gave arsenic to a young woman who put it in a cake for her husband. Unfortunately, not only did the husband die but so did her father who ate some of the cake as well. She was found to be pregnant while waiting for her execution and although the child was born, she was hanged in Norwich.

Finally, readers may recognise some of the names of people mentioned in the book. Harold Davidson was really the Rector of Stiffkey who caused a scandal in early thirties Britain. The story is as Rosemary describes in her journal and he really did end up displaying himself in a glass coffin on Blackpool seafront after being defrocked by the Church of England. His death was also tragic as he was killed by a lion in Skegness Amusement Park.

Rosemary's journal also mentions Oswald Mosley and Diana Mitford, who became Diana Mosley, whose affair and subsequent marriage were also hot gossip at the time. Oswald Mosley was famously the leader of the British fascists, the BUF. All the details are from the historical record, although I don't know if he ever came to Norfolk.

All the titles of the pamphlets mentioned in the novel and the quotes from newspapers are real ones.

One more influence on the novel came from the book *The Story of a Norfolk Farm* by Henry Williamson. Before he came to Norfolk, Williamson was famous as the writer of *Tarka the Otter*. Although he arrived in Stiffkey in 1937, so after the time covered in this novel, his story overlaps with many of the places and themes. He took over Old Hall Farm which is adjacent to the Old Hall, and was a supporter of Mosley.

I received inspiration on East Anglian folk tales from many sources, but I would recommend Kevin Crossley-Holland's *Between Worlds: Folktales of Britain & Ireland* for further reading.

Finally, most of the details of The Big Freeze of 1962–63 are historical fact, apart from one key detail: the snow began on Boxing Day, not 23rd December as in the novel. But this is fiction.

Acknowledgements

This novel was partly written during the Covid-19 pandemic and has therefore had a strange genesis. I would like to thank my agent, Laetitia Rutherford, for her calm steering during a time of stress. In addition, the novel has been subject to a series of twists of fate that mean I owe a great debt of thanks to not one, but three talented editors: Madeleine O'Shea, Charlotte Greig and Sam Boyce. I am extremely grateful to each of them for their guidance and expert editing. In addition, thanks must go to all of the team at Head of Zeus, including Kate Appleton, Anna Nightingale, Jade Gwilliam, Clare Gordon and Kathryn Colwell. And I can't forget the designer of the beautiful covers for both my books, David Wardle.

I would also like to thank some amazing early readers and supportive friends: Lily Dunn, Charlotte Packer, Rosie Smith and Lucy Tallis.

Other friends who've been a source of support this last year have been the ever-wonderful Anna-Marie Crowhurst, Gemma Thomas, Jean Stewart and Claire Kendall Muniesa. And a particular and heartfelt thank you must go to all of the D20 writers' group, all writers whose debuts came out in 2020, and who have been such wonderful sources of laughter and sanity during this extremely bizarre and tumultuous time.

Thanks to Jain, whose knowledge of flora, fauna and herbal remedies was an inspiration.

Love and thanks to all of my family in Norfolk and Wiltshire. I must add a particular thank you as ever to Will for his unwavering support, his critical reading and everything else.

This book is dedicated to my children, Alex and Jessie, who both love books and who are brilliant writers.

About the Author

Zoë Somerville is a writer and English teacher. Born and raised in Norfolk, she has lived all over the world – Japan, France, Washington – and now lives in Bath with her family. Her debut novel, *The Night of the Flood*, was inspired by the devastating North Sea flood of the 1950s and is also published by Head of Zeus.